"I told you. This is not your problem," T.J. said.

Kate straightened up to her full height. "Why don't you go back where you came from? You're not here to help Bobby. You've got your own agenda. Whatever it is you need to work out, do it on your own time. All you're doing is making things worse."

T.J. stared at her for a long moment and then finally blinked. "All right," he said.

"All right, what?"

"I'll talk to him."

"Talk? Or yell?"

The edge of his mouth quirked up in a slight smile. "You are one tough cookie, you know that?"

"I eat tough cookies for breakfast...."

Dear Reader,

There's a nip in the air, now that fall is here, so why not curl up with a good book to keep warm? We've got six of them this month, right here in Silhouette Intimate Moments. Take Modean Moon's *From This Day Forward*, for example. This Intimate Moments Extra title is a deeply emotional look at the break-up—and makeup—of a marriage. Your heart will ache along with heroine Ginnie Kendrick's when she thinks she's lost Neil forever, and your heart will soar along with hers, too, when at last she gets him back again.

The rest of the month is terrific, too. Jo Leigh is back with *Everyday Hero*. Who can resist a bad boy like T. J. Russo? Not Kate Dugan, that's for sure! Then there's Linda Randall Wisdom's *No More Mister Nice Guy*. Jed Hawkins is definitely tough, but even a tough guy has a heart—as Shelby Carlisle can testify by the end of this compelling novel. Suzanne Brockmann's TALL, DARK AND DANGEROUS miniseries continues with *Forever Blue*, about Lucy Tait and Blue McCoy, a hero as true blue as his name. Welcome Audra Adams to the line with *Mommy's Hero*, and watch as the world's cutest twin girls win over the recluse next door. Okay, their mom has something to do with his change of heart, too. Finally, greet our newest author, Roberta Tobeck. She's part of our WOMEN TO WATCH new author promotion, and once you've read *Under Cover of the Night*, you'll know why we're so keen on her.

Enjoy—and come back next month for six more top-notch novels of romance the Intimate Moments way.

Leslie Wainger,
Senior Editor and Editorial Coordinator

Please address questions and book requests to:
Silhouette Reader Service
U.S.: 3010 Walden Ave., P.O. Box 1325, Buffalo, NY 14269
Canadian: P.O. Box 609, Fort Erie, Ont. L2A 5X3

EVERYDAY HERO

JO LEIGH

INTIMATE MOMENTS

Published by Silhouette Books

America's Publisher of Contemporary Romance

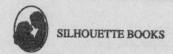

SILHOUETTE BOOKS

ISBN 0-373-07740-8

EVERYDAY HERO

Books by Jo Leigh

Silhouette Intimate Moments

Suspect #569
Hunted #659
Everyday Hero #740

JO LEIGH

is a relocated Texan who began her professional career in the motion-picture industry. After years of collaborative film efforts, she decided to strike out on the solitary road of novel writing. Much to her delight, she's found enduring friendships, generous mentors and a thriving community of romance writers. She loves to hear from readers. You can write to her at: P.O. Box 720361, Houston, TX 77272-0361.

To my nieces and nephews: Lena, Paulie,
Avigail, Rachel, Rami, Trysa, Sara, Yael,
Daviel, Jack and Breetel.
I love you all so much.

And to my wonderful critique partners who made
writing this a dream: Debbi Quattrone, Bonnie Tucker,
Kathleen McKeague, Kim Rangel and Jan Freed.
My heartfelt thanks.

Chapter 1

What the hell was he doing back here?

T.J. Russo grimaced as he looked around the town where he'd grown up. The trees were bigger and the streets were dirtier. The auto parts shop where he'd worked when he was fourteen was now a thrift store and he'd counted five new fast food drive-throughs. He parked his car by the youth center, in front of the entrance where everyone hung out. The building was even more worn down than the rest of the town. The once-white paint was dull and dirty, weeds stuck up between cracks in the paved entryway and two windows were no longer glass but boards covered with sprayed graffiti. It still reminded him of a prison.

And it still attracted a great deal of the teenage population of Harbor Bay. Thirty or so young men, dressed in a uniform of baggy jeans and baseball caps with the brim in back, milled around the front entrance. In his day it had been chinos and cigarettes rolled up in T-shirt sleeves. Half as many girls stood in small groups just near enough the boys to cause trouble. The females wore too much makeup and oversized bomber jackets, not the tight skirts and sweaters he remembered so fondly. Even so, there wasn't that much difference between this gang of teenagers in the yard of the youth center and the gang he'd hung with twenty years ago. Same insolence. Same desperate need to belong. Same fear that this was all you'd ever get out of life no matter what you did or who you prayed to.

He didn't want to get out of the car. He wanted to put it in gear and head straight back to Hollywood. Instead, he pushed open his door and stepped out. The cool air hit him and he remembered the only thing he'd ever liked about Harbor Bay. The ocean. Eleven blocks from his mother's house. He'd gone to the beach a lot those last years. Before he'd been locked up.

A bus roared by and T.J. looked again at the group of teenage boys. He didn't see Bobby, at least he didn't recognize him. Just how lousy was that—his own damn half brother and he hadn't seen him in nine years. Bobby had grown from a kid to a young man and T.J. hadn't been around to see any of it.

He stepped up onto the curb and moved toward the gang. Rap music bombarded him from inside the building.

He knew the instant the group outside honed in on him. He didn't see anyone look at him, he hadn't expected to, but as he approached the front entrance he felt them check him out. He wondered how many of them had already guessed he was a cop.

A short, beefy Hispanic kid moved his shoulder. That's all. Just eased his shoulder forward, keeping his hands in his pockets. He met T.J.'s eye with a cold stare and told him, without speaking a word, that he was carrying a gun.

That was another difference. They were all armed now. Not just with switchblades, but automatic rifles and high-caliber pistols. The stakes were life and death. And Bobby was right in the middle of it.

"You lost or something?"

It was the big one talking to him. He was their head man—the gang leader.

"I'm looking for Bobby Sarducci."

"Don't know no Bobby Sanduski, man."

T.J. didn't say a word. He stared at the big kid and moved in closer. He knew the type. Nothing at home but poverty and trouble. Nothing to look forward to but more of the same. The only place to feel like a man was with other boys who were in the same boat, all of them clinging to their sarcasm and their loaded weapons as if they were drowning.

"You tell Bobby his brother's looking for him."

"You deaf? Don't know no Bobby." The teenager's eyes were black and cold and the warning in them was greater than the words. His thick Latino accent seemed exaggerated and filled with scorn.

"Tell him I'll be calling his mother. Tell him I'll be looking for him." He stood a foot away from the center of the crowd. No one looked over eighteen. T.J. didn't want to start anything here. He wanted Bobby to know where to find him so he didn't have to spend the next week hunting him down.

"Why don't you go back where you came from, man?"

T.J. ignored the remark and skirted the edge of the group as he headed for the door. He knew every eye was on him. He also knew that five minutes from now, Bobby would know he was in town.

He went to the entrance of the center and looked inside. Kids were in there, too, but not as many as were behind him. The music pounded, the bass so loud he felt the vibrations in his feet. He took off his sunglasses and looked around.

Four pool tables, all busy, took up the most of right side of the room. Long tables and plastic folding chairs that made him think of school cafeterias dominated the left. Posters of hockey players and basketball stars were interspersed with anti-drug-and-crime messages. Magazine racks

and bookcases lined the wall of the far side of the room—
the empty side of the room.

No sign of his half brother. He walked around the pe
riphery of the room, studying the teenagers, rememberin
all the afternoons he'd come to this place. There hadn't bee
pool to play back then. No music, either. Excitement the
had meant sneaking smokes in the alley.

But the feeling was the same. Nothing to do but hang ou
and try to make time with the girls. He didn't see any adult
around, which surprised him. Where were the nuns wh
used to run this place, who used to pray for all those littl
lost souls?

He'd almost reached the bookcases when he got the feel
ing something was wrong. Seriously wrong. There was n
movement in the room. Everyone had grown still. The mu
sic seemed even more intrusive. He turned slightly and
caught the gaze of a girl with teased hair. She stared at hin
blankly as she chewed a large wad of gum. Then she turned
her head to look at the front entrance. The big kid, the
leader of the pack, stood in the doorway. The others were
behind him, all straining to get closer. T.J. sighed. It mus
really be boring around here if they needed to stir some
thing up with a cop.

As the gang moved forward, the kids inside faded to
ward the walls. T.J. knew his gun was loaded in his shoul
der holster, but he wouldn't pull it unless he absolutely had
to. Damn it. This town was nothing but bad news.

"Hey, po-lice man."

T.J. didn't move a muscle.

"Hey, why are you still here? Didn't you believe me? You
think I'm a liar?"

"Nope."

"Then why are you in here? This ain't no doughnut
shop."

The others laughed.

T.J. lifted the corners of his mouth.

The kid moved inside. The pack behind him stayed close on his heels. T.J. shifted so he faced the group head-on. He kept his hands loose and open. He didn't want to hurt this boy.

"Why don't you leave, man? Go shake down some jay-walkers."

T.J. saw the teenager's hands were by his sides, the fingers slightly curled. Something bulged in the pocket of his jacket. It couldn't be a big weapon. Probably a .22. Small, but at this distance, the punk might get lucky. A .22 in the heart would kill you just as effectively as a .45.

"Why don't we both take it outside," he said, keeping his voice low and calm.

The kid didn't respond. He just kept walking.

T.J. held his hands up. "Come on, Ace. Nobody wants trouble."

The music stopped. The boy reached in his pocket.

T.J. went for his gun.

Then a woman stepped between them.

He grabbed her by the waist. She was lighter than he expected and he lifted her clear off her feet. She yelped. He turned, putting her down so she was nearly in back of him. With one step he blocked her from the line of fire. His hand was on his gun, but before he could pull it out she was beside him, then in front of him again.

"He doesn't have a gun!" she shouted. "He's unarmed."

T.J. stopped, his hand resting on the butt of his pistol, and looked over her shoulder. The kid was staring at him. He held a cassette. No gun.

T.J. let his hand drop. He turned his attention to the woman. She was tall, nearly as tall as he was and she had long, thick, dark red hair.

"Who *are* you?" she asked. Her fists were on her hips, her feet planted firmly apart.

"I'm a cop."

"Not a very bright cop," she said, her voice low but filled with sarcasm.

"When you've been shot at as often as I have, then you can talk to me about how bright I am, okay?"

She stared at him. He watched the anger ease from her body, first from her shoulders, then down to her hands. Finally the crease in her brow disappeared.

"Okay," she said. "I can see where you might have thought Danny had a gun. But I assure you, no one comes to this center with a weapon."

"Hey, he could have killed me, man," Danny whined.

The woman spun to face the boy. "You're lucky he didn't."

"What!"

T.J. watched Danny's theatrics for a moment, then turned his attention to the woman. She had to be almost six feet tall. Her body was slim and straight, her face dramatic. Her eyes were an astonishing green and her skin clear and tan. He wouldn't call her beautiful, she was too powerful looking for that, but she was striking. She wore jeans—straight legged and tight. The denim showcased her behind and those long, long legs. Now that he looked, he could see she wasn't quite as boyish as he'd previously thought. There were curves there, all right. Her green sweater was a bit loose and he could see the swell of her breasts. They were on the small side, nothing to call the paper about, but nice just the same.

"What are you trying to prove, Danny?" she said. "That you're tough? You're not tough. You're just a punk. And one of these days you're going to get yourself killed."

"Punk? Where did you hear that, on TV?" Danny's voice was loud enough so all his friends could hear. "You watch all those cop shows so you'll know how to be *hip?*" He turned his head briefly so he could see his crowd behind him.

T.J. wanted to wipe that smug smile off his face.

The woman moved closer to the teenager. Danny held his ground, but not for long. She kept coming at him, forcing him backward until his back hit the side of a pool table and he was stuck. His grin became a memory. She raised her right hand and poked him once in the chest. She leaned so close to his face that T.J. was sure the boy could feel her breath.

"Don't screw with me," she said, her voice even and dangerous. She poked him again. "You are no match for me, Arcola. Not in any street fight, not with any weapon. I simply will not tolerate rude behavior in my center, you got that?" She used her finger one more time. "You are a guest here and you will act like one. This is your last warning."

The teenager wanted to strike back. T.J. could tell by the way his fists curled at his sides. He was desperate to get away from the woman. But something made him stay and take it, for now. She didn't seem to notice the thin thread that held him back. When she was good and ready, she let him go.

Although T.J. admired her spunk, he wondered if she'd just bitten off more than she could chew. The Danny Arcolas of the world were dangerous. Young, foolish, with a reputation to uphold. It wasn't a question of whether they would explode, only when. But right now, if he had to set odds, he would bet on the woman, double or nothing.

She looked at the crowd around them. "Show's over," she said. "If I don't see some homework being done pretty soon, I'm going to kick all of you out of here and lock the doors."

Danny smiled at the woman, his anger reined in for the moment, but when she turned her back, his smile faded, leaving behind a look of malice so tangible T.J. nearly went for his weapon again. The boy was armed. It didn't matter that he'd had a cassette in his right pocket. Somewhere—his other pocket or behind his back—he had a gun and he was prepared to use it. Their eyes met and the look of hate focused in on T.J. He realized Danny wasn't angry with the woman. His fury was directed at one target—him. T.J. knew if he came back here again looking for Bobby, Danny wouldn't let a tall redhead stop him.

The teenager turned and moved slowly toward the exit. Most of the others left with him. Still, several kids stuck around, mostly to play pool. A small group did sit down, but no books made an appearance.

She turned from the boy and stared at T.J., no sign of the altercation marring her strong features.

"Do you have business here?" she asked.

"I'm looking for Bobby Sarducci."

"What for?"

"Not that it's any of your business, but he's my brother." She looked surprised. "You're his brother...?"

"Half brother," T.J. said. "I haven't seen him in a while."

"So you're Detective Russo."

"He's talked about me?"

She stared at him with a disapproving glint in her eye. But that was okay. They really were pretty eyes. Damn, she was a striking woman. He had the feeling if he told her that, she *would* strike him.

"No, he's never said a word about you. But his mother has. She told me you haven't been to see him in years."

He noticed one of the girls, a blonde with thick, dark eyebrows, had stopped to listen. He took a step closer to the woman. "I'd rather not talk about my deficiencies as a brother right now, Miss, uh..."

"Kate Dugan. I run the place. My office is right over there."

Kate led him toward the west side of the center. He followed close behind and she knew he was checking her out. She shouldn't complain. She'd done some checking out herself.

T.J. Russo had been the subject of several conversations with Teresa Sarducci. He'd left years ago, without a back-

ward glance. Did he know how much he'd hurt his mother
by not coming home? Did he know how much Bobby
needed him now? Should she tell him where his brother was?
No. She would leave that up to his mother. It wasn't her
place.

It seemed hard to believe he was Bobby's brother. Bobby
was a wiry boy, short, with a tendency for trouble. Now that
she thought about it, he did look something like the man
behind her. They both were too good-looking.

She reached her office and pushed open the door. After
Russo entered, she closed it behind her. She could still see
the kids outside through the large windows, but this way
they could talk undisturbed. "So what do you want to discuss, Detective?"

Kate pointed to one of the plastic chairs against the wall
while she pushed some papers to the center of her desk and
perched on the edge. She kept her back straight and tall so
when he sat, he would have to look up to meet her eye. She
still rankled from his exhibition in the main room. He'd actually lifted her in the air. No man had ever done that to her.

He ignored the chair and walked around the room,
checking out the framed permits on the wall. He stopped
when he saw her degree. "His mother seems to think he's
hanging out with the wrong crowd," he said.

"*Your* mother's right. I can't say for sure, but I think
Bobby is trying to hook up with Danny's posse. I've seen
him with Danny a few times. Enough to make me nervous."

T.J. didn't face her. He just kept looking at her things.
The basketball on the chair in the corner, the plaque from
the city commending the center for their big-brother proj-
ect. He seemed bigger in here, even though she knew he was
only a few inches taller than her. Why should that bother
her? He wasn't going to pick her up now. She remembered
the feel of his big hands on her waist and felt herself flush.

"Tell me about this posse."

She hesitated. T.J. now stared at a corkboard on the wall across from her desk. Pictures of kids and supervisors—past and present—covered the surface and she guessed he was looking for a picture of his brother.

He ran a hand through his dark hair in a gesture she knew instantly was familiar and unconscious. The back of his jacket went up and she stole a quick glance at his rear end. Not bad.

She smiled, sure he would be embarrassed if he'd seen her. Then he turned to face her and she knew he wouldn't be embarrassed at all. He was used to having women give him the once-over. He was relaxed and composed in this stranger's office. His dark brown eyes looked at her with interest and not a little amusement. The hand-through-the-hair routine was probably his version of a peacock showing his feathers. The ironic thing was, it worked. She felt a flutter in her stomach and a ridiculous urge to bat her eyelashes. She held back.

"I don't know much about Danny's posse," she said. "I've just heard things secondhand."

"What kind of things?"

"That they're like every other gang in the country," she said. "Reckless. Dangerous."

"That's it?"

She wondered briefly if she should tell him that they're the kids responsible for the rash of racketeering and arson spreading through Harbor Bay. No. Everything she knew about T.J. Russo was negative. He'd left his hometown to go to college and had never come back, even though he lived only fifty miles from here. He'd done nothing but hurt his mother and his brother. She wasn't quite sure why he'd come back now. Guilt probably. But that wasn't her problem. Bobby was, and she wasn't going to confide in T.J. until she could determine if he was here to help.

"That's it." She got to her feet. "I think it's commendable that you're taking an interest in Bobby. He's a bright kid. He could use a good role model."

T.J. laughed. She hadn't expected that. She grew even more puzzled when she saw the look of derision on his face. She was glad now that she hadn't opened up to him. If he wasn't here to help Bobby, why was he here?

"Thank you, Ms. Dugan," he said, his face once again poised with a hint of arrogance.

"No sweat," she said. She walked to the door of her office, but when she turned to see him out, he wasn't behind her. He still stood by her desk, but now he was staring through the glass at the kids in the big room. She almost said something, but his expression stopped her. The tough cop was gone and in his place was an ordinary man filled with extraordinary regret. The eyes that had been so full of the devil a moment ago now looked as if he'd just lost everything that mattered in the world. She followed his gaze. All she saw was the familiar center with the shoddy carpet and peeling paint. The kids who had nowhere else to go. But T.J. Russo was seeing something else. Something painful. Whatever it was, he was staring with so much sorrow she could feel it ten feet away.

"Detective?" Kate waited for T.J. to turn away from the window. When he didn't, she cleared her throat and repeated, "Detective?"

He turned toward her and she saw a remarkable thing. He donned his mask, as clearly as a man puts on a shirt in the morning. One second his eyes were wide with confusion and sadness, the next, they were cool, even insolent. But he'd changed too late. She'd seen the other side. The raw pain of the man. It took all her control not to go to him, which was as surprising as anything else that had happened today. She wanted to reach out to this stranger. This cocky bastard who knew women like he knew breathing.

"Why are you here?" he asked.

She took a moment before answering. "To help," she said.

He smiled, but there was no humor in it. "Do you?"

She shrugged. "I try."

"But does it do any good?" He walked closer to her, staring at her hard. "Have you saved even one of them? Has any kid ever turned his life around? Left all this behind and made something of himself? "

"You did."

His lip curled in a cruel grimace. "Sure. Sure I did. I'm a cop now, one of the good guys. I'm just a goddamn model citizen."

"So you're not perfect. Who is?"

He didn't say anything for a long moment. He simply looked at her as if he'd just now noticed her. She felt his gaze pry beneath her skin and she crossed her arms over her chest.

"No," he said, his voice low and gruff. "I'm not perfect. No one's perfect and no one ever will be. Especially not here. Not in this place."

She walked over to her desk, still burning from the fire in his eyes. "People do change, Detective. All the time."

"They get worse."

"No. Not always. If I believed that I'd quit right now."

He looked away. Finally she could breathe again. She rubbed her arms against a sudden chill. "Why are *you* here, Detective? If that's what you believe, why did you come?"

He walked to the corner of the room and picked up the basketball. He turned it over and over in his hands, squeezing it so tightly his fingers became pale. "The hell if I know," he said.

She stared at him, straight in the eyes. He didn't turn away, didn't retreat, yet she knew the pain was still there, hidden behind the brick wall of cynicism. She made her decision. "Your brother isn't here, Detective. But I'll tell you where he is. I was going to see him in a few minutes anyway."

His hands stilled.

"He's in jail. Your mother called me a little while ago. She's at work in Santa Barbara and she can't get down here to bail him out. She asked me to get him."

"What's he in for?" His voice was cold as ice.

"Vandalism. He tagged an office building."

"That's all? I'm surprised."

"You have so little faith in him?"

He put the basketball back on the chair. "I don't know the kid. I do know his father."

She knew Gus Sarducci, too. He was a vulgar man, gruff, drunk most of the time. She was sure he beat up on Bobby and his mother, although she could never get either one of them to admit it. He hadn't held a job for as long as she'd known him. That's why Mrs. Sarducci was in Santa Barbara. She worked two jobs, just to keep the family going. "He's not like his father, Detective."

He turned his head to look at her again. "No? How's that?"

"He's bright, he's young, he's still got hope. Don't condemn him yet. You said yourself you don't know him."

"What is that expression? The fruit doesn't fall far from the tree? Bobby doesn't stand a chance."

Something told her he wasn't just talking about Bobby, but himself. "I'm sorry for you if that's what you truly believe."

He looked down. "I'd give a lot to be wrong," he said.

"Let me show you," she said. "Come with me now. Talk to Bobby. Show him you care what happens to him."

"You think that's all it will take? Lady, you watch too much television."

"Sarcasm won't win any points with me, Detective. Either you have a stake in Bobby's future, or you don't."

Something flickered in his brown eyes. A glimmer, a tiny shred of hope.

He swiped his mouth with the back of his hand. "Why not? I came here to see Bobby. I might as well see him in jail."

"Good," she said. "Good." She picked up her phone and dialed. When her assistant, Molly, answered, she asked her to come up to take her place. She hung up and turned to T.J. He was watching the teenagers in the big room again, that same sadness pressing him down so hard his shoulders bent from the weight. Suddenly it became very important to her to show this man he *could* make a difference.

Chapter 2

At the police station, T.J. parked his car next to Kate's beat-up station wagon. He sat for a moment, looking at the brick building, remembering the last time he'd been there. Not as a cop but as a criminal. Even now he could hear the echo of the cell door closing. He could feel the fear in the pit of his stomach eating away at his insides. He'd never been that scared since, not even when he'd been shot. He'd been Bobby's age.

Bobby. It was hard to imagine him old enough to do anything bad. T.J. still pictured him as a little kid. He'd been a pistol, that one.

The year before T.J. had left Harbor Bay for good, Bobby had discovered the Christmas presents in the hall closet and had opened every one. His attempts to wrap them up again had been as goofy as his smile had been when he'd seen that baseball glove. The boy had slept with it for weeks after. When T.J. had told him he was leaving, Bobby had thrown the glove into the trash.

"Are you coming?"

Kate's voice startled him. She was right next to his car, leaning down to speak to him. She pushed her hair behind her ear, then behind her shoulder, leaving the long line of her neck exposed. He sniffed, then shook his head at his own stupidity. She was outside. He was inside. What did he expect to smell?

After slipping the key from the ignition, he stepped out of the car. They walked toward the entrance, Kate leading the way. He studied her tall, lean body. She walked quickly but smoothly, not afraid to use those long legs. But it was her neck that kept his attention. That spot right below her ear. He was dying of curiosity now, wondering what perfume she wore, if she wore any. He moved ahead of her to push the door open. She looked at him quizzically as she passed him by.

"Not politically correct, eh?" he said.

"No, it's all right. Just unusual." She turned her attention to the front desk.

T.J. wondered what kind of guys she was used to.

Two uniformed officers stood behind a long, high desk. Behind them were cubicles for messages, large posters informing citizens of their rights and a desk overflowing with paperwork. Just like home, T.J. thought. Police stations around the country all had an air about them that was unmistakable. Fear. That and the elitist attitude of the cops themselves. That need to have the brotherhood stand together against the "civilians." There was a lot of survival involved in that perspective. He knew that firsthand.

"Derrick, how are you?" Kate addressed the younger of the two desk officers.

"Hi, Kate. Hold on a minute. I'll be right with you."

T.J. leaned closer to her. "You know him?"

She nodded. "We've met."

"So Bobby's not the only kid you've bailed out."

"Unfortunately, no."

He thought about taking another step toward her, just so he could get near her neck, but if he did, he had the feeling she would swat him away.

The older officer caught his attention. There was something familiar about him. Not just familiar, but uncomfortable. He must be close to retiring, from the look of him. Gray, thinning hair, paunchy middle. The broken blood vessels around his nose told T.J. he spent a lot of his off hours with a bottle. Where did he know him from? Had he been part of the Hollywood P.D.?

Derrick hung up the phone and smiled at Kate. It was a big smile. Real friendly. "You here about the Sarducci boy?"

Kate nodded. "Did Mrs. Sarducci call you?"

"Yep. She said you would be by. You can go see him now." He looked at T.J. and gave him the once-over. "Who's your friend?"

"This is Bobby's brother. Detective Russo."

Derrick's eyebrows rose. "Detective?"

T.J. put out his hand. "Hollywood homicide."

The young officer shook his hand enthusiastically. "You know Nick Castle? He's in homicide, too."

T.J. nodded. "You could say I know him. He was my partner for six years."

"No kidding? I went to the academy with him."

"I'll give him your regards when I talk to him." T.J. pulled his ID from his wallet and flipped it open. He stuck it in his pants, so his badge would show. "You think I can talk to my—"

"Russo?" The older cop interrupted. "I remember you. Well, I'll be damned."

"You do, huh?" T.J. still couldn't place him.

"Yeah. I busted your ass. Car theft. That's it. Thought you were tough. Busted your old man, too."

T.J. stared hard into the red-rimmed eyes. Now he remembered. The man had changed a lot over the years. He'd gotten fat and he'd lost his hair, but the eyes were the same. Mean. The son of a bitch was responsible for a lot more than busting him. T.J. still had a scar on his back where the bastard had used his club on him.

"Still beating up on kids, Fleming? Or have you grown bored with that game?"

The cop's face flushed red and his eyes narrowed. "You want me to show you?"

Derrick stepped in front of his desk partner. "Hold on," he said. "Kate, why don't you take Detective Russo back to the cells?"

Kate touched T.J.'s shoulder and he jerked free. He held himself still, waiting for the rage inside him to stop building. He had to get a grip. It wouldn't do any good to get into a fight with this jerk. Bobby was in his custody. That was the important thing. He turned to Kate.

"Let's go."

He walked toward the door that led to the heart of the Harbor Bay Police Department.

Kate said something he didn't catch to Derrick, then she was next to him, pinning a visitor's badge on her sweater. She had the good sense not to mention what had just happened, although he saw the questions in her eyes. It was easier not to look at her.

"When was the last time you talked to Bobby?" she asked as she led him past the watch commander's desk.

"About a year ago. On his birthday."

"So he'll be glad to see you."

"I wouldn't say that." He followed her past desks swamped with papers, plainclothes officers, the signs overhead with Burglary and Narcotics and all the other divisions that competed for attention. It *was* just like home. He felt comfortable in a police station. In his element. Hell, this had always been where he belonged. On one side of the bars or the other.

He kept moving past the ringing phones and the stacks of files, following Kate toward Bobby. The anger he'd felt seeing Fleming was easing out of him slowly, leaving behind a feeling he disliked even more. Why was he here? What was he trying to prove?

"Hi, Ken."

His attention went back to Kate and once again he wondered what the deal was with her. Why she gave a damn what happened to Bobby. He saw her nod to a young black officer who smiled at her, just as Derrick had. And not just him, either. Two other guys, one old enough to be her father, grinned like idiots as she passed them by. She was obviously running for Miss Congeniality. "Just how often do you come down here?" he asked.

"Too often," she said. "Turn right up there. That's the hall that leads to the jail." She pointed to a corridor on his right.

He let her go first. Now that he was close to seeing his brother he wondered what he was going to say to him. What could he say? The last time they'd talked, Bobby had barely been civil. T.J. doubted he'd warmed up any in the ensuing year.

They stopped in front of a thick, locked door. The top half was safety glass. Behind it, the jail officer commanded the booking room.

It was just like the Hollywood jail, only smaller. He lifted his badge from his waistband and flashed it at the officer inside. An earsplitting buzzer rang out and Kate pushed open the door. This time, she held it for him. He smiled at her.

"Not politically correct?" she said, grinning back.

"No, but hell, I'm used to it."

Kate was relieved to hear him joke around. It was clear that Fleming had opened a can of worms back there. Obviously T.J. hadn't just stayed away because he was too lazy to drive the fifty miles between Hollywood and Harbor Bay.

This was where his bones were buried, where he kept his secrets.

He'd been arrested for stealing a car, Fleming had said. How long ago? she wondered. When he'd been Bobby's age? His father had been busted, too.

The only thing Kate knew about T.J.'s father was that he wasn't Bobby's father. And that he'd been shot and killed while robbing a liquor store. Teresa had told her the story in bits and pieces. Kate had gathered that the man had been a habitual criminal. But that had been T.J.'s father, not Bobby's, although Gus Sarducci wasn't much better, from what she could see. Just knowing him had taught her a lot about his son.

She wondered what kind of a life it had been for T.J. with that father and stepfather. No wonder he'd been in trouble. The real question was how he'd gone from grand theft auto to homicide detective. What a trip that must have been.

She led T.J. past the booking desk into the central jail area. On her right, a man in a torn T-shirt and jeans sat handcuffed to a low bench. Posters, explaining the rights of the citizens, were plastered on every wall. She could hear the odd echoed voices of inmates as they spoke in the concrete cells.

She nodded to Jenny Teague, a policewoman Kate had known for many years. It didn't surprise her when Jenny's gaze moved past her to lock onto T.J.

Jenny, ever the pragmatist, eyed him as if he were a saletable sweater. She liked what she saw, too. Her normally obdurate face softened and Kate wondered if she was going to sigh.

When T.J. figured out what was going on, he flashed Jenny a killer smile. His confidence, shaken by the exchange with Officer Fleming, was back with a vengeance. Kate finally knew what *cocksure* meant.

She wanted to dislike him. She saw what he was and who he was. Dangerous. A classic bad boy. Still there was something else inside him that belied all his posturing. She felt sure that if she could understand what it was that made T.J. Russo tick, she would be able to understand Bobby. The brothers shared a common wound. Something had happened in that family that had alienated T.J. from his home, from his past—from his only brother. The same thing was happening to Bobby. If she could find out what, she had a chance to help the boy. She doubted anything could be done for the man.

"Where is he?" T.J. asked, looking into the cells that faced the center of the room.

"Back there, I think," she said, guiding him toward the rear of the building. They would put Bobby away from the others, being a juvenile. Sure enough, he was in the farthest cell. Alone. Staring at his high-tops. He looked small in the concrete room. The only decor a lone cot, inhospitable metal covered by a too-thin mattress, a sink in the corner and the etched testaments of hapless criminals on the scarred walls. T.J. slowed before he reached the cell door.

"Hi, Bobby," she said.

His head came up and she could tell he was glad to see her. It wasn't exactly a smile on his lips, but it was close. His eyes widened with relief to see a friend. Well, at least someone familiar. Then he looked past her and a cloud descended. Surprise, hurt, anger. All that and more played on his young face. He hadn't learned yet to shutter his feelings. Not completely.

"What's he doing here?"

She glanced back at T.J. He held himself still as a statue. His face was unreadable. Bobby could take lessons. "He's here to see you."

"Why?"

She waited to see if T.J. would answer. The silence just grew. She closed her eyes briefly, wishing she knew what to say.

"How are you, kid?" T.J.'s voice was soft, strained.

"Why'd you bring *him?*"

He spoke to Kate, but the message was to T.J. The bitterness in Bobby's tone cut right through all pretense. He'd been betrayed and it wouldn't be easy to win back his trust.

"I heard you were in some trouble," T.J. said, as if it weren't crystal clear that his brother wouldn't talk to him, wouldn't even look at him. Bobby stood several feet from the bars. He was still rigid, as if relaxing his muscles would disarm him.

Kate moved forward and wrapped her hands around the steel bars that separated them from the teenager. The more she looked at him, the more she saw the resemblance between the brothers. Bobby also had dark hair, although he wore his long, pulled back in a ponytail. He was several inches shorter than T.J. and he was much leaner. His face was where the real clues were. Those large, dark eyes with the thick lashes. The straight nose and even white teeth. The kind of male beauty that leads only to trouble. They both had that in spades.

"Tell him to get out of here. I don't want him in my business." Bobby stood up. He paced to the back of the cell and leaned against the wall, his left side toward Kate.

"Can't you just listen?" she asked, her words echoing off the concrete. "It seems to me you could use a friend right now."

Bobby snorted and hunched his shoulders.

"Damn it," T.J. said, his voice loud now and sharp. "You're in trouble, little brother and I'm here to get you out of it. If it's not too late."

Bobby swung around. "Too late? How about by nine years, *brother.*"

"You know why I left."

"Yeah. I do. I woulda left, too, only I was just a kid. So I had to stay. While you went off to Hollywood to screw movie stars."

"It wasn't like that." T.J. moved closer to the cell.

Kate didn't think he realized she was still there.

"Get outa here," Bobby said. "I got nothing to say to you."

"You damn well better have something to say. You think I can't leave you here in jail to rot?"

Kate spun on T.J. "What are you doing?" she whispered, sure Bobby could hear her anyway.

T.J. looked at her and she stepped back to get away from the anger.

"Keep out of this."

"You think you can just waltz in here and take over?"

"He's my brother."

"He's my responsibility."

"Not for long."

T.J. left her standing by the cell. He walked down the hall, his boot heels loud in the empty room. She glanced back at Bobby, then took off after his brother.

She caught up with him at the booking desk, although he didn't acknowledge her.

He called the officer on duty over. "What's your name—Reynolds? What are you doing about the Sarducci kid?"

Reynolds turned to some stacking trays behind him and shuffled through papers. He found the documents pertaining to Bobby and brought them to the desk. He read for a moment, using his index finger to guide his eye. "He's a minor."

"I know that," T.J. said sharply.

Reynolds glanced at T.J.'s badge. "You should also know that someone has to sign the Notice To Appear and then he can go home."

T.J. leaned forward, his eyes narrowing dangerously. Before he could speak, Kate grabbed him by the shoulder. "I told you I'm taking care of this," she said.

He spun, turning on her with fire in his eyes. "This is not—" He looked behind him, only to see Reynolds watching them with interest. "You enjoying this?"

Reynolds's face hardened. "This is *my* desk, buddy. Who the hell are you?"

Kate stepped closer to T.J., taking him by the arm. "Excuse us," she said to the cop behind the desk. "We'll be back."

She led T.J. down the corridor, stopping by the drinking fountain where they wouldn't be overheard. "Are you crazy? You're worse than Danny Arcola. I've never seen—"

"I told you. This is not your problem," he said.

She didn't flinch. "I didn't have to bring you here."

"But you did. So back off."

Kate straightened up to her full height. "Why don't you go back where you came from? You're not here to help Bobby. You've got your own agenda. Whatever it is you need to work out, do it on your own time. Don't come in here and bleed all over the floor. All you're doing is making things worse."

He stared at her for a long minute, his dark eyes still filled with a rage that was as old as he was. She could see he was ready to bolt, to put as much distance between himself and Bobby as he could. She couldn't help but feel disappointed. She'd hoped that T.J. could help his brother. With a little patience and some luck, Bobby wouldn't have to come back here again. He could make something of himself. It wasn't to be. That's all.

T.J. finally blinked and she waited for his excuses.

"All right," he said.

"All right, what?"

"I'll sign him out."

"Then what?"

"I'll talk to him."

"Talk? Or yell?" She could see she was making him angrier, but she couldn't back off now. Not when she was so close.

"Look, I said I'd stick around."

"For how long? Until it gets uncomfortable again?"

Just when she thought he was going to lash out at her, the edge of his mouth quirked up in a slight smile. "You are one tough cookie, you know that?"

"I eat tough cookies for breakfast. Answer the question."

"I'll see it through."

"It won't be easy."

"Nothing ever is."

She nodded. He'd surprised her. That hadn't happened in a long time. "Let's get Bobby out of here, okay?"

He stepped back and rubbed his face with his open palm. He looked at her again, as if he didn't quite know what to do with her, then held that same hand out in front of him. "After you."

She walked past him toward Reynolds's desk. She'd won that one. All she could do was hope it was Bobby's victory, too.

Reynolds was on the phone. While they waited, T.J. leaned back against the desk and looked around the booking area. His anger had disappeared as if by magic. He seemed calm and cool, but she knew it wasn't that simple. It was all still there—anger, bitterness, rage. But if she'd met him right now instead of a few minutes ago, she would never have guessed.

This one is a master of disguise, she thought. A shapeshifter.

T.J. turned around as Reynolds hung up the phone. "I'll sign that NTA, if you've got it," T.J. said.

Kate waited to see if the officer would be satisfied with T.J.'s conciliatory tone. Reynolds didn't look happy, but he seemed assuaged.

"Can you tell us how long a wait it will be for his court appearance?" Kate asked.

Reynolds went through some more paperwork. "Tomorrow, probably. Judge Hammond is quick."

"Good," she said, then turned to T.J. "He's strict, but fair."

Reynolds handed her a form to fill out. Of course, she knew the drill. She'd done this before. Normally the parents came to spring their kids, but often she would get a call from a single mother who couldn't get off work, or who was just too frightened to go through the procedure alone. The parents had to show up in court, but for misdemeanor offenses, her role as social worker allowed her to sign the Notice to Appear.

"I'll sign it."

She turned to T.J. "If you sign it, you have to appear in court with him."

He nodded. "I know." He slid the triplicate form closer.

Kate heard someone behind her. She turned, expecting to see a police officer. Instead, she saw trouble.

"What the hell are you doing here, Russo?"

T.J. spun around. The moment his eyes settled on Gus Sarducci, Kate saw T.J.'s hackles rise. His back stiffened and his right hand, still holding his pen, curled into a tight fist.

"Go back to your bottle, old man," he said, his voice deceptively soft. "Bobby doesn't need you to start any trouble."

Gus Sarducci was a bear of a man. He wasn't fat, just thick. His neck, his arms, his legs, all were outsized. Even his fingers were like bulging sausages. She guessed he'd been drinking. His eyes were bloodshot and she thought she saw a slight waver in his step.

"You're the one that don't belong here. He's my son. Mine."

T.J. barely moved. She could hardly see him breathe. He stared at the old drunk through narrowed eyes, but the quick anger she'd seen earlier had been replaced by something more dangerous, more controlled.

"Look what that's got him," he said.

Gus took a step toward T.J. "You button your lip, you son of a bitch. Or I'll button it for you."

"Hey." Reynolds moved quickly. In an instant, he'd come from behind the desk and positioned himself between T.J. and Gus. "Take this out of here, or I'll lock you both up."

Gus pointed a beefy finger at T.J. "He's got no business here. Tell him to go back to the hole he crawled out of."

"Wait a minute," Kate said. "Just stop this right now. *I'm* signing Bobby out. And I'm taking him with me."

She turned to face Gus. He was several inches shorter than she, which made her job easier. "Go home. Bobby will be at the youth center. If you want to come and talk with him there, be my guest. But if you've been drinking I'll have you arrested on the spot."

His eyes darted from side to side, as if he were scanning his options on some private screen. Not that he had many. It wouldn't be hard to press Reynolds to lock him up right now and he knew it.

"Just so long as *he* don't take him. That's all I'm sayin'. He's just like his father. He'll steal the bread from your table. He don't give a damn about anybody but himself. Go ahead, ask his mother. See what she has to say."

T.J. turned his back on Bobby's father and on her. She should have been relieved to see his self-control. Instead she grew more uneasy.

Kate held up her hand. "Officer Reynolds, would you please see Mr. Sarducci out? I'll finish up the paperwork here."

Reynolds looked from Gus to T.J., then nodded. He took hold of Gus's arm. "Let's go."

"Hey, you can't do this—"

"I can do whatever I please," Reynolds said.

Gus turned to stare at T.J. "Don't you go near him. Or you know what will happen." Then he shook his arm free and walked down the hall. Reynolds followed him, his hand resting lightly on his holster.

"So," Kate said. "You two are pretty close, huh?"

It took a minute for T.J. to register what she'd just said. He gave her a half smile, although there was damn little that was amusing about any of this. Seeing Gus had been worse than he'd anticipated. It was as if time had stopped in this small coastal town, stopped dead the moment he'd left.

He remembered the feel of that thick fist pounding his gut and his face. He remembered the filthy words spewing from those lips, the lies, the taunts. The threats. The accusations that he was just like his father. That he would end up bad. He remembered his mother, too drunk herself to intervene.

"He hasn't changed. Nothing's changed."

"You have. You're not a helpless kid anymore. He can't touch you. But he can still get to Bobby, so I need him cooperative."

T.J. shoved his memories aside and eyed her carefully, letting his gaze linger all the way down her body and back up again. "I don't get you. One minute you're Robocop, the next you're Pollyanna. Which one is it?"

Kate shook her head. "Neither. I'm just trying to do my job."

He shook his head. "We've just put off the inevitable. The minute Bobby goes home, Gus will beat the crap out of him, just like always. Worse. He'll beat Bobby twice—once for him, once for me."

Kate turned to the booking desk and reached for the Notice to Appear form. "Bobby won't be seeing Gus. Not for a while at least. I'm going to take him to the center. He can stay there until his court appearance."

"What then?"

"I'm going to ask the judge to remand him to me. Bobby's going to be given community service. At least a hundred hours. I want him to work with me. Where I can supervise him every inch of the way."

"You think if you get him under your roof, you can save him?"

She met his eyes. Her gaze was clear and impassioned, full of conviction. He recognized that look. He'd seen it in rookies at the precinct. In young lawyers and brand-new D.A.'s. But it never lasted. The world beat the idealism out of those Young Turks, just like Gus beat the future out of Bobby.

"I can try," she said. "Someone's got to." She turned back to the form and picked up a pen from the desk.

"Hold it."

She stopped, but she didn't look up at him.

He placed his hand over hers, then slid the form from beneath her fingers. When he put the pen to paper, he got the feeling he was signing up for a lot more than just a court appearance. Against his better judgment, he was going to throw his hat into the ring. It was probably a huge mistake. One both he and Bobby would have to live with for a lifetime.

T.J. waited none too patiently while the booking officer finished up the paperwork on Bobby. His gaze kept returning to Kate. Did she really believe she could save his brother? That she could offer him more than the prestige and danger of Danny's posse? He would have thought the whole idea ridiculous, coming from most of the social workers he knew. But Kate was different. He'd watched her stand up to Danny Arcola, to Gus, even to him, without hesitation. Her physical presence was only a part of it, her strength went much deeper than that.

In some ways, she reminded him of his old partner, Nick Castle. Nick was a hell of a cop—sharp, quick and as tough as petrified wood. But Nick had lived by a moral standard that set him apart. He'd held on to his beliefs long after any other man would have thrown in the towel.

How many times had he told Nick to wise up? To forget about changing the world? But Nick hadn't listened to him. And he didn't think Kate would listen to him, either.

The difference was, Nick had been lucky. He'd met Joanna and she'd taken him out of Hollywood and out of homicide. He knew Kate had no plans to leave. Which meant the rock-hard core that made her stand tall and shoot straight would be chipped away, day after day, year after year, until there was nothing left inside. Until she was just like him.

"They've gone to get Bobby." Kate walked toward T.J. from the back of the room, where she'd been talking to Reynolds.

She pushed back her hair and he looked at her neck again. That lovely hollow spot at the base, the curve under her ear. He'd never been interested in necks before. Not to say he ignored them, they just hadn't been high on his hit parade. But damn, if there wasn't something about *that* neck.

"Come on. We can meet him out back."

T.J. pushed himself away from the booking desk. He was anxious to be out of this place. Away from cops and criminals and bars and handcuffs. He should have gone to Hawaii. He would have wasted his time there, too, but at least he would have come home with a tan.

"Do you have your copy of the NTA?" Kate asked.

He patted his back pocket. "Right next to my heart."

She gave him the smile he deserved before heading toward the back entrance. "We need to go get Bobby's clothes. And I want to talk to your mother. I'm sure she'll agree to let Bobby stay at the center."

"Yeah, why not?" he said, not even trying to hide the bitterness in his voice. "More time for her to pursue her little hobby."

Kate stopped short and he nearly bumped into her. "Is there anyone you do like?"

He looked straight into her green eyes. "There was this guy, once. He died."

Well, glory be. The steely-eyed cop had a sense of humor. It didn't seem to be fully developed, but with some work there just might be hope.

"So," she said. "Are you coming with me?"

"Where?"

"Back to the center, after we get Bobby's stuff."

"I guess. I don't have anything better to do."

"Have you ever thought of becoming an inspirational speaker?"

He smiled, but not so she could see it.

They got to the back entrance to the station, which led to the official parking lot. One of the guards would bring Bobby here and then they could leave. He wanted it over with. Not just the waiting, but the next part, too. He hadn't seen his mother in years. Their phone conversations were always stilted and made him feel like hell. Teresa Sarducci had made guilt an art form. To be in the same room with her was to sit at the feet of the master. The pitiful looks. The sighs. The tremble of her lower lip.

"This whole thing is a mistake," he said.

"No, Reynolds said he would bring Bobby here in a minute."

"That's not what I'm talking about. Look, you go on and take Bobby home. Get his stuff. It'll be easier for everyone if I'm not there."

Kate's fisted hands went to her hips. "Trying for the world land speed record of broken promises?"

"Don't have a kitten. I'm not leaving town. I just think it would be better for Bobby if I wasn't there with him. I'll meet you guys back at the center."

"Better for Bobby? You are so transparent I can see what you had for breakfast." She took a step closer to him, close enough that he could make out the individual eyelashes and count the freckles on her nose.

"This is the deal, Russo. You either knock off the crap, or you're out of here. I've already got one kid to take care of. I don't need two."

He started to give her a smart-ass answer, but stopped the second his gaze met hers. He studied her face. The determination there, the fervor. When she looked at him like that, he could almost accept that his being around could have a good effect on his brother. That coming here hadn't been a mistake.

He closed his eyes briefly, just long enough to break the connection between them. There was a decision to be made and he needed to make it for himself—not just to please Pollyanna.

If he stayed, he would have to give it everything he had. All of it. He would have to face things he'd been avoiding for nine years. He would have to put aside his own feelings and concentrate completely on proving to Bobby that he could make it.

"Let me ask you something," he said.

She nodded.

"What makes you think my sticking around won't make things worse?"

She thought about it for a long time. Her brow creased and she got hold of a tiny bit of her lower lip with her teeth. Finally she nodded once more and said, "If you screw it up, Bobby will join up with Danny. Statistically, that means in the next five years he'll be killed, or go to prison. When he's older—that is if he lives—he'll know just how to play the game, because he'll have had good teachers. Of course, by then he'll have fathered several children and if he bothers to take care of them at all, he'll poison their lives, too. But that's likely to happen even if you decide to leave right now. So, to answer your question, I don't think you can make it worse."

"What about you? I thought you believed you could save him?"

She looked down and he saw her lashes fan lightly across her cheeks. "The chances of Bobby listening to me aren't very good," she said. "I'll try and I'll keep trying, but he has no stake in me. He might respect me a little. But that's not enough. Bobby doesn't love me. I've got a hunch, though, that he does love you. That's why, if you stay, he's got a chance."

Behind them, a door opened and Bobby stood next to Reynolds. The boy had a plastic bag in his hands and T.J. could see a brown wallet and a key. His worldly possessions.

Looking one more time at Kate, at the plea in her gaze, he knew he would stay. And fight.

Chapter 3

Kate poured herself a second cup of coffee, then slipped back into the quiet of the morning. No one was up yet. The kids who stayed here were still asleep, the troops wouldn't arrive for another hour and a half. It was her time, a precious few minutes when no demands were made, no arguments needed settling. She sat at the big wooden table, leaving her morning paper folded for now. Of course, her thoughts went to T.J.

That had been happening all too frequently in the past two days. He'd shown up, as promised, at the hearing. He'd played it smart with the judge and even smarter with Bobby. He hadn't pressed, hadn't made a big production of staying in town for the rest of the summer. He'd given his word, that's all. To the judge, to his mother and Gus, to Bobby. He'd sworn to do his best and she believed he would. What she didn't know was if it would be enough.

Bobby was belligerence personified. All his anger and hurt were directed at his older brother. Years of hurt and neglect had left him scarred and his need for revenge was honest, if not healthy. What on earth had she let herself in for?

This center was supposed to be a refuge. A safe haven for the kids—and for her. T.J. Russo's appearance threatened to change all that.

She sipped her coffee. He would be here in a little while. She wasn't prepared. Oh, there was work for him to do, God knows she needed all the help she could get. It was the idea of him so close for long stretches of time that made her nervous. He unsettled her. Big time. What she couldn't figure out was why?

Okay, okay, so he was gorgeous. Big deal. Gorgeous men were nothing but trouble. They got away with murder because they knew they could. She'd never been a sucker for a pretty face or even death-defying shoulders. Except yesterday, when she'd watched him talking to the judge. She should have been going over her paperwork, or comforting Teresa Sarducci, but no. She was too busy staring at his shoulders, his back, the way his jacket fit, the creases in his carefully pressed slacks. She'd lost four minutes looking at his jaw. When he'd turned and glanced her way, she'd blushed. Blushed!

"Get a hold of yourself, girl," she said aloud. "He's just a man."

"Who's just a man?"

Kate nearly dropped her coffee cup as she spun around. Molly stood just inside the kitchen. Barely awake and still in her old chenille robe, her assistant shuffled toward the coffeepot in ancient, wounded bunny slippers. "Talking to yourself is one of the first signs of old age," she said, her voice raspy from sleep.

"Thanks for the insight."

"No problemo."

Kate watched as Molly followed her morning ritual. First coffee, black, then a bagel, sliced carefully and toasted long enough to burn the edges. No butter, God forbid she should add one ounce to her eighteen-year-old, one-hundred-five-pound body. Then she shuffled to the table and grabbed the paper, quickly finding the sports section to check up on her beloved Dodgers.

"What did you and Bobby talk about last night?"

Molly took a sip before she turned half-opened eyes toward her. "Same old, same old. No one understands him. Life isn't fair. Yadda, yadda, yadda."

"And you agreed with his analysis, of course."

"Well, yeah. You know. Us against them, down with the establishment."

"Hey, I'm the establishment."

"I'm just trying to make his transition easier. You know he'll come around."

"No, I don't know that. He's got some real problems."

"They all have real problems and they all come around. If you bring 'em here, that is."

"I'm inspired by your faith in me."

"Well, you could still screw up. There's always a first time."

"Thank you. I'm touched."

Molly snorted in a most indelicate way.

"God, that turns me on."

Kate grinned at the sound of Peter's voice.

"Bite me," Molly said.

Peter came around in back of Molly and nipped her quickly on the neck. He moved like lightning then, because her elbow came back sharp and high. Just like every morning.

These kids were her joy and her headache and she wished summer would never end so they would stay with her, just like this, forever.

Peter made it to the coffee machine and while he poured himself a cup, he turned to Kate. "There's a guy out back. Sitting in a Camaro. Thought you might like to know."

He was here already? She looked at the clock above the sink. Seven-fifteen and he was here? Grabbing her cup, she got up and put it in the sink. She wasn't dressed yet, for God's sake. What was he thinking?

"Is this the guy you have the hots for?" Molly asked.

"What?"

"You know. The one who's just a man?"

"Yes. No. I mean no. He's Bobby's older brother, that's all."

Molly's dark eyebrows raised. "Is he as studly as brother number two?"

"Molly, read your paper. I've got to go get dressed."

"Pardon me, but I'm not the one who was talking to myself."

"What did she say?" Peter asked as he took his seat across from Molly.

"I think it was 'Take me, take me hard, you hunka hunka burning love.'"

Kate lightly thwapped her assistant on the back of the head as she walked past her.

"Hey!"

"Do me a favor, Molly. Stuff it." She got past the kitchen door, then backtracked. "And get Bobby up, would you, Peter?" Then she headed down the hall toward her room.

She didn't make it.

T.J. watched Kate walk down the hall and all he could do was admire the view.

She wore gray sweats and a tank top, no shoes. Her hair was down, tousled from sleep, sexy as hell. The nearer she got, the more aware he became of her size. Nearly as tall as he was, but in the genderless outfit, she was more woman than he thought possible.

"You're here early," she said, stopping a little too far away from him.

"Might as well get started."

She nodded. "Bobby's not up yet. The others are in the kitchen, though. Go introduce yourself while I get dressed."

"Don't change on my account."

She took a small step backward. "It's not on your account. I'm running late."

He walked toward her and when he was at her side, he glanced into one of the rooms. Dozens of supermodel posters on every available surface made him suspect this was not her boudoir. "Who lives here?"

"That's Peter's room." She stepped closer to T.J. to share his view. "He likes girls."

T.J. nodded. "So it seems. Who is he?"

She brought her right hand up and threaded her fingers through her hair, pushing the red strands back, revealing that long neck of hers. A pull at his groin took him by surprise and he quickly looked away. His gaze lit on Cindy Crawford and he sighed in relief. Of course he'd be turned on by her. What red-blooded heterosexual male wasn't?

"Peter's staying here for the summer. His mother was killed in a drive-by shooting last October and he was having some trouble at home. He's in charge of the grade-schoolers. It's been good for him. I expect it will be good for Bobby, too."

T.J. studied the walls in Peter's room, remembering the cramped cells from long ago. "I thought, with the Sisters gone, that this place had changed. But it's still the same way station, isn't it? Only without the religion."

"We don't discourage religion, but yes, you're right. What Father Xavier and the Sisters did here was wonderful. They helped a lot of young people find the right road."

She paused and he could feel her watch him. "But you knew that, didn't you?"

"You have any coffee in this place?"

She nodded and pointed down the hall. "In there. I'll join you in a minute."

As he passed her, his arm brushed hers lightly, just a hint of contact. The sensation traveled straight into his chest and he picked up his pace, just as she did. When he looked back at her, she was walking, fast, rubbing that small section of bare skin with her hand. It was going to be interesting working with her all day.

He moved on down the hall and glanced in the other two rooms to his right, but Bobby wasn't in either. Then he reached the kitchen.

It hadn't changed much. Functional and ugly, it seemed half the size after all these years. A young man close to Bobby's age sat at the table reading the comics. He looked up, nodded, then went back to the paper. Next to him, a girl with very blond hair, cut so short it stood straight up, sat nursing a cup of coffee. She eyed him up one side and down the other and when she reached his face again, the corner of her mouth lifted in a crooked smile.

"Do I pass?"

She nodded. "You'll do."

"T.J. Russo."

"Molly Tyson." She pointed to the young man. "Peter Warren."

"You two live here, huh?

"For the summer. I'm in charge of the nursery. We have a day-care center here for infants and toddlers."

"I'm with grade one through six," Peter said.

"Kate does the rest?"

"We have volunteers most of the time. Like you."

"Yeah. Just like me." He spied the coffeepot on the counter. "May I?"

Molly nodded. "Help yourself."

He found a cup that wasn't chipped and poured.

"Your brother's going to work with me," Molly said. "With the little ones."

"You're kidding." He walked to the table and pulled out a chair. "Bobby?"

She nodded. She was really a pretty girl, despite the unorthodox haircut. Big blue eyes, a generous mouth. Young, maybe eighteen.

"Kate says taking care of the little kids encourages responsibility."

"I'll bet," he said. "Somehow I can't imagine Bobby changing a diaper."

"He'll get used to it."

"Right."

"You'll be working with Kate. I hope you're in shape. She'll run you ragged."

"I think I can hold my own."

"Uh-huh. You know she runs five miles a day. And plays basketball. Baseball, too."

"She likes to wipe everyone out," Peter added. "Make 'em too tired to cause havoc on the streets."

"It's a good plan."

"Most guys can't keep up with her," Molly said.

"I see."

She leaned forward, staring intently into his eyes. "Do you think *you* can? You know, she's six feet tall. She says she's five-eleven, but she's not. She's strong, too. Tough."

He worked hard at keeping a straight face. "I'll keep that in mind."

Molly leaned back. "Okay, then."

So, Kate had her own Praetorian guard. One thing T.J. understood was loyalty. It meant the leadership was fair, the working conditions satisfying. A good police captain got this kind of devotion from his officers. From what he'd already seen of Kate, it wasn't surprising that her assistants felt protective. He would do his best not to disappoint any of them.

Molly had gone back to reading the paper and Peter started doing the crossword puzzle. He must be pretty good at it, using a pen instead of a pencil. T.J. drank some coffee and looked around the room he hadn't been in since high school. It was a damn peculiar world to bring him back here. Damn peculiar.

Kate looked in the mirror above her dresser. What harm would a little mascara do? She lifted the wand to her eye, then brought it back down. No. Why should she put on makeup? She never wore it during working hours. How would she explain it to Molly and Peter, let alone the whole tribe? On the other hand, what did she care what anybody thought? She lifted her hand again and this time she darkened her lashes with the black makeup. Before she lost her nerve, she did the other eye, grabbed a broken piece of rouge and pinked her cheeks. She even took the lipstick from her top drawer and did her lips.

There. She didn't look too, too. Just nice. Like a girl. Hell, Molly wore makeup, didn't she? Most women wore makeup. It didn't mean anything. So put that in your pipe and smoke it, Mr. Russo.

She grabbed her brush and attacked her hair, pulling the bristles through with a vengeance. What was she so upset about? He was only a man! Not even a particularly nice man. He was trouble, hadn't she figured that out yet? The only reason he was in her center was because Bobby needed him. Period. End of story.

She bent double, tossed her hair forward and brushed some more. Damn it, she had rules about men, didn't she? Rules that had served her very well, thank you. Number one—keep your distance. Number two—well, number one pretty much covered it. All her life, men had been nothing but a pain in the behind and T.J. Russo was no exception. She had the center. And the kids. That was enough for anyone. No need to complicate matters.

She rose again, tossing her hair back. He was nothing to her. Nothing. Not even worth a second thought. Grabbing her scrunchie, she tied her hair in a ponytail, then went to the closet and got her running shoes. Another moment and she was finished, ready to start the day. Just like any other day.

She grabbed her whistle from the nail by her door, then went down the hall, feeling the old confidence in her legs and in the strength of her back. She looked forward to her run. To the basketball game she would play this afternoon. To shaping young lives and molding some character.

She reached the kitchen. T.J. looked up at her. His eyes widened and he opened his mouth to speak.

"Excuse me," she said, then turned on her heel. She couldn't get back to her room fast enough. Once there, she slammed the door behind her and went back to her dresser. Plucking a handful of tissues from the box and the jar of cold cream, she attacked her makeup, wiping it away as quickly as she could.

"What were you *thinking?*" she said to the mirror. "Are you out of your mind?" She rubbed harder, practically taking a layer of skin off with the cosmetics. When she was through, she looked a little pink, but not, thank God, from rouge. Now she was Kate. Not some prissy little princess. If he thought for one moment that she was going to change anything for him...

Well, he'd just better not, that's all.

"I don't know nothing about changing no diapers."

T.J. struggled not to laugh at the look on his younger brother's face. His terror was real—and justified, in T.J.'s opinion. Babies were a form of life that was necessary but best left to the experts. Bobby was no expert.

"It's easy," Kate said, walking to the large changing table against the back wall. "Just use a little common sense and be gentle. Nothing's going to hurt you."

Bobby looked at her through narrowed eyes. He'd been unpleasantly awake for about fifteen minutes, refusing coffee and conversation. When Kate had told him that he was to help Molly with the littlest children, he almost made a run for it.

"You can't make me do this," Bobby said, crossing his arms over his chest. "I got rights, you know."

Kate smiled at him. It was the kind of smile one tends to see on prison wardens and math teachers. "But you do have to do this. Or go to jail."

"Maybe I want to go to jail."

"Okay." Kate walked past Bobby toward the door.

T.J. couldn't decide where to look. Bobby was pretty entertaining, what with his dilemma playing across his face like a silent movie, or Kate, who looked sensational in her running shorts and tucked-in T-shirt. Kate won. He'd seen Bobby before.

"Hold it," Bobby said, just as Kate reached the door. "Why can't I work somewhere else?"

Kate stopped and turned. "Because I want you to work here."

"Who died and made you God?"

"The court. You have one hundred and fifty hours of community service to do in little over a month. If you don't do it, you're going to jail for a long time. It won't be pleasant there. Large men will ask you to dance, if you get my drift. So, I recommend that you stop whining about this and listen up. I'm not going to go over this twice."

Bobby turned his gaze from Kate to T.J. All the blame in the world was in his eyes. "You put her up to this, didn't you? You thought it would be funny, huh?"

"Me?" T.J. settled his back against the plastic jungle gym that took up most of the left corner of the room. "Nope. I just work here."

"That's right," Kate said. "He'll get his assignments next. Now, though, I'm going to show you how to change a diaper. Then we'll show you how to work the washer and dryer. By that time, the kids will start arriving. Molly will be in charge and you'll do exactly as she says with no guff. Is that clear?''

T.J. could see Bobby's jaw grind from across the room. Finally, though, he nodded. Kate went back to the changing table and picked up a realistic-looking doll. She proceeded with the lesson, but T.J. preferred to watch the teacher.

Years ago, there had been a comic book that T.J. had liked, even though he didn't dare read it in public. The main character was a woman, a strong, sexy woman who dispatched criminals with an ease that would make Superman weep. Kate reminded him of that character. It wasn't just her physical attributes, although God knows they were legendary in their own right, but her attitude. He'd seen it that first day, when she'd cornered Danny Arcola and he'd seen it again in court yesterday. Her confidence was a tangible thing and it was easy to see how she'd come to gain the respect of not only the kids she worked with, but the police and the judicial officers.

Bobby couldn't be in better hands. As a matter of fact, T.J. wondered what part he was going to play in this soap opera. Maybe he'd overreacted about this whole thing. Bobby didn't need him and his presence here was likely to cause more damage than good.

Molly arrived and joined Kate and Bobby at the changing table. She'd donned a pair of cutoff jeans and a green army T-shirt. He hadn't seen her figure in that oversized robe of hers, but now he noticed that she was exceedingly buffed. Her arm and leg muscles were clearly defined. Not too much bulk, but a hell of a lot of strength there. What was it with the women in this place?

"Molly, you can show him the rest, can't you?" Kate asked.

"You got it, boss. No problemo."

Kate touched Bobby lightly on the arm and he jerked away. She didn't make a big thing of it. She just left him with Molly and walked over to the jungle gym.

"You're really going to trust him with babies?" T.J. asked.

"Not right away. He'll be too busy washing clothes and chasing the toddlers. Molly's awfully good with the kids. And she can keep him in line."

"I'll bet."

Kate nodded toward the door. "Come on. We've got to get you ready. The troops will start arriving soon."

They walked together from the nursery through the grade school area where Peter was setting out clay on long tables, to the big room.

"You were pretty good with him in there," T.J. said.

"It was nothing." She dismissed the compliment with a wave of her hand. "I usually start off the morning with a run. We do about five miles." She looked him over, frowning at his white button-down shirt and pressed jeans, stopping completely at his boots. "Those won't do. You're going to need running shoes, shorts and comfortable clothes. T-shirts, old jeans. That kind of thing. Do you have them?"

He nodded. "At the motel."

She started walking again, moving quickly toward her office. "Can you be back here in fifteen minutes?"

"Whoa, hold on there, skipper. We're moving a bit too fast."

"If you think this is fast, wait till the place is packed with kids."

He reached over and grabbed her arm. The second he touched her she stopped. Her gaze went to his hand then, slowly, she lifted her eyes to meet his.

The effect was unsettling, to say the least. There was fear there, in those green eyes. He could see she wanted to bolt, to get away from him and his touch. It didn't make sense. Not coming from the woman he'd seen in action. Why would she be afraid of him?

Chapter 4

"I'm not going to hurt you," he said softly.

She broke contact, turning her head away and easing out of his grip. "I don't know what you mean."

"Sure you do."

"Look, I've got work to do. Are you going to go get changed or not?"

Her voice seemed higher, faster. What was going on here? Was it the touch? Was she that skittish?

"We need to talk," he said. "How about we go to your office?"

Before he even finished the sentence, she was moving, fast. He followed, curious as hell about her. When she got to her office, she went behind her desk and sat down. He thought about sitting on the small plastic chair across from her, but changed his mind. He stood to the side, forcing her to turn to look at him.

"You wanted to talk," she said. "So talk."

He waited a few beats, trying hard to catch her eye. She wouldn't look at him. "What's all this?"

"I don't know. This is your meeting, remember?"

"I don't mean about that." He took a step closer to her. "I mean about us."

"Us? There is no us."

"Sure there is. There's me...." He moved closer still, wondering when she was going to give in and push her chair back. "And there's you."

She didn't push back. She stood. As tall as she could, right in his face. "Knock it off, Casanova. I'm not one of your Hollywood bimbos. That kind of talk doesn't wash with me."

They were only inches apart. Close enough for trouble. "What kind of talk is that?" He leaned in even farther. He could hear her sharp intake of breath.

"Back off. Or—"

"Or what?" he whispered.

Kate put her hands on his chest, intending to push him away. But when her fingers made contact with the warmth of his skin beneath the shirt, she couldn't move at all.

"The kids will be arriving any second," she said, cringing at the breathy quality in her voice. She cleared her throat. Her hands, seemingly with a mind of their own, lingered on his chest for a second and instead of sensibly dropping to her side, trailed down his shirtfront, feeling the rough texture of hair and the hard muscle beneath the fabric.

"They can play by themselves for a few minutes."

"The door is locked."

"It's nice out."

"Don't do this."

"Do what?"

She couldn't seem to look away. His brown eyes held her steady and close. Heat swelled up from her solar plexus until she felt her cheeks burn, and still she stared into those eyes. She had never been more aware of her own heartbeat.

Then he touched her. With his fingertips, on her arm. She jerked back, out of his reach. Her legs hit the chair, sending it scooting back toward the wall. She turned and put her hand on her desk to steady herself.

His low chuckle chased all her embarrassment out the window, leaving plenty of room for pure, unadulterated anger. She spun around again and this time there was no hypnotic spell or whatever the hell that had been. He was just a guy with an attitude, in her territory.

"Back off, hotshot," she said. "And don't try that little gimmick again. Next time, I'll flatten you. Don't think I can't."

T.J. held up both hands. "Hold on there, Red. I'm innocent. I didn't move a muscle."

She took another step back, preferring the distance between them to be as great as she could make it. "There's you," she said, mimicking his low, seductive tone, "and there's me." She picked up her clipboard and brought it to her chest. "Is that how you talk to your captain?"

He grinned. "The rumors about that are completely untrue. We're just good friends."

"If you want to be friends with me, you'll keep your distance. Got it?"

He nodded. "It's a shame, though. You would've had a lot of fun."

"I'll live." She turned her back on him to retrieve her chair, feeling as though she'd just escaped from a head-on collision. What she couldn't understand was her own reaction. What had happened to her? She'd put that part of her life away for good, hadn't she? No batting eyelashes or heavy breathing for this babe. The decision had been a sound one and she wasn't going to let brown eyes over there change one thing.

She sat and looked at the day's schedule. "After the run, I want to set up teams for basketball. You'll be a captain and so will I. Do me a favor, don't let your glands pick your team. This isn't so much about winning as it is about sportsmanship, so I want everyone to play. Girls, boys, nerds. It doesn't make a difference. They all get a chance.''

"And what makes you think my glands would have any part of this?''

She sighed. "You and I both know that when the testosterone gets moving, winning is all you men can see.''

"Okay, fine. Does that mean when you have PMS, we don't play?''

"What?'' How dare—'' She stopped. "Touché. I apologize. It wasn't fair of me to make that assumption.''

"Damn straight.''

She smiled, but only a little. It wouldn't do to let him get a swelled head. "We can go over the rest of the schedule later. If you hurry, you can get changed and back here before we run. If you're late, we're going without you.''

T.J. walked to the other side of her office and picked up the basketball. "I did want to talk, you know. About Bobby.''

She leaned back, glad to have the conversation move to something completely safe. "Shoot.''

"I think it might be a mistake. Having me here, I mean. I think it's great that you have him in the nursery. It'll be good for him. He'll have to be responsible and he'll have to put his own feelings aside.''

"But . . . ?''

He tossed the basketball lightly into the air and caught it. "Don't you think he'll mellow out a lot faster if I'm not here?''

"Probably.''

"Exactly. So while it's been swell—''

"He'll mellow out, all right. He might even come to like it here. But he'll keep on hating you. You'll lose him forever. Is that what you want?''

His hands stilled on the ball, but he wouldn't look at her. "Can I tell you a secret? Now that we're such good friends and all?"

"I'm listening."

T.J. put the ball down and moved back to the desk. He sat on the edge and folded his arms across his chest. He looked at her, but not in the eye. He focused instead on her mouth. Even that seemed to be too much. He turned away. "I don't know what to do. I realized that last night. I don't know what to say, or how to behave."

"Just be yourself."

He gave her a curt laugh. "Thanks very much, Ms. Manners. That clears everything up."

"I wasn't being flippant. I meant it. You don't have to do anything special. What you're forgetting is that he already loves you. Your job now is to show him you'll be there for him. Running away is the worst thing you could do. He needs to know that no matter what he's like, you'll stick around. It won't be easy. He's going to test you every way to Sunday. But it'll be worth it in the end."

"You sound pretty sure of yourself."

"I am." She stood up and walked to the side of her desk so she could face him. "I'm very good at what I do. I've seen kids like Bobby before. Scared, alone, unsure of who they are and what they want. They're ripe pickings for gang members who offer them solidarity and a place to belong. I can't stop you from leaving, but if you do, Danny's going to win. He's going to be the big brother Bobby needs."

T.J. didn't speak for a long while. He studied her face, but she felt no desire to look away this time. It wasn't a predatory stare, just curious.

"You know what? I think I do want to become friends with you."

The flutter in her stomach caught her off guard. "I'm thrilled beyond measure," she said, making sure the sarcasm was thick. "Now get the hell out of here. We've got a job to do."

He stood and once again the nearness of him seemed to draw the breath right out of her body. But then he stepped away and went to the door.

"I'll be back in ten," he said.

"Do that."

"Then, after our run, I'll show you how the game of basketball is supposed to be played."

"Give me a break."

His laughter lingered after he'd closed the door. Encouraging him to stay was the right thing to do for Bobby. But that meant she was in for a very rough five weeks. Being near T.J. was going to be a lot tougher than any basketball game she'd ever played. And she wasn't even sure which side she was rooting for.

By the time T.J. got back, the center was packed. He thought he recognized some of the kids from his last visit, but he wasn't positive. He didn't see Danny and for that he was grateful. That meeting was not going to be fun. He still remembered the look of unbridled hatred and, more than that, the certainty that Arcola was carrying a weapon. It was bad enough that T.J. was here against his brother's wishes—if Danny and his posse wanted to, they could cause some real trouble.

He hadn't reached Kate's office yet when he heard her whistle. The activity around him came to a faltering halt and all eyes went to the front door.

Kate, head and shoulders above the crowd, waved her clipboard in the air. "Everybody who's going to run, line up here," she yelled.

The noise picked up immediately as kids shuffled around to either get in line or find other things to occupy their time. He heard the crack of billiard balls at the break, the high laughter of young girls, the slap of running shoes on the paneled floors. For some reason, the cacophony made him feel good—hopeful. He made his way through the crowd, mindful of all the stares and comments he incurred. Twice he heard "nice butt," and at least one appreciative whistle.

"Just in time," Kate said, as he reached her side.

"Nice crowd."

Kate looked him over and nodded at his gym shorts, T-shirt and running shoes. "Better," she said. "We run for five miles. Can you keep up?"

"I'll struggle along."

She turned from him and faced the line of kids. "Okay, team. Everybody put on sunblock? Let's go."

"Who's going to stay here to supervise?" he asked.

She pointed to a teenage girl with long, almost white hair. "Jeanne." Then he followed her outstretched finger to the other side of the room, right by the pool tables. "And Joanne."

His brow went up when he saw an exact duplicate of the first girl. "Twins?"

She turned to him with a look that screamed *moron*. "No. They're just good friends."

He gave her a dazzling smile. "Don't try to pull any fast ones on me. I'm a brilliant detective, remember?"

"Right, Sherlock." She shook her head, then hooked her clipboard on a nail by the door and headed out.

They started slowly, with a very gentle pace to warm up. The sound of twenty pairs of feet coming up behind him was disconcerting at first, but soon he was too busy concentrating on his own gait, and the woman next to him, to care.

She ran beautifully, like a Thoroughbred. Head high, shoulders back, easy long strides. It was difficult to keep his eyes off her. His gaze moved down to her chest and the soft bounce of her breasts was as intoxicating as a bottle of champagne.

He opened his mouth to tell her how much he liked her style, when his foot caught on some damn thing and he nearly fell flat on his face. The wild gyrations of his arms kept him upright. The sound of Kate's laughter got him moving again.

"Smooth move, Grace," she said, as he caught up to her.

"You think that's funny, huh?"

"What do you do for an encore?"

"Catch me and find out." With that, he was off. No more of that sissy jogging. He ran, hard, fast, and with a purpose. She didn't have to know that he needed some privacy. That if she were to look down at the front of his gym shorts, she would see that his little stumble had done nothing to quell his reaction to her.

He'd reached the street corner and turned, heading toward the beach. It was only a few blocks away and he felt the need to hear the ocean and feel the spray. She could take her entourage on whatever route they usually followed. He'd meet her back at the center when he'd cooled down.

The light was green at the next corner so he pushed himself to move faster, to feel the strain in his legs. He regulated his strides and took slow, deep breaths. When he reached the next corner, he felt in control enough to ease back. Only one more block to the beach.

He hit his rhythm. Not full-out running, but close. He used to run regularly at home, at a nearby high school. It was a ritual he'd come to enjoy, but after Nick left town, he didn't get down to the track much. The gym either, for that matter. Damn, where had the months gone? He let the guilt go and turned his thoughts to Kate.

What had he been trying to prove back there, in her office? He had been coming on to her, she'd been right about that. It had started off as a kind of test, a lark, to see what she'd do. Everything had gone according to plan, until the moment she'd touched his chest.

There was no explanation for it, but he could swear he still felt her fingers trailing light as a feather down the front of his shirt. The whole way to the motel, he'd thought about it. He'd even rubbed the spot, just to get rid of the phantom sensation, but it hadn't worked. The entire time he'd talked to the desk clerk, he'd kept picturing Kate's eyes. The fear, followed by the flash of desire that had flared then vanished without a trace.

He reached the edge of the pier and took his speed down another notch. He was breathing harder now and once he got on the sand he would need the energy.

He went down the long flight of concrete steps, taking in the familiar view. The old place looked just the same, down to the graffiti on the pilings. How many times had he taken girls here, under the wooden walkway, and kissed them till the world tilted sideways?

His meanderings were interrupted by the sound of running feet behind him. When he hit the sand, he turned his head to see who was coming so quickly and he nearly fell down when he saw it was Kate! What the hell?

She hit the sand at a run and shot past him like a bullet. He'd left her in his tracks two miles ago. Had she caught a cab? He looked back once again. No kids. Had she ditched them, like he'd ditched her? Picking up his pace, he followed Kate right down to the breakwater.

Man, she was moving. He could feel his heart thumping in his chest, his throat burn with each intake of oxygen. She was still several yards ahead of him and she didn't appear to be straining any important muscles. At least not from this angle.

She'd have to slow down soon, he thought. No way she was going to keep up this pace. He was starting to hurt now and he pressed his side with his palm to ease the beginnings of a stitch. If he had any brains at all, he'd ease up. But he'd rather have a stroke than let up before she did. Only she never did.

Going back to the sidewalk through the soft sand was pure torture. His calf muscles burned, his thighs, well they just plain screamed for mercy. Still, she didn't slow down.

Thankfully they reached the sidewalk and he was positive she was going to stop. But no, she crossed the street and kept on going. Damn it all to hell, she didn't even look back. Which was a good thing, because he didn't want her to witness his actual death.

He stopped. There was no choice. He gasped for air like a fish out of water, each oxygen molecule burning his throat all the way down to his lungs. His side pulsed with pain and his legs trembled. If he could have spoken, he would have cussed a blue streak.

Bent double, massaging his thighs with his thumbs, he didn't hear the kids until they were on top of him. The whole pack, every one, passed him by. Their laughter was louder than his gasps and he raised a fist at their backs, but he had to drop it. He was in shape, damn it! No way he was going to let this happen.

He started in again. So what if he had a heart attack? It would be better than straggling back into the center. It wasn't too hard to catch up and pass the kids, but he didn't even see Kate.

Turning the final corner, trying to remember if he'd ever made out a will, he spotted her. She was a block and a half ahead. But not for long.

There was no energy left to have a single thought, let alone plan his race. He just ran. Pumping his arms, keeping his head low and streamlined, blocking everything from his view but one nicely shaped rear end, he jammed.

The rear end got closer. Closer. He kept his eyes on it, aware in some primitive part of his brain that although he was surely about to die, it would be all right if he could just keep looking at that derriere.

Then he looked up and saw they were almost at the center. Loath as he was to give up the view, he switched his gaze to the door. He ran full bore and God help anyone who got in his way.

* * *

She beat him.

He'd run with his whole heart and soul and the woman had passed him by. She crossed the threshold three full paces ahead of him. Oh, she was breathing hard, but who cared. She'd beat him.

He bent over, not sure if he was going to throw up or not. Kate stood next to him, doubled over herself, hands on her knees. He heard her gasps for breath over his own. Good, he hoped she'd pulled two hamstrings.

"I—" He took another breath. "I—" He swallowed and wiped his brow. A few more breaths, until the ability to speak returned. "I—really hate you."

"Then—" She stopped, shook her head, shook her arms, leaned down again and turned to face him. "Then my work here is done."

Damn if she didn't get a smile out of him. Damn.

When her breathing became steady and normal, which took considerably longer than she'd liked, Kate retrieved her clipboard from the nail on the wall. She stared at the schedule, but her eyes didn't focus. She was still too busy thinking about her sweet, sweet victory.

Sure it was childish. But that didn't take away one iota of pleasure. The look on his face when she'd passed him at the pier was something she would treasure forever.

She was used to beating the boys. Hell, her five brothers had given her all the practice she needed. The basketball scholarship that had sent her through school was no token. She'd worked incredibly hard, taken her body and mind to the limit, until they'd won the national championships and she'd gotten her degree. But winning today's race was nearly as satisfactory.

Detective Russo had just been taken down a mighty big peg. Maybe now he wouldn't be so all-fired cocky. Nah. She shook her head. It would take a lot more than a footrace to knock the wind out of his sails. But she wasn't going to let that spoil anything. At least he knew who he was messing with.

Next on the agenda was basketball. Although T.J. was slightly taller than she was, she knew he didn't have her years of experience on the court. She could wipe the floor with him, if she chose.

He was still walking the perimeter of the room, working off his leg cramps. He'd been a real good sport about her win—for a guy, anyway. What the heck. She'd take it easy on him for the rest of the day. Let him get a little bit of his pride back.

"Kate?"

Peter was standing near her, looking at the front door.

"What's up?"

"I heard a rumor that Danny Arcola was coming here, looking for trouble."

"Great. When?"

"Don't know. Look, I gotta get back to the muppets. I just wanted to warn you."

"Thanks." She searched the room until she found T.J. He was near the drinking fountain talking to Alice Dee. That meant trouble, right there.

Threading through the crowd, she realized she should have briefed T.J. on some of the more challenging kids, including Miss Hot Pants. It didn't seem to matter how hard Kate tried, the girl was determined to get her self-worth from men. Any men.

As she neared, T.J. caught sight of her and raised his eyebrows. Then Alice said something else and he faced her again.

"...so boring. I mean, come on. High school boys? As if! I wouldn't be caught dead with any of them. Not even Cody Stevens. He's the football captain and everyone says he's so cute, but I don't think so. He's totally immature. Not like you.''

"You'd be surprised how immature I am," T.J. said with a perfectly straight face.

The girl giggled and flipped her hair back in an ancient and honored mating dance.

"Alice."

At Kate's word, Alice spun around. Her cheeks infused with pink and her gaze immediately shifted to her shoes. "Hi, Kate," she said, her voice filled with guilt.

"Joanne is starting her knitting class in about five minutes. You'd better hurry if you want a seat."

"Knitting? I don't—" Alice looked up and saw Kate's expression. "Oh, yeah," she said, backing away. "I did want to go to that." She turned and walked so quickly she bumped right into the famous Cody Stevens. "Oh, God," she cried, putting her hands to her face.

"You okay?" the boy asked.

Alice shook her head and ran straight toward the rest room.

It served her right, Kate thought.

"Now, was that nice?" T.J. wasn't smiling, although she heard the humor in his tone. "She was just trying to make me feel welcome."

"She's seventeen, Russo. In these parts, that means jail."

"You shock me, Ms. Dugan."

"I'll bet."

He grinned then and it was so good-natured that she had to grin back. Then she remembered why she'd come to get him. "Rumor has it that Danny Arcola is on his way here."

"How nice for him."

"This isn't a joke. He can be hell on wheels."

"I think I can handle it."

"You have to do more than that. For six or seven hours a day, I know where Danny and his friends are going to be. Here. Which means they're not out there. Get it?"

He nodded. "In other words, don't chase him off?"

"Right. He's safe here and the rest of the city is safe too. I'd like to keep it that way."

"Whatever you say, Red."

"Quit calling me that. The name is Kate. It only has one syllable, so it shouldn't be too hard for you."

"You flatter me."

"I know."

"Are we doing basketball now?"

She nodded. "Remember—"

"No glands."

"Right.

He held his arm in front of him and bowed slightly from the waist. "After you."

She shook her head and turned toward the door. He came up next to her and touched her lightly on the small of the back. Her whole body shivered and the flesh on her arms and legs rose in a mass of goose bumps. She walked a little faster, but he kept up, his hand still hovering right above her waist.

She wanted to jerk away, to make him stop. It shouldn't have bothered her.

Certainly she'd been touched there before, by men she'd liked a lot better than him and nothing like this had happened. But then her body had been acting strangely for a few days now. Maybe she was coming down with something.

"Anything you want to tell me before we reach the court?" he asked, his voice as calm as could be.

At least he hadn't realized how jumpy she was. "Yeah. Don't pick Alice."

He laughed and her stomach fluttered, just like this morning. She must be getting the flu. She'd double up on her vitamin C starting tonight.

They reached the front door and Kate stopped briefly to put up her clipboard and take a second whistle from the hook. "Here," she said to T.J. as she held out the long cord. "You'll need this."

He took it from her and lifted his arms to put it around his neck. His T-shirt pulled up, exposing an inch of his belly. She saw he was an "innie," and that the hair she'd touched from outside his shirt tapered to a thin line just above the waistband of his shorts.

"What's wrong?" T.J. lifted his shirt a little higher and bent to stare at his stomach. "My fly can't be open, 'cause I don't have one."

She felt her cheeks grow warm as she started outside. "Nothing's wrong," she said. "I was thinking, that's all."

He hurried to her side, leaned close to her and whispered, "I'd like to hear those thoughts."

She stopped, put the whistle in her mouth and blew for all she was worth.

T.J. put his hands to his ears and cringed. "Jeez. Now *that's* effective birth control."

"Line up, everyone," she yelled, turning away from T.J. so he wouldn't see her grin. "Karl," she called to a young man by the door. "Go tell Jeanne to announce that basketball teams are forming out here."

Karl took off and a river of young people flowed through the doors. The chatter was loud and friendly and spirits were high and clearly excited. They all loved the basketball games, none more than she. Some of the kids were great and some couldn't shoot a basket if their lives depended on it, but everyone had a good time. That was her goal. To make every one of these kids feel important and part of a team.

"Hey, who's the old guy?"

Kate grinned and shouted, "The old guy is Detective T.J. Russo. He's going to be the other team captain."

"What?" T.J. cupped a hand over his ear. "I can't hear ya," he said, his voice high and quavering. "Anyone seen my cane?"

The laughter from the kids sounded wonderful. This might just work out, she thought. For Bobby and for T.J.

She looked up and he winked at her. It tickled her in a way that was completely uncalled-for. It wasn't as if she were Alice Dee, trying to get the good-looking cop to notice her. For heaven's sakes, she was beyond that nonsense.

"How many teams are there going to be?"

"Can I be on the team with Tony?"

"I want to be a guard."

"You couldn't guard me on your best day, you little squirt."

Kate blew her whistle for silence. After a few seconds, it worked and all eyes were focused her way.

"Okay, we're going to pick players for four teams. Remember, everyone gets to play. No exceptions."

Several of the taller boys groaned.

"If you don't like the rules, you don't have to participate. There's a knitting class starting inside. I'm sure Joanne would love to have you there, Darnel and Frank."

The miscreants shoved each other good-naturedly, then settled down.

"Darnel, why don't you come be on my team," she said.

The young man slapped his friend on the back of the head and jogged to her side.

It was maybe seventy-two degrees, the breeze was coming in from the ocean and her kids were all happy. It was good to be alive. "T.J., you need some help?"

He shook his head, then pointed into the crowd. Sly "Stallone" Richardson started toward him, but T.J. said, "Nope, sorry, I meant the pretty girl right next to you."

Sly and everyone else in the crowd turned to face the girl. Kate had to move to see who he was referring to. It was Pam Greer, a shy, slightly overweight fourteen-year-old. Blushing furiously, Pam inched her way toward T.J. When she got close enough, he leaned down and said, "You can be my assistant, okay? Help me pick the winning team?"

"I don't know how," she said softly, her cheeks still rosy.

"Have you watched these guys play before?"

Pam nodded, unable to look him in the face.

"Well, I haven't. So you've got that one up on me."

"I—" She took a little step back, then tried again. "I'm not a very good player."

"That's okay. I'm not, either. But I can tell, just by looking at you, that you have a good head on your shoulders. Trust me, you'll be great."

Kate smiled. T.J. couldn't have done anything better for the girl. What Pam needed was a good dose of self-esteem and it looked to Kate as if she were going to get it. She glanced at T.J., wondering if he realized just what he'd done.

He was laughing at something and for the first time, she noticed how much laughter changed him. She couldn't put her finger on it, it wasn't anything physical. Looking at his smile, seeing the kids smile at him in return, she wondered what had happened to the angry man she'd met just a few days ago. Had that been an anomaly? Was this the real T.J. Russo?

"Hey, how about picking me, police man."

Kate froze. She followed T.J.'s gaze to the back of the crowd. To Danny Arcola and his gang. They must have just turned the corner.

"No, Danny," she called out. "I need you on my team."

Danny didn't look at her. He kept staring at T.J. The crowd sensed trouble and moved apart until there was no one between the gang leader and the detective.

"How 'bout you and me doing a little one-on-one, police man."

"This is team basketball, Danny," Kate said.

"Wasn't talkin' 'bout no basketball, lady." He nodded toward T.J. "You here to teach Bobby how to steal cars, man? I heard you was good at that. I heard you was good at armed robbery, too. Or was that your old man?'' Kate watched as T.J. transformed once again. His back stiffened, his hands curled into tight fists and the red-hot anger in his eyes could have melted steel.

Chapter 5

T.J. stared at Danny Arcola's insolent face. He wanted to wipe off that smug expression. He might have, if it wasn't for Kate and the kids.

"I'm not going to tangle with you, Arcola. You either shut up and play the game, or get out. I don't have time for this."

"You'd better make time, police man." Danny moved toward him slowly. His clothes were familiar to T.J.—jeans three sizes too big, a dirty T-shirt that hung nearly to his knees. The way he walked, with one leg stiffened to cause a sway, was as much a part of the gang uniform as the backward cap on his head.

"You want to fight?" T.J. asked. "You're kidding, right? You think I'm really gonna fight with you? Here?"

"Not if you send Bobby out."

T.J. shook his head. "Get serious."

"You better take me serious, man."

"Or what?"

T.J. saw Kate in his peripheral vision. She was moving toward Danny. He stepped forward, trying to intercept her before she reached the boy. Just in time, he reached his hand out and grabbed her arm. "I've got this."

She whipped around to look at him and he was taken aback at the anger in her face. "Let go of me," she said, her voice low and fierce.

He did. But he moved closer to her at the same time. "This is inevitable," he whispered. "We have to get it over with now."

"No fights. I told you what I expected of you."

"So have a little faith. I know what I'm doing."

She stared at him, hard. He could see she didn't trust him. But if they were going to do this for the next five weeks, she'd have to.

The decision came slowly, but finally she nodded and stepped back. T.J. looked again at Danny, who'd watched the little drama with great interest.

"You better listen to her, man," Danny said. "She don't want me to hurt you."

T.J. kept moving until he was inches away from Danny. The boy held his ground, even though he had to look up into T.J.'s face.

"Why don't we take this conversation around back," he said. "Just the two of us."

Danny glanced behind him at his gang, then shook his head. "They go where I go."

"You don't want them to see this."

"Why, you afraid they'll see you beg for mercy?"

T.J. smiled. "Let me tell you a little story."

Danny snorted and moved his hand, presumably to push T.J. back. He never got the chance. T.J. grabbed his arm and pressed his flexor muscle with his thumb just hard enough to make the kid sweat. He'd turned to make sure no one could see the maneuver. As far as the rest of his gang was concerned, they were having a nice intimate chat.

"See, there was this kid, once. In Hollywood." He kept his voice low, speaking so only Danny could hear. "He had a gang, maybe you've heard of them. The Crips?"

Danny jerked, trying to get his arm free, but T.J. just increased the pressure. He knew that the boy was hurting, that the muscle he'd dug his thumb into was so close to the nerves that the pain must be excruciating. "He called me out. Told everyone he was going to put me in the ground. Made a promise, in front of God and everybody that I would go down and not get up again."

Danny's anger was as palpable as the ocean breeze. T.J. could smell his fear, his rage, and he knew if he didn't do this right, there was every chance this punk would try to kill him.

"Let go of me, man. I don't give a shit about your story."

"You'd better, son. You'd better listen and learn. That boy, that gang-banger, was tougher than you. He had better weapons and three hundred boys behind him. He's dead now. Got it? There was no discussion. He didn't stand a chance. You know why? Because I learned to kill when I was ten years old. I'm not a bleeding-heart liberal. I'm your worst nightmare. I've got a gun and permission to use it. No one's going to blink an eye if I shoot you. No one's going to ask questions. They're just going to breathe a little easier because another scumbag's off the street."

He leaned closer, so his mouth was right next to Danny's ear. "So you got a choice. Back off, play nice, don't get in my way, or you won't be playing in this yard. Ever again. What's it going to be?"

Danny's eyes were narrow and a sheen of perspiration covered his forehead. His breathing was rapid and T.J. didn't think that was all from pain.

"I'm even gonna give you a deal. No one has to know about our little chat. It'll be between you and me. You can tell them all that you decided to back off, for Kate's sake. Do something nice for the lady. Okay?"

T.J. wasn't sure what Danny was going to say. He hoped it would be the right answer. Despite what he'd said, he had no desire to kill this kid. But boys like Danny couldn't be reasoned with, despite Kate's Pollyanna attitude. They understood fear and they understood death.

"Let go."

"What's it going to be?"

Danny tugged at his arm, but T.J. gave no quarter. "All right," he said, through clamped teeth. "Let go."

"You gonna leave Bobby alone?"

"If he wants to come with me, that's his business."

T.J. stopped for a second. It was true. He couldn't expect Danny to abandon everything. It would be T.J.'s job, not Danny's, to make sure Bobby didn't join the gang. "Fair enough. Now," he said, letting go of Danny's arm. "Go tell Kate that we've worked everything out. Make it good."

Danny rubbed his arm and stared at T.J. with hatred. But something had shifted. The rage was tempered with a drop of respect. Not enough, he'd wager. But the battle wouldn't be with guns or knives. It wouldn't be a physical contest of strength between the two of them.

They would be playing for Bobby's soul.

Danny would do everything in his power to get Bobby in his gang. And if he fell and joined, Danny would take his anger out on Bobby. All that was in his eyes. Right there, for T.J. to see.

He nodded once and Danny turned to Kate, but not until they both understood that the new rules were in place and it was every man for himself.

"Hey, Kate," Danny said, loud this time, so his posse could hear. "Police man here tells me you don't want me to hurt him. That right?"

Kate looked from Danny to T.J., then back again. "That's right."

Danny nodded and stuck his hands into his pockets. "So okay. I won't hurt him. As long as he keeps in line, you know what I mean? Nobody touches my boys. Got it?"

"I see," she said, even though she didn't. What had T.J. said to him?

"Okay, then. We gonna play basketball or what?"

Kate wasn't convinced that this was the end of their troubles with Danny. A postponement, maybe. But the tension was still too thick to believe everything had been worked out. "Why don't you be on my team, Danny?"

He turned to face his posse. She could see his grin. It was sexual, feral. She had been made part of this truce, but she wasn't quite sure how.

Danny walked toward her, strutting like a peacock. When he got close, she noticed the mark on his arm, where T.J. had held him. A bruise was already starting to blossom.

Danny took off his cap, wiped his hair with his hand, then put it on again. "I'm gonna be center, Kate. Got that?"

Normally she would have told Danny that she would decide who played what, but something told her he needed this little victory. "Of course," she said, and did her best to smile.

She moved back toward the middle of the court, darting another glance at T.J. He seemed subdued, as if his victory hadn't been all he'd hoped for. But at least they weren't fighting. For now.

"Who should we pick?" T.J. said to Pam. She looked from him to Danny, and Kate could see she'd been frightened. They'd all been frightened.

"Cody," she whispered.

T.J. turned around, facing the crowd. "Cody? Who's that?"

Cody Stevens, Alice Dee's football hero, moved forward through the crowd. "That's me, coach."

T.J. leaned sideways, toward Pam. "You really think he's good?"

"He's the football captain," she said.

"But this is basketball."

"Hey, you think I can't play?"

"Quiet. I'm discussing this with my general manager." He leaned down again. "Well? Are you sure?"

Pam smiled shyly. "I think so."

"Done," T.J. said. "Son, you've made the team."

"It's about time," Kate said. "Is it going to take you this long to pick each player? We'll be here till tomorrow."

"This is serious business, Ms. Dugan. Because my team is going to whip the collective butt of your team."

"Not in this lifetime, Russo," Kate said, laughing. She looked around. The spirits that Danny Arcola had managed to snap were rallying again. Laughter, banter, good-natured shrugs. Slowly but surely they were getting back to normal.

T.J. had asked her to trust him. She had, but as soon as this game was over, she was going to find out the terms of this peace treaty. Something told her this had only been a battle, not the war.

Kate blew her whistle and Danny grabbed the ball from Cody, holding it tight against his stomach until the guards settled down.

"Foul," she called. "On Franco. Holding."

"What?" Franco, the accused, put his hands on his hips and glared at Kate. "I didn't hold nothin'."

T.J. walked across the court to Kate's side. "Knock it off, kid," he said as he passed the boy. "You heard the lady."

"I can handle my own calls," she said as soon as he was close enough. "Thank you."

"You're welcome."

"I didn't mean thank you."

"Sure you did. Besides, he wasn't holding."

"What?"

T.J. blew his whistle to get the game started again. He watched the play intently, not sparing her even a brief glance. "I said, he wasn't holding. But that's okay. You've been pretty accurate with most of your calls. We can let this one go."

"Of all the stupid, egotistical—"

The blare of his whistle made her wince and before she knew it, T.J. was in the center of the court, holding the ball, telling Danny Arcola that it was his fifth personal foul and he was now out of the game.

Her pulse accelerated as she jogged over, keeping her eyes on Danny, cursing T.J. Russo for distracting her. The game had been going so well, too. Almost everyone had played, there were ten minutes left in the fourth quarter and now this.

"I didn't do no foul, man. You're blind."

"You grabbed Cody's shorts and practically ripped them off. You don't consider that a foul?"

"It was an accident!" Danny turned to Kate. "Tell him. You saw it."

She hadn't. She'd been too busy grousing at T.J. "If Coach Russo says you fouled, then that's it. You're out."

"No way. He's crazy. I didn't do nothin'."

"You call the king of all wedgies nothing?" Cody moved to face Danny. He towered over the gang leader, yet he still kept a respectful distance.

"Get outa my face, jock itch."

"Don't you call me—"

Kate blew her whistle this time. It served its purpose and stopped the argument. But it didn't make her feel any better about how she'd dealt with things today.

T.J. was disrupting everything. Her morning coffee, her run, the game. If this was an indication of how things were going to go for the next five weeks, they were all in serious trouble. As soon as this game was over, she was going to have a talk with the handsome detective and do a little humility enhancement work.

"Danny. You're out." She held up her hand when he started to speak. "Don't argue. I was going to pull you out anyway. It's Sherryl's turn to be center."

She waved the tall brunette onto the court, then turned to Cody. "You're out, too."

"What?"

"What?"

T.J. and Cody yelled in stereo, but she kept her eyes on the football star. "That's right. It's time for Pam to play. She's hasn't been in yet."

"But—"

Kate gave him *the look*. It worked. His curse was detailed and clinical, but he did leave the court.

"That's my team, you know."

Kate shivered as T.J.'s breath hit the back of her neck. He stood so close to her his arm touched her side.

"It's *my* team. You're here on a guest pass, buddy, and don't forget that."

She expected a smart-ass retort, but when the silence stretched, she turned to face him. The look in his eyes made her want to take back her words.

"I'm sorry. I didn't mean that."

He nodded. "Yes, you did. You're right. I've overstepped. I'm sorry."

"Wait a minute."

"Hey, are we gonna finish this game or what?"

Kate turned to Franco and nodded, then took hold of T.J.'s arm and led him to the sidelines. She blew her whistle, but didn't watch the play. Her gaze was on T.J.'s face, on the hurt she'd put there. "I was kidding around."

"No, you weren't. I don't belong here. I don't know what I'm doing."

"You're doing great. Honest."

He gave her a limp smile. "I think I'll go check on Bobby. You can end this up alone, right?"

She almost said no. "Sure. Go on ahead. It'll be lunch soon."

He took the whistle from around his neck and handed it to her. She watched as he walked slowly around the court, not once looking at the furious action beside him. He just stared straight ahead and went inside.

The game went on and she shifted her attention to the ball, but her thoughts stayed on T.J. He was a curious mixture of bravado and helplessness. So secure in his masculinity and in his humor and, she was sure, in his job. But when it came to this—to caring for the young people, for giving a gentle, guiding hand, he had all the right instincts but none of the confidence. No wonder he kept trying to back out of his promise to Bobby. He was just plain scared he would screw it up.

She still intended to talk to him after the game, but the agenda had just changed.

T.J. leaned against the nursery door. He had no idea how long he'd been there, just that he had no intention of moving. Not while Bobby was playing with the baby.

His half brother was sitting in the corner, near the changing table. His back was to Molly and occasionally he would turn to make sure she wasn't watching him. Then he would go back to the little one. T.J. couldn't see if it was a boy or girl, just that it was bald and smiling toothlessly at Bobby. Despite the racket around him, T.J. heard the squeal of laughter coming from the corner. Bobby held a little doll of some kind and he was using it like an airplane—zooming it from far above his head, down and around the baby until finally tickling her tummy. The sight was a revelation for T.J. He'd known Bobby would be working with the babies, but never in his wildest imagination had he pictured Bobby enjoying himself like this. He'd figured that his brother would pout most of the time, give Molly a hard time and generally make a nuisance of himself. Now, here he was, acting as if playing with the pre-verbal set was a walk in the park.

As much as he was enjoying the spectacle, it brought home again that he didn't know Bobby at all. He didn't know what the kid wanted from life, what made him laugh—hell, he didn't even know if Bobby had a sense of humor. All he'd meant to T.J. these past years was guilt. And anger.

He *was* on a damn guest pass. Not just in the center, either.

"Hey, Sanduski. Finally found yourself a chick who wants to be wit' you?"

T.J. heard Danny's voice, but he didn't turn to look at him. His eyes were on Bobby. His brother had spun at the first word, dropped the little doll from his hand and stared at the gang leader. His face reddened as he took in the sight of his big brother and Danny Arcola, who'd watched him play with the infant. T.J. could see the shame wash through him, followed quickly by a rage that made his hands tremble.

"We don't take no *women* in the gang, Sanduski. No wonder you brought your big brother to stay here with you. He can wipe your nose when it gets runny."

Bobby started toward them and T.J. wasn't sure if his brother was going to bolt or fight. Either way, he was going to stop it.

"Don't listen to this jerk, Bobby." T.J. turned to Arcola. "Get lost, before I turn you inside out."

Danny's laugh was filled with derision. "Sure thing, police man. I don't like hanging around all these babies anyway."

Danny walked away and T.J. turned back to Bobby, but not quickly enough. Bobby was already at him and both hands hit T.J. square in the chest, pushing him backward, nearly costing him his balance.

"What'd you have to bring him here for?" Bobby was yelling, his voice shaking with his humiliation. "It's not enough you have to make a fool of me in the jail, but you have to bring *him* here? Why the hell are you doing this to me? I hate your guts, you bastard. Just keep away from me."

After Bobby darted into the hall, T.J. set off after him, cursing Danny Arcola and the bad luck that had followed him all day. He caught sight of Bobby just as he reached the main room.

It was crowded and Bobby shoved his way through toward the door. T.J. heard the protests of kids being pushed aside, even recognized Alice Dee's high-pitched squeal as T.J. struggled to catch his brother before he made it outside.

He was too late. He stepped into the sunlight and looked right, then left, but Bobby was nowhere to be found. "Damn it all to hell."

"What's going on?"

Kate was beside him and when he looked at her, he saw a crowd had gathered in back of her, which wasn't surprising considering the spectacle he and Bobby had just made.

"He split. Do you know where he went?"

Kate shook her head. "I don't have a clue. Not if Danny is still here."

"Danny is why he left. He found Bobby in the nursery, playing with one of the babies."

"I see," Kate said.

If she was worried, she sure wasn't showing it. He was struck again by the strength of her as she stood tall beside him, staring down the empty street in front of the center. She seemed all grace and composure and he found his pulse slip into an easier rhythm just watching her.

"Maybe he went home."

"To Gus?" T.J. asked. "Not likely."

"Gus may be horrible, but he's familiar. Bobby's afraid. He's going to go somewhere he can feel safe."

"There's no safety at his home. Believe me."

"We aren't talking about you."

He met her gaze and in that glance he knew she saw right through him, down into the secrets he used to think he kept hidden. He looked away. "I'll go. I'll bring him back."

"Maybe," she said.

"I don't want him in jail."

"You may have no choice," she said gently. "Sometimes, it just doesn't work out the way we want it to."

He smiled and sighed. "If it were only sometimes, that would be enough."

He walked across the street, not looking back at Kate or the kids or the center. He could have gone back inside and changed, grabbed his car keys and driven to his mother's house, but he wanted to walk. He needed the time to think.

What the hell was he going to say to Bobby if he ever found him? Right now it was hard to come up with one reason Bobby should come back to the center. It wasn't going to do any good. The cards had been dealt and all any of them could do was play out the hand.

Kate locked the front doors, grateful the workday had come to a close. Exhaustion made her muscles ache and her eyes gritty. Where the hell was T.J.?

Neither he nor Bobby had returned to the center. Only now, when the last kid had been picked up, did she realize how many times she'd thought about the detective and his brother.

She'd tried to picture where they were, if they'd met, if they'd fought. The truth was, she didn't know either of them well enough to make any guesses. She'd find out the truth when they came back. If they came back.

"Are you gonna stand there all night? I'm starving to death."

Trust Molly to put a smile on her face. "I'll trade you dinner duty tonight," she called. "Even better. I'll do your laundry all next week if you cook tonight."

"Deal."

"You haven't heard from Bobby, have you?"

Molly shook her head. "He did pretty good with the kids today. Better than I thought he would."

"Yeah?"

"I think he kind of liked it. Of course he didn't do any diaper changes. That, we'll have to work up to."

"I hope so."

Molly turned to leave but stopped before she got to the door. "You sure about that laundry thing? A whole week?"

Kate's nod earned a huge smile.

"Sucker!"

She laughed. Molly was getting the better of her, but she just couldn't face the kitchen. Not right now. It was all she could do to walk around the big room and pick up. Odd bits of paper, a broken cassette, three brand-new number two pencils and a silver condom packet—unopened. Well, at least someone had *thought* about safe sex. She tucked the packet into her pants and threw the rest of the garbage in the big barrel just before she turned off the lights.

Peter had already cleaned up from the grade-school kids and Kate was sure Molly had done the same in the nursery. Trust her crew to be efficient without complaint. She was the one who felt whiney tonight.

What she wanted was a bath. A real bath where she could soak her whole body at the same time. Bubbles up to here. A glass of wine. Pink candles. Pavarotti singing *Nessun Dorma*.

She sighed. The only part of that equation she had any hope of actually getting was the wine. There was a bottle in the back of the fridge. At least it was there a month ago.

Molly was chopping veggies when Kate made it into the kitchen. As usual, her assistant was cooking with the finesse of a bull moose. Pots, pans, knives and food were spread around her on all available surfaces. Kate thought about helping, but discarded the idea immediately. Without saying a word, she turned down the hall and went back toward her room. She'd change, wash up. Try not to think about T.J.

She reached for her door, then stopped. She heard a sound coming from Bobby's room. Crossing the hall quickly, she pushed his door open, wondering what she was going to say to the boy.

It didn't matter. Bobby wasn't there. T.J. was. He held one of Bobby's baseball caps in his hand. For a long time, he didn't move and she didn't, either. Finally he looked at her. His gaze held nothing but sadness.

"I didn't find him," he said softly. "I should have, but I didn't."

"He'll come back."

T.J. shook his head. "There's been another fire. Bobby was seen near the store. I don't think he'll ever come back again."

Chapter 6

Kate took a step toward T.J., but stopped when she saw him flinch. It was a subtle move and she might have missed it in another man. Not with T.J., though. For whatever reason, she was able to read him. At least when he let down his tough-guy facade.

Right now, there was none of the brash, cocky cop. Only a big brother who'd made some big mistakes. Who didn't want or need her comfort.

"I'll call the station," she said.

He nodded, fingering the lettering on the cap, tracing the *L* of Lakers with his thumb. "I went to the house. No one was there. I waited for a long time."

"How did you find out about the fire?"

"Gus. He showed up about forty minutes ago."

"Damn," she said.

"You got that right."

"Well, how did he hear about it?" She kept wanting to move closer to him, even just to see him better, but she forced herself to stay perfectly still.

"I never asked. It was a pretty one-sided conversation. He wasn't particularly interested in my opinions."

She looked him over carefully, studying the knuckles on the hand she could see—his right hand. There were no bruises or cuts. So they'd avoided a fistfight. This time.

"What were his?"

"Don't know. Maybe he expects Bobby to run away. He sure doesn't think he'll come back here."

"Do you?"

He tossed the cap onto the bed. "How the hell would I know?" He turned to her, sticking his hands into the pockets of his jeans and she wondered when he'd changed clothes. The last time she'd seen him, he'd still been in his running shorts.

"I was the idiot out there all day," he continued, "thinking we had this thing wrapped up. That Bobby was going to get one look at those little babies in there and grow wings. All day I've been real busy patting myself on the back for my insight and wisdom."

His gaze found hers and the accusation there let her know he wasn't confining his ill will to himself. He blamed her, too.

"You didn't do anything wrong. For God's sake, it's the first day."

"And last."

"Not necessarily."

He seemed to have no response to that, except the cold stare. She thought of this afternoon, the look on his face when they'd raced back to the center. The sound of his laughter when one of the kids made a joke. She wanted that man back. "I'm going to the phone," she said. "Molly's working on dinner. Why don't we meet in the kitchen and plan from there."

He shrugged his shoulder in as noncommittal a way as possible, but she couldn't help that. Right now, she had to talk to her friends on the force and get the real skinny. "If you want to stay here and pout, be my guest," she said. "It's up to you."

With that, she left Bobby's room and went quickly toward her office. When she sat at her desk, she reached for the phone but didn't pick it up. She'd sounded so sure of herself back there, but that had been some kind of reaction to T.J.'s indifference. The truth was, she was deeply disappointed, too. T.J. hadn't come up with those dreams. He'd gotten them from her, special delivery. Good old Pollyanna strikes again.

Sighing, she picked up the receiver and hit the speed dial number for the Harbor Bay police. She didn't recognize the voice on the phone and asked to speak to the desk officer. A few moments of piped in music and then, "Tucker."

"Randy. It's Kate. What's this about another fire?"

She heard the sound of a siren in the background. That and shuffling paper. Odd that those two noises were all it took to form a complete picture of the station.

"They hit the Stop-N-Go on 7th and Fortuna. Gutted the place, but no one was seriously hurt. Mr. Calloway, the proprietor, was beat up, but not enough to put him in the hospital."

"Did he recognize who did it?"

"Nope. Never saw a one. At least that was his story."

"You think he's afraid to talk?"

"Wouldn't you be?"

She nodded, even though she knew he couldn't see her. "What do you think? Who was it?" No use planting the seed of Bobby's being there if it didn't already exist. She held her breath while she waited for his response. Two, three seconds while she struggled not to cross her fingers.

"Odds are on Arcola. Maybe this time we'll get something on him. But then again."

"That's it? Nothing special about this one?"

"What's going on with you, Kate? Is something wrong?"

So much for her acting ability. "No, nothing."

"You know something we don't?"

"No. No, trust me. Thanks. I'll speak to you later, okay?"

She heard his goodbye faintly as she hung up the phone. Randy was a good guy. He would have told her if Bobby was under suspicion.

Had Gus made the whole thing up to bait T.J.? Having seen the two of them together, she wouldn't doubt it. It didn't matter now. Bobby's whereabouts did, however. It wouldn't surprise her if he'd run to Danny's camp. There was something charismatic about Arcola. If he'd had the right opportunities, he really could have made something of himself.

"Dinner's ready, Kate."

She looked up to see Molly standing at the office door.

"What's wrong with Captain Marvel? He's pouting like someone took his fire truck."

"Bobby."

Molly waved away the word as if it were a gnat. "He'll be back. He didn't have any money and it's past his dinner-time."

Kate stood and joined her assistant in the walk to the kitchen. "Why are you so sure? You know something I don't?"

"Yeah."

"Well?"

Molly ran a hand through what she jokingly called her golden tresses. "He's got the hots for me. Bad."

Kate smiled. "You just met him this morning."

"Doesn't take but a minute."

"Really? You're that good?"

Molly grinned as they entered the kitchen. "Better."

"What's better?" Peter was standing at the table, handing a fistful of silverware to T.J.

"Molly has this idea that Bobby will come trotting back any minute."

T.J.'s eyebrow came up. "Why's that?"

"Because he wants me," Molly said, moving to the stove. "I can't help it. It's this thing I do to men."

Kate kept her eyes on T.J. She was used to Molly—well, sort of. The girl still surprised her with her incredible self-confidence and a wisdom way beyond her years. But T.J. hadn't been exposed to "the Molly factor" as Peter so eloquently put it.

"All men? Or just the men in my family?"

She turned to T.J. and gave him a critical once-over. "You don't have to worry. It only works with young guys."

Kate burst out laughing and to his credit, T.J. did, too.

"It's the second time today I've been accused of being a geezer," he said. "This place is hell on the ego."

"Don't get your panties in a bunch, T.J.," Molly said. "I'm just saying we're from different worlds. What cassette is in your car stereo right now?"

T.J. blinked a few times. "The Eagles' live album."

She nodded. "When's the last time you stayed up all night, drinking beer and shooting pool?"

He shook his head slowly and Kate could almost see him search his data banks for an answer. "Last July. No, wait. That was something else. It wasn't that long ago. Hold on, I'll remember—"

"Uh-huh," Molly said, cutting him off. "And what was the big controversy over the last Salt-N-Pepa video?"

T.J. frowned. "Too spicy?"

Molly shook her head. "Cute." She gave him a weak, pitying smile. "Don't be depressed. Really. It's not so bad. You have your memories."

T.J. pulled out a chair and sat down. "Damn." He looked up at Kate and smiled wryly. "How do you take it?"

"First off," Peter said, "we don't listen to her. She's completely insane."

Kate went to the cupboard to get the plates and to keep her grin hidden from T.J. She was disproportionately pleased about this turn in the conversation. Leave it to Molly to snap him out of that ugly mood.

Brushing off the small whiff of jealousy that it was Molly and not her who had the magic touch, she got four bowls, two of them from the same set, and brought them to the table. "What is that luscious smell?"

"Chili," Molly said. "Prepare your gullets. This be hot stuff."

"She means that," Peter said. "Don't be fooled by her size. The girl has an evil streak a mile wide."

Kate held out a bowl for T.J. He took hold, but stilled his hand. She didn't let go. Not after he'd caught her gaze. His slow smile had lost all irony and was as genuine and real a thing as the floor beneath her feet. Swallowing hard, she thought she should say something. Assure him that things would turn out okay, that Bobby would return and that he wasn't wasting his time. But she couldn't make her mouth work.

It was his eyes that stopped her. The dark gaze that didn't waver, the small lines at the corners that signaled his pleasure and no small measure of surprise.

"Is this some new dinner ritual?"

Molly's voice snapped her back to the room and she let go so quickly the bowl nearly fell to the floor. T.J. seemed to recover his senses, too, and they both turned to get on with the meal.

She sat down across from him and concentrated on Molly as the girl brought the big cast-iron pot to the table. While Molly dished out the chili, Kate thought about what had just happened. How, with a simple look, T.J. had somehow managed to stop time. What was the deal here? Was she really interested in him? Had she completely lost her sense of reason?

She took a bite, burning her tongue for her trouble. Grabbing her water glass, she doused the fire, then noticed T.J.'s panicky reach for his glass. He'd done the same thing.

Was he thinking the same thoughts, too? She's the one who needed to think. To straighten things out in her head. But she couldn't do that while he was so close to her. She took another sip of water while the questions circled.

"So, T.J.," Molly said. "The bedroom next to Kate's is empty. Why don't you move in?"

Kate spit.

Molly jerked back and looked at her wet T-shirt. "Ewww, God. That's so gross."

"I'm sorry," Kate said, reaching with her napkin to dab Molly's shirt.

Molly grabbed the napkin and did her own wiping. "I said the bedroom *next* to yours, Kate. Don't get hysterical."

Kate felt the heat radiate from her cheeks. "I coughed. I'm sorry. It had nothing to do with—I mean, I don't care—I'm sure T.J. has a place to stay."

"No, I don't. I checked out of the motel this morning."

She turned to look at him. His grin was entirely too smug. "Then you'll have to check in again tonight. This isn't a rooming house."

"What if Bobby comes back late?" Molly said, giving Kate her wide-eyed, little-Miss-Innocent stare. "We can't expect T.J. to keep coming back and forth."

"Didn't you say just last week that you were going to get another counselor to move in there?" Peter asked. "Isn't T.J. a counselor for the rest of the summer?"

"Yeah," Molly said. "That's right."

All eyes were on her. The two mutineers continued to eat as if they hadn't just pushed her out on the gangplank. T.J. was no better. He wasn't grinning, but only on the outside. She could tell that inside he was doing a little victory dance. This was a plot, plain and simple. They'd all ganged up on her. They enjoyed watching her squirm.

"If and I mean *if* he stays, it means he has to work. Just like the rest of us."

"Hey, just tell me what to do," he said.

"Okay, hotshot. But you're on probation. I run this ship tight."

"Yes, ma'am."

"After dinner, you can help Peter—" Kate caught sight of Molly in her peripheral vision. The girl was staring past her, toward the kitchen door. She turned.

It was Bobby.

Her gaze swung from the boy to his brother.

All the good humor from a moment ago vanished. "Where the hell have you been?" he said, his voice sharp and bitter.

Bobby took a step back and for a minute, Kate thought he was going to bolt. Instead, he looked at Molly. "I needed some time to think."

"So you ran off to find Danny?" T.J. pushed himself back from the table, although he didn't stand up. "Does he do your thinking for you now?"

"You don't know what you're talking about. I shouldn't have come back here. You—"

"Bobby," Kate said, cutting him off. "Go get washed up for dinner."

He looked at Kate through narrowed eyes, but he didn't move.

"Now." She turned to Molly. "Get him a bowl of chili, would you, Molly?"

Molly stood up and that seemed to be enough to send Bobby to the back to clean up.

Kate turned to T.J. "Come on. We're going for a walk."

He ran his hand over his face. Suddenly he looked old, as old as Molly had teased him of being. Why couldn't he keep his temper in check around Bobby? What buttons did his half brother push?

"Why?" he asked.

"We need to talk."

"I don't need your counseling. I didn't torch the store."

"We don't know that Bobby did, either," she said, as firmly as she could.

"Right. He was probably out there helping old ladies cross the street."

"Don't you ever get tired of that cynicism?"

"Don't try and take that from me, honey. It's all I've got."

"How can you get through a day believing that?"

"It ain't easy."

He looked her in the eye, finally. She inhaled sharply at the plea in his face.

"That isn't fair," she whispered. "I can't do that for you."

He nodded once, slowly, then stood up. "A walk is a hell of an idea. But I think I'll go it alone, if you don't mind."

"Wait—"

He didn't. He walked out of the kitchen toward the back door.

"Go on," Molly said. "I can handle the kid."

Kate looked at Molly, so sure of herself, so sure of everything. "Don't let him run out again. See if you can find out where he's been."

"No problemo."

Kate smiled at the breezy reply. When had anything in her life been no problemo?

T.J. got to the pier, but he didn't go down the steps. There were a lot of people on the beach. Moms in their floppy hats, dads with their transistor radios, little kids with sand in their bathing suits. And all those teenagers looking for hot summer sex.

It was a stupid thing, thinking about the past. What good did it do? It just made him miss things that never were. Still, he longed for the summers of his youth, even while he knew they were nothing great when he'd gone through them. He wanted someone else's childhood. Beaver Cleaver's, maybe.

Or Greg Brady's. No, he would have had to shoot himself if he'd been a Brady. Who was that kid on "Flipper"? Yeah, that would have been cool. Living in Florida, having a dolphin for a friend. Ten-to-one, Flipper never once thought of joining a gang. A few fish, maybe a lady Flipper and that was one happy mammal.

But no. He got Teresa and Ed Russo. Gus the Wonder Drunk. Bobby, who hated his guts. "Those are the breaks, kid," he said aloud. "Deal with it."

"I want to help."

He spun around at the sound of Kate's voice. She stood several feet away, at the edge of the stairs.

"Go back to the center. Bobby's the one who needs you." He turned and started down the concrete steps.

She came up behind him. He already knew the sound of her shoes.

"Cut it out, T.J. Things aren't that bad."

"What do you know about it?" he said, over his shoulder.

"What?"

Her pace picked up and then he felt her hand on his shoulder. Resisting the urge to jerk away, he settled for standing still. Not turning around. Not looking at her.

"Please," she said. "Don't shut me out."

He closed his eyes. The sound of the waves filled him up. The salty smell of ocean and sand, the breeze coming strong from the west. It all hurt.

"Talk to me."

He opened his eyes and the first thing he saw was her face. The gentleness there hurt most of all.

He walked past her, grabbing her arm as he went down the steps. "I want to show you something." Leading her from the concrete onto the sand, he was keenly aware of the cool skin beneath his fingers. The softness as foreign to him as a baby's cheek.

He took her under the pier, the air temperature dropping several degrees the moment they were out of the sun.

"Where are we going?"

"Hold on," he said, staring at each huge round piling, at each scrawled word of graffiti. He didn't let her go as he walked closer to the shoreline. The odds of his mark still being there were astronomical. The wind would have blown it away by now, the sand scratched it out of existence.

He hurried her until they reached the last pole that was completely free of the water. There it was, after all these years.

Pointing up, just under the pier itself, he showed her. His initials. T.J.R. Underneath that, the remnants of what had once been a dagger. A crude dagger at that.

"I was twelve," he said. "That dagger was my brand. Like Zorro, you know? I'd read a book when I was a kid. It was about a soldier who thought of himself as his own sword. Sharp, deadly, a real piece of art. Sheathed until someone messed with him. Then watch out."

He looked from the weathered crest to Kate.

She stared up at his dagger, saying nothing for a long time. The surf kept creeping in, then slipping out, over and over. The gulls landed in the sun, searching for food.

"Now you have your badge," she said.

She understood. The fact revved his pulse, made him stupidly glad. "Yes. I have my badge."

"Bobby doesn't have either one."

"I don't know how to give it to him."

"He has to get it for himself. Just like you did."

"I owe him."

She reached across the distance between them and touched his arm with her fingertips. "Let's walk."

One more look at the dagger, a flash of anger, then release. It did no good to fight with dragons. They always had the home-field advantage.

He took hold of the hand still resting lightly on his arm and led her out into the sunlight.

"What are you going to say to him?" Kate asked.

"You know what? I'm sick to death of this whole subject. I don't want to talk about Bobby or Danny or anything remotely connected to them. As a matter of fact, I don't want to talk at all. How about you tell mc something?"

"What?"

"I don't care. Anything. A slice of your life."

Kate bent and slipped her shoes and socks off, one at a time. "Come on. We don't have all afternoon."

"I don't want to go swimming."

"Your shoes, Sherlock. Just the shoes. And you'd better roll up your pant legs, 'cause I may want to splash."

Shaking his head, he reached for his right shoe, lost his balance in the sand and sat down. Kate laughed and the sound of it was like a tonic. She made it hard to stay mad. Which wasn't necessarily a good thing. He liked being mad. It gave him something to do with his hands.

"Will you get a move on?"

He nodded and took his shoes off, then his socks. Putting them aside, he rolled his jeans to his knees. They wouldn't go higher. Then he grabbed his gear with one hand and held out the other. Kate took it and pulled him up.

They stood facing each other. Very close. The sound of the surf diminished so he could hear her sigh. The wind died so he could feel her soft breath on his cheek. The sun moved down an inch to make her hair glow like fire. He moved his head toward her, never letting go of her gaze. It was as if the kiss had already begun. He could almost taste her, feel her lips and the heat of her.

A gull screamed from above; its shadow crossed Kate's face. She pulled back, dropped his hand and his gaze. The moment passed and he wondered if it had really happened at all.

"So, when I was a little kid," she said, "I don't know, eight maybe, I was in love with horses." She was moving already, walking closer to the surf, her feet sinking into the moist sand, leaving perfect prints in her wake. He hurried to catch up, the mystery still unsolved.

"I wonder why it is that little girls love horses so much? Anyway, I was mad for them. I collected plastic replicas, read every book I could find. God, how I loved Misty." She looked at him, a smile curving her lips. "I don't suppose you ever read *Misty of Chincoteague,* did you?"

He shook his head. "*Hardy Boys.* And *Playboy.*"

"What an intriguing combination," she said. "I wanted a horse so much it consumed me. I don't think I've ever been that passionate about anything since. I begged for a horse. A pony. I was sure a pony could live in our backyard. Finally my father sat me down and told me that when he made his third million, he'd buy me a horse."

They stepped around a little girl who was dumping wet sand in a bucket. She didn't even look up.

"I got so excited. I planned out everything. I was certain that third million was just around the corner. It was all I could think about."

A wave came up, higher than most and they both scurried sideways. Cold water washed over his feet and it felt good.

"Did you ever get the horse?"

"My father was a coach. A high school coach. There was never a chance. Only I didn't understand. It was a good year before my brother Craig clued me in. I cried for days."

"That's depressing as hell."

She laughed again. He liked it when that happened.

"Well, I got over it. Expecting the horse, I mean. But I never did stop dreaming."

"So, uh, you still want a pony?"

She shoved him. "Be serious. This is a heartwarming story, damn it."

"Sorry. Go on."

"It's ruined now. You've spoiled it."

"No, no. I want to hear the moral. Please. Don't make me beg."

Her smile, the way the last rays of the sun played on her face, the wind, the air—it was all perfect. He wanted to stop time. That laugh. Low, throaty, uncomplicated. He wanted that to last forever, too.

"There is no moral. It was a slice of my life, that's all. Isn't that what you asked for?"

He shook his head. "I'll tell you a story now. There was this dead guy—"

"Oh, nice beginning."

"Shut up and listen. There was this dead guy and he was sent to hell. Or maybe it was purgatory, I don't remember. It doesn't matter. Anyway, so he lands in this big room that was filled with manure."

"Oh, God—"

"Will you be quiet? So it was filled with manure. He finds a shovel and starts digging. He digs and he digs and he digs. Finally this other guy comes in and asks him what he's doing. Why's he digging so enthusiastically? So the first guy says, 'There's gotta be a pony in here somewhere.'"

Kate stopped and folded her arms across her chest. "That's it? That's the worst joke I've ever heard."

"Joke? That wasn't a joke. That was a character sketch."

"A what?"

"A character sketch. Of you."

"Please do go on, Doctor."

"Don't you get it? That's who you are. At the center. With the kids. You keep looking for the pony."

Another wave came up and washed their feet. The sun had an inch to go. Then Kate laughed. Big time. Her whole body got involved. He watched her until he couldn't help but laugh, too.

Finally, when she'd finished wiping her eyes, she said, "You're exactly right, Detective. I do keep looking for the damned pony."

Chapter 7

Kate sat on her bed, her sleep shirt in her hand. She was very still, listening.

A bump against the wall, then silence. T.J. was unpacking, moving into the room next to hers for the rest of the summer. A wall, not a very thick one, the only thing between them. This, she thought for the third time in as many minutes, was a very bad thing.

Against her better judgment, she was starting to like T.J. Russo. No use denying it, or blaming it on the flu. He had hooked her when she wasn't looking. Was it the walk on the beach? The run this morning? Or was it when he'd looked into Pam Greer's eyes and listened to her advice as if every word had been golden?

What about the other side of him? The dark half? That was there, too, which was no little thing. He was a damaged man, with a whole troop of skeletons in his closet. He couldn't handle Bobby, he was enraged at Gus and his mother—and that's just the stuff she *knew* about. This was not the mental health poster boy.

Dating him would be no walk in the park. He would test her over and over, just like Bobby was testing him, to see if she would stick around. Then, likely as not, he would leave her without so much as a goodbye.

Sighing mightily, she reached down and grabbed the bottom of her T-shirt and pulled it up over her head. That spurred her into changing the rest of the way, although her clothes didn't quite make it into the hamper. She would pick up tomorrow. Tonight, all she wanted to do was slide between her sheets and go to sleep.

He'd been here one day. One day! And already she was thinking about him as if he were boyfriend material. Was she stupid, or what?

She had ground rules, damn it! So he knew she was still looking for the pony.

Big whopping deal. One acute observation does not a husband make.

Reaching over to her bed table, she switched on her radio. Whitney Houston was telling Kevin Costner that she would always love him. See? There's a perfect example of how relationships didn't work out. If Kev and Whitney couldn't make it work, what made her think she and Russo could? It was impossible. Ridiculous. Just plain dumb.

She turned the radio off and then the light. She climbed under her comforter and closed her eyes, commanding herself to go to sleep.

But the damn song kept playing. At first she thought it was all in her head, then she realized she was hearing the radio in T.J.'s room. He'd turned to the same station. Had he also been thinking the same thoughts?

She put her hand on the wall. He was just on the other side. A few inches away. Oh, God.

T.J. stared at his hand on the wall. She was just on the other side, probably sound asleep by now. So why couldn't he stop thinking about her?

It was bad enough that his family had screwed up his life by forcing him down here. He wasn't about to let Kate Dugan mess things up even more. This was not his life. This was not his home. His job waited for him, his apartment waited for him, even Debbi Q, the woman he'd spent a good many pleasurable, no-strings-attached nights with waited for him.

He needed Kate like a hole in the head. That was the given. But that didn't mean he couldn't dream about those long legs wrapped around his waist. Which is just what he intended to do.

The alarm woke him thirty seconds later. At least it felt that way. Despite his last conscious thought, he hadn't dreamt of Kate. Instead, there had been fire.

He flung the blanket off and sat up. The coarse stubble on his chin scratched him as he rubbed his face. He thought about the day to come and, for the first time in a long time, he had no idea what he was going to do.

Of course, back home he'd never known when a murder would crop up, but even with that, his days had been remarkably similar. He was a man of routine—everything from his morning coffee and newspaper to his parking place was mapped out to suit him. This was like a vacation. A very bad vacation.

He stood. And moaned.

His leg muscles were angry. Vicious. They let him know in no uncertain terms that he hadn't been quite truthful about his state of fitness. He'd been a slug for the past six months and clearly that was a crime punishable by pain. Moaning again, louder this time, he hobbled over to the wooden bureau in the corner. He pulled on his robe, the plaid number Joanna had given him for his last birthday.

Someone banged on his door. The sound startled him and that made him jerk, which pulled his muscles yet again.

"Hey, Sleeping Beauty. You gonna be in there all day?"

It was Molly. She would have to die.

"I'm coming, damn it all to hell," he said, but not loud enough, because she pounded on the door again.

"If you don't get out here now, I'm going to take your turn in the bathroom."

Turn? He had to share? He hadn't thought about that little detail. He didn't even know where the bathroom was. Surely the staff didn't use the big rest rooms in the main center.

He heard Molly clomp down the hall. Thoughts of a shower danced in his head. A long, hot, soothing shower. He grabbed his bathroom kit and went into the hallway, then walked gingerly past Kate's room. She wasn't there.

Checking first to make sure he was alone, he entered her sanctum sanctorium. She'd made her bed. The comforter was plaid or maybe that was tartan, he wasn't sure what the difference was. The blue, green, yellow and red rectangles looked nice, though. The top of her dresser had a hairbrush, a stand-up mirror and a box of tissues on one side and three paperback books on the other. One small bottle of perfume hid behind her copy of *The Stand*. He picked it up and sniffed. Flowers. Kate flowers. The combination of this scent and her neck was really something to think about. Putting it down, he noticed a snapshot half hidden by the hairbrush. He lifted it from underneath.

It was Kate. Kate and a man. He was taller then her by several inches and wore UCLA sweats. His arm was around her waist and she'd rested her head on his shoulder. She looked beautiful. Long and slim, like some vision from a Greek myth. The guy, on the other hand, looked like a schmuck. There was a territorial glint in his eye and a smirk on his thin lips.

T.J. checked himself in the mirror. Yep, he was so much better looking than this schmo, it wasn't worth thinking about. He didn't know who the jerk was, but he hoped Kate had sent him packing. She deserved better.

The sound of laughter filtered in from down the hall and T.J. quickly put the picture back where he'd found it and left the room, feeling only a little guilty for snooping.

The next door was closed, but he remembered that was Molly's room. The door after that was the bathroom. It was small—a stall shower, a commode, a sink. One shelf with a cup full of toothbrushes and a half-squeezed tube of toothpaste with the cap off next to it. Down below that was a cupboard, and to his relief there were fresh towels inside. He locked the door and dropped his robe, itching to feel that hot spray.

The water was cold. Not completely, but enough to make him wish he'd kept that motel room. The only thing he could do was wash. And swear.

"Captain Marvel found the shower," Molly said. "Think there's any hot water left?"

Kate grinned at her. "Nope."

"Think he'll get up earlier tomorrow?"

"Nope. He'll just complain about it."

Molly sat down with her second cup of coffee. "You know so much about men. I'm impressed."

"Five brothers. I don't recommend it."

Peter, sitting in his usual seat next to Molly, grunted but didn't bother to look up. He just went on with his crossword puzzle.

"Five-letter word for a guy who grunts but doesn't speak," Molly said. "Begins with an *M*, ends with an *N*."

Peter grunted again. Kate noticed, however, that the fingers around his pen shifted so to that one stuck out prominently. "I love that you two kids get along so well," she said. "It gives me goose bumps."

"So does your shower."

Kate turned to see T.J. standing at the doorway. His hair was wet, his cheeks smooth from his shave. The T-shirt he wore said L.A.P.D. on the breast pocket. It was the same blue as his shorts.

"That's what happens when you get up late. The water's only hot for the first two customers. After that it's all downhill."

"Thanks for telling me." He walked over to the coffee-pot.

Kate saw his stiff-legged movement and smiled. "So, you ready to run again today?"

T.J.'s cup slipped, he played a little volleyball with it, then lost it to the counter. It didn't break. "I think I'll pass."

"How come?" She shouldn't goad him. It wasn't nice. "Sore, are we?"

"*We* are not sore. We just have better things to do than run to the beach every day."

"Yeah? Like what?"

"Like talk to Bobby. Find out what he was doing yesterday on his field trip."

"Speaking of Bobby," Kate said. "Someone go make sure he's up, okay?"

Molly looked at Peter. Peter looked back at her, then turned once again to his puzzle.

"Sheesh," she said. "What a maroon."

"You're the one he's in love with," Peter said.

She stood up, walked behind Peter and bent low so her mouth was close to his ear. "Don't be jealous, Peter darling. He's too young for you anyway."

"Get out of here, you little twit."

Molly scooted away from him, laughing.

"Is it always like this?" T.J. asked as he sat down at the table.

Kate nodded. "Mostly. Did you sleep all right?"

He shrugged his shoulders and flinched at the movement. "Sure."

"I've got some deep-heating rub if you want."

He gave her a look that told her what she could do with the rub.

"Suit yourself."

He drank his coffee, keeping his gaze down. She looked down, too, at her white shorts and her impossible legs. Molly always said she wished she were tall, like her, but Kate figured that was just foolishness. Being a giant was great on the basketball court, or on the track, but anywhere else it was uncomfortable. Her gaze moved back to T.J. Did he think about her height? Did it bother him?

"He's up," Molly said, walking back to her chair. "But he's not happy."

"Is he going to join us?" Kate asked.

"Yep. As soon as he gets dressed. He sleeps in the nude, you know."

Kate laughed and T.J. turned a surprised eye toward her.

"I'm not even going to ask how you know that," Kate said. "I just hope you didn't embarrass the boy to death."

She shrugged, then ran her hand through her crew cut. The movement lifted her tank top, revealing her brown, flat stomach and her belly button ring.

Kate quickly looked at T.J. to see if he'd noticed. He had. "What is that about?" he asked, pointing to her pierced navel. "I mean, what's it good for?"

"It's decorative. Like pierced ears."

"It's barbaric," he said.

Molly shook her head. "Poor old Captain Marvel. It might do you some good to get yourself a navel ring. Or a tattoo."

"How do you know I don't have one?"

"You? Tattooed? Don't make me laugh."

He stood up, gingerly, and pulled his T-shirt off. He turned to the side and there, on his shoulder blade, was a dagger, the same dagger Kate had seen at the beach. It was faded, but the image was still discernible.

"A dagger," he said. "As deadly as it is silent."

Molly rose. "Oh yeah?" She pulled down the right side of her tank top, exposing the top of her breast. She was decent, but only just.

"Black widow spider," she said. "She mates, then she kills."

T.J. checked out the spider and the web. He nodded, then turned again so his other shoulder came into view. There was a small rose, with three thorns on the stem and a teardrop of blood on one petal. Below that was the name, in script, Rosie. "My first girlfriend. She left me for a sailor named Troy."

Molly pulled down the waistband of her running shorts and pointed to a curled snake on her rump. "Cobra. He was a biker. He left me when he realized he would never truly satisfy me."

"What the hell?"

Kate and the others turned toward the door. Bobby, still tousled from sleep, stared at Molly's exposed flesh. "You all perverts, or what?"

Kate burst out laughing and so did Peter and T.J. Molly simply raised her eyebrows as she raised her waistband. "See what you miss when you sleep late?" she said. "Tomorrow, get up when you're supposed to."

Bobby shook his head in wonderment, his gaze locked on Molly. He swallowed, the movement lifting his Adam's apple up and down and Kate realized her assistant hadn't been kidding last night when she'd said Bobby had it bad for her.

Kate's gaze moved back to T.J. He still had his T-shirt off and while she meant to give him a head's-up about Bobby, she got sidetracked there. How come she hadn't realized he looked like that? His broad shoulders and his arms were perfectly developed, with clear definition. But they didn't hold a candle to the chest. He was like someone out of a magazine. Just the right amount of hair over smooth, rippling waves of muscle. Her mouth went dry as she looked at his stomach.

"Hey, Kate," Molly said. "Put your eyeballs back in."

Heat filled her cheeks and she got up quickly. Grabbing her empty coffee cup, she walked to the counter, making sure she made eye contact with no one. "We've got half an hour till the troops arrive. Bobby, you work with Molly again today, got it?"

"I ain't goin' back there," he said bitterly.

She didn't bother to look his way. "You say that as if there's a choice involved."

"Don't sweat it, Sarducci," Molly said, her words muffled through her mouthful of bagel. "You did pretty good yesterday, until you bailed."

"I don't want to be no nursemaid. Put me somewhere else."

Kate turned back with her full cup just as T.J. said, "You heard the lady. Your job is in the nursery and that's final."

Bobby turned angry eyes to T.J. "You want to bring everyone by to watch me change diapers? Is that it?"

Bobby hadn't moved from the door. Kate pulled out the chair next to Peter's then went to her own. "There's a cup in the cupboard. Get yourself some coffee and sit down. We'll discuss this thing calmly."

Bobby stared at her hard. She could see that he wanted to bolt again, that a discussion was the last thing he had in mind. But something else was going on there, too. He eyed the "family" scene in front of him, lingering over Molly, of course, but also the spread newspaper, the bagels, Peter's Pop-Tarts, her bowl of cereal. It was as if he were standing outside a big window, wanting to come in from the cold to a warmth he couldn't quite feel. She smiled at him and nodded again at the chair.

He turned the seat so his back would be toward T.J. and sat down. However, he didn't really join the group. He kept himself apart. His body language was tense and mistrustful and she found herself regretting that she hadn't warned T.J., before Bobby had gotten up, to keep his cool.

"Tell me what bothers you about working in the nursery?" she asked, hoping her voice sounded kind to him.

"It's a girl's job," he said. "I ain't no girl."

Kate could feel Molly tense beside her and she sent silent kudos when her assistant kept her mouth shut. "Taking care of infants isn't just for women, Bobby. Lots of men do it."

"Yeah? Name one."

"Well, the most famous baby doctor of them all was a man named Spock."

Bobby's eyes narrowed. "Don't give me that. He's on that "Star Trek." I've seen it."

"That's Mr. Spock. I'm talking about Dr. Spock. Another person altogether. He's been the leading expert in infant care for over forty years. I've got some of his books, if you'd like to read them."

"So?"

"So I'd like you to continue to work with Molly. I think it's the right place for you."

"What about what *I* think?"

"You're going to have to trust me on this. But I'll tell you what. You work the whole day in the nursery and you don't give Molly any trouble and tonight, you can join her at the movies."

Molly looked up then, but to Kate's everlasting gratitude, she still kept her cool.

"What movie?" he asked, his voice just a bit less hostile.

"Whatever," Molly said. "I'm not picky."

Bobby continued to look at Kate, waiting for the kicker. She sipped her coffee and struggled to keep her eyes on Bobby, not his brother.

"Why?"

"Why not? Molly says you're good with the kids. She needs someone to help her. You're elected."

"No. Why should you let me go out? I ran off, remember?"

"That was yesterday"

The silence grew then and in the quiet she could feel T.J.'s gaze pull at her. There would be time for him in a minute. She put her cup down and waited. Then it happened. Bobby's shoulders relaxed and he moved forward in his chair. He'd given up the warrior stance—for now.

Molly, bless her little tattooed heart, caught the signal. She stood. "So come on. If you're going to get coffee, do it now. You can take it with you. We have to get ready."

Bobby stood slowly. His gaze moved from Kate to T.J. and his shoulders stiffened, but not too much. He walked, or maybe *slunk* was a better word for that god-awful gang strut of his, over to the counter. Getting his coffee was a production, with a lot of banging drawers, complaints about the sugar, the milk and finally the coffee itself. Then it was done and he followed Molly out of the room.

Peter looked up, caught the silent signal that she and T.J. needed to be alone and then he, too, was gone.

"You want to tell me why you did that?" T.J. asked, his voice low and angry.

"Did what?"

"The bribe."

"That wasn't a bribe."

"What do you call it?"

"A beginning."

He got up and walked over to her, forcing her to look up at him. It didn't work. She wasn't intimidated. Not about Bobby at least. However, there was something about being that close to T.J., to his bare legs and that incredible, unfortunately covered, chest.

"That sounds poetic," he said, with a tinge of sarcasm. "What the hell does it mean?"

She couldn't keep looking up at him. She didn't like what he was trying to do and when she stood, she made sure she rose to her full height. Things weren't so one-sided now. They were eye-to-eye and she could stare with the best of them. "If you want to talk about my techniques, Detective,

I'll be happy to. What I won't do is justify myself in *my* center. Are we clear about that?"

He didn't say anything. His eyes narrowed in the exact same way his little brother's had just a moment ago. But where she knew Bobby had wanted to bolt, T.J. wanted to pounce. He came closer to her and suddenly she wasn't at all sure that this was about psychology. No, this was basic chemistry.

His lips parted and she could see a hint of his even, white teeth. His nostrils flared as he took a deep breath, and she knew he was inhaling her scent. He scanned her face with rapid movements, his gaze darting from the top of her head to her mouth, where he stopped and stared for a long time.

"Are you planning on following him around the rest of his life," he said, never moving his gaze. "Giving him little rewards whenever he does the right thing?"

She shook her head slowly, still mesmerized by the closeness of him. "This isn't about rewards, it's about consequences. Good consequences."

"Semantics. That's—"

"No, it's not semantics. It's about believing in your own worth. Knowing that doing the right thing means something."

He shifted his weight, moving a quarter of an inch closer to her. She noticed a scar, a tiny one, above his right eyebrow and wondered where he got it.

"All his life," she continued, "Bobby has only known disappointment. In school, at home. With you." She said that last softly, but said it nonetheless. T.J.'s only reaction was to close his mouth and press his lips together.

"What we need to do now is replace those negative reinforcements with something positive. Give him a reason to succeed."

"Not going to jail seems like a damn good reason to me."

She shook her head. "Try it my way, okay? What do you have to lose?"

His eyes captured hers again and the urge to step back was nearly unbearable.

"I stand to lose everything," he said, his voice low and dangerous.

"Bobby—"

"I'm not talking about Bobby."

He moved closer and she knew what was coming. For a second, she felt the urge to flee. Then it was too late. His lips came down on hers, hard, hard and oh, soft, too.

Her eyes fluttered closed and she acquiesced as the ground beneath her seemed to slip away. His scent was masculine and indefinable. His taste, hot coffee and sin. When his arm came around her back and pressed her to him, she felt the hard parts of him. His chest, his naked thighs. And more than that, she felt his sex. Rigid, thick, pressing her at the juncture of her thighs.

The sound of laughter came from somewhere far away. She tried not to hear it, to keep her concentration on now, this instant.

Then the choice was gone as he stepped away and all contact was lost between them.

"I'd better go get ready," he said. She barely recognized his voice.

"The kids..."

He nodded.

"I—"

He didn't give her a chance to speak. He turned quickly and headed for the door. Just as he was about to go down the hall, he stopped and looked back at her. "It's too risky," he said. "I don't belong here."

Then he was gone.

Chapter 8

T.J. didn't go running. Not because of his aching muscles, although that was a hell of a good reason, but because he needed to keep his distance from Kate.

He stood in the back of the big room, watching the swarm of kids buzz around the pool tables and each other. The noise was almost loud enough to drown out his thoughts, but not quite.

He hadn't meant to kiss her. It had been the last thing on his mind. Until she'd gotten close. Damn it, she'd shanghaied him, that's what it was. He wasn't sure how, something to do with female magic or voodoo. He'd looked into those green eyes, smelled that Kate smell and then "Mr. Happy" had taken over.

What was he supposed to do now? He'd been here only a couple of days and he was ready to do the horizontal bop with the Amazon queen. Was it just last week he'd thought her *mildly* attractive? Not his type? Yeah, right.

Well, it couldn't happen. In four and a half weeks, he would be out of here, back in Hollywood, back in the real world. Bobby would be in school or in a gang—either way, T.J.'s conscience would be assuaged and this little vacation would be nothing but a sidebar.

In the meantime he needed to keep both his mouth and his jeans zipped. Concentrate on convincing Bobby that he had a chance at life. Let Kate try her Dr. Spock methods and her fancy Gestalt therapy. No one would ever be able to say he hadn't given this experiment a chance. But he didn't want to be around for the inevitable failure.

Kate would be devastated and as sure as his name was Russo, she would end up blaming him. That would make it unanimous. Well, not for this cop. He had enough of that from his mother. Not to mention good ol' Gus.

All T.J. had to do was remember who he was and the problem with Kate would disappear. Sure, he would have a few laughs, shoot a few hoops, keep Danny at a distance. Why not? Hell, at the very least, he could use the time to get himself back in shape. There were worse things.

"Hey, Mr. Russo. Aren't you even going to say hi?"

T.J. looked to his right. Alice Dee stood there, wearing itty-bitty shorts, a tube top and a practiced pout. Her hands were on her hips and a flash of a lady he'd once known for a couple of blurred nights back in San Francisco crossed his mind. "How you doin'," he said, keeping his voice firmly in neutral.

"Not so good. Everyone's gone out running, except for you, of course."

His gaze swept over the sixty or so kids milling about. "Everyone, huh?"

She nodded. "Everyone who matters."

"So why didn't you go, too?"

"I get my exercise in other ways."

"Uh-huh. Well, nice talking to you, Alice." He made a quick getaway, backing up until his legs hit a study table, then he did a cross-court dash to Kate's office.

Fifteen more minutes and Kate would be back. Then basketball. He went behind her desk and sat down, keeping an eye out for Alice. At least it was quiet in here.

He pulled open Kate's bottom desk drawer with his foot and got himself comfortable. With his feet up and his hands behind his head, he could lean back just enough to see most of the crowd through the windows. He found the twins, what were their names? One was busy with some sort of arts and crafts, the other was dressed in a cheerleading outfit, leading a group of girls in some energetic routines.

He felt calm for the first time this morning. Maybe kissing Kate hadn't been such a bad idea. It helped him get clear, focused. He was back in control, which was just how he liked things. No complications, no involvements. Just because Kate made him laugh and had legs that could stop traffic, was no reason to discard the lessons life had taught him. He was a big boy and he didn't have to let his libido lead him around. There were plenty of fish in the sea, right? Hell, maybe if he worked on it, he could come up with a few more clichés.

He brought his head back farther with a sigh, but then the chair skidded backward and he lost his balance. Quickly dropping his hands to brace himself, he nearly tipped over before he could get his feet down squarely on the floor.

Cursing the way his old man had taught him, he scooted back toward the desk while adjusting the bottom drawer. He stopped when he caught a flash of pink, then pulled the drawer out all the way.

In the back, behind the files, was a doll. It sure wasn't anything fancy. Most of the hair was gone, one eye was open, the other shut. Even the little pink dress was torn around the collar. He wouldn't have given it another thought, except for the name embroidered on the apron: Katie's Little Angel.

He reached for the old toy, bringing it out into the light, somewhat surprised that Kate would keep a memento like this for all these years. He hadn't thought about it much, just assumed she'd been a tomboy. With that athletic build, he would have pegged her for a hellion, a real jock. So what was this about?

"What are you doing?"

He jerked up, banging his funny bone on the desk for good measure. Kate stood in the doorway. She looked hot from her run. Her hair was damp around her face and her cheeks were tinged with pink. Not to mention how her T-shirt clung to her various highs and lows.

"I needed someone to play with." He cradled the doll in his arms. "Someone who wouldn't snap at me."

She came the rest of the way into the room, moving purposefully toward him. "Put her back," she said. "You have no business looking through my things."

"Hey, it was a joke," he said, surprised at the vehemence in her voice. "I wasn't snooping. I came across it by accident."

Kate stood right beside the desk and she reached over and grabbed the doll from him. Before he could say a word, she'd shoved him, chair and all, to the side and put the doll back in the drawer. "You had no right."

"I'm sorry." He stood up and touched her arm. When she finally looked at him, he said, "Honest. I'm sorry. I didn't mean to pry."

The anger seemed to leave her, at least the muscles in her arms relaxed. Clearly he'd pushed a big button here. "She means a lot to you, huh?"

Kate swallowed and then she looked down. "My mother gave her to me. Just before she died."

"Ah. I see."

"Yeah, well, it's time for basketball. That is if you're not too sore."

"How old were you?"

She flashed him a "back off" look. "The kids are waiting."

"I bet you were a real beautiful little girl," he said. "A handful, but a beauty, right?"

Kate sighed and moved just far enough away so that his hand dropped. "What do you care what I was? You're just visiting, aren't you?"

"You and I both know I shouldn't have kissed you. Not that it wasn't great, it was just a mistake."

"Right. A huge mistake. A colossal, giant error. Now, can we leave?"

"Wait a minute. What's with the anger? I thought we were friends?"

She stared at him once more and he felt slapped by the look in her eyes. "Friends? I don't even know you. You're here for Bobby, nothing else. I'm not interested in you, got it? I'm sure you're a real stud-muffin back in Hollywood, but here, you're a guest. Don't abuse the privilege."

He didn't say anything for a long while. He just watched her, trying to think of some way to respond with at least a bit of dignity. It was no use. "Stud-muffin?" he whispered. "You really think so?"

She didn't laugh. But she did smile. A little. "Get out of here, Russo. Stop being a jerk."

"You can't have it both ways, babe. Frankly, I think stud-muffin suits me."

"I don't believe you," she said, and he noticed a trace of weariness in her voice. That bothered him more than the anger of a moment ago.

"I'm nothing special," he said. "Ordinary run-of-the-mill guy with all the attendant guy problems."

"No, you're not. That's my point."

It was his turn to back off. He walked around the desk, over to the small plastic chair by the wall. It was too small to sit in, so he kind of kicked it. "Look, I meant it about this morning. I don't know what happened, except of course that you're a very attractive woman. I know I've got a job to do here, which doesn't include seducing the boss. We both have our own lives and whatever happens is going to be over in a few weeks.'' He turned to her then. She was leaning against the back wall, fiddling with her whistle. It was clear she was uncomfortable.

''But that friendship thing has a lot of possibilities,'' he said. ''I haven't had many, but none of them have given up on me.''

The corners of her mouth moved up slightly, then she pushed off the wall and came around to the front of the desk. ''The only way we can be friends is if there's mutual respect. I may not succeed with Bobby, but I'm going to try my damnedest. My methods might not be comfortable for you, but I still need your cooperation.''

His gaze kept wanting to move to her mouth. It was wildly inappropriate, especially after the speech he'd just given, but the urge to kiss her was back. Stronger than it had been this morning. He cleared his throat, looked her square in the forehead and nodded. ''You've got it.''

''All right then. Let's give it another try.''

''Basketball?''

''And after that, dancing.''

His gaze moved down to her eyes, looking to see if she was pulling his leg.

''Dancing?''

''Once a week. Mostly to rap music, but sometimes they let me sneak in an oldie.''

''Dancing.''

''Don't be so scared. *You* don't have to do anything but supervise.''

''Okay then.''

She walked to the door and opened it, then hesitated. ''Watch out for Alice today,'' she said. ''I caught her ogling.''

''Well, us stud-muffins are used to that kind of thing.'' He walked past her without looking her in the eye.

"I'm gonna regret that remark for the rest of my life, aren't I?"

He nodded. "Till the day you die."

Kate grabbed a clean white T-shirt from her drawer and pulled it on. The music had already started; even here in the staff quarters the loud percussion made her mirror quiver. She was glad that it was Wednesday and that the kids would have a chance to wear themselves out on the dance floor. They had so much energy that the strenuous basketball games only left them raring to go. She was another story. The run, then the million laps up and down the court had left her exhausted. What she wouldn't give for some quiet time to take a nap. Or to think.

She didn't want to admit it, but she was still shaken up from this morning. The kiss had caught her completely off guard. She hadn't wanted it or expected it, but when it had happened, she'd been utterly floored at her reaction.

She'd thought about it on her run, during the game, even when she and T.J. had that little heart-to-heart in her office. The only conclusion she'd come to was that she'd liked it. A lot. Way too much. Damn it.

Every time it came to mind, which seemed like every twenty seconds, her active little brain sent signals straight to all her erogenous zones—some she hadn't realized existed before today.

The other surprise was that all that running hadn't done a thing to cool her off. Usually she zoned while running. It was her form of meditation. She'd used it on occasion to rid herself of troubling thoughts and it worked like a charm. It had been a convenience she'd taken for granted since high school and now, for some inexplicable reason, it was failing big time.

Try as she might, she couldn't blame the phenomenon on the time of the month or the phases of the moon. It just was. The obvious thing to do was to not think too much about it.

Some women might obsess about a guy like T.J., but they didn't have a job like hers, or a life plan set in concrete. They certainly hadn't had her experiences with men. No, it was important to see T.J. as a friend, just like he'd suggested. A buddy. A pal. You didn't have sex with a pal, right?

Her reflection nodded in agreement and she left her room. The music swelled as she neared the main room.

She stopped for a moment at the nursery to check up on Bobby. He didn't say much, just a sort of snarl actually, but Molly gave her the thumbs-up, so she thought things must be all right.

Then through the toddlers' room, where Peter had all the muppets dancing on the floor cushions. At least that brought a smile.

When she reached her final destination the sound crashed in on her, nearly visible in its intensity. She must be getting old. She could remember going to concerts and not giving one thought to the decibel range. Now she went straight to her office and got a couple of pairs of earplugs, bought strictly for Wednesday afternoons. Once her pair were in place, she snaked her way through the swaying, jerking, bouncing bodies. No one touched—that was a cardinal rule—but the dancing was sexual and raw just the same. She could practically feel the oozing testosterone floating in the crowd, which reminded her that she had to go out and get more condoms for the bathroom. She tried to discourage the teenagers from having sex, but she was a realist. At least, with a proper education, no one would have to die from it.

She was edging her way around Darnel and Alice, bumping their way to paradise, when she spotted T.J. He was standing casually by the back wall, elbows high, index fingers planted firmly in his ears. It took her several minutes to get to him and by that time, she'd stopped laughing.

"This is hell!" he screamed. "We'll all be deaf for the rest of our lives."

She held out her hand, offering him his own brand-new pair of earplugs. He grabbed them as if they could save his life. A moment later, he had them properly installed and his grin said all the thank-yous she needed.

"You don't like Dr. Dre?" she said, leaning close to him so he would have a chance to hear her.

"Who?"

"Dr. Dre. The singer."

"This song has a singer?"

She smiled and leaned back against the wall, keeping her gaze moving over her charges. No one seemed inclined to break the rules. They'd all been here too long for that.

T.J. moved close, so his mouth grazed her ear, sending yet another unwelcome signal to points south. "How long does this go on?"

She turned, making sure no part of her body touched his. "Another two hours."

He maneuvered back. "I have about six thousand in the bank. If I give it to them, will they stop?"

Shaking her head, she shouted, "You can leave and come back if you want."

"You calling me yellow?" he yelled.

"Yes!"

He waited a minute, adjusted his earplugs, then leaned once more. "You're right. I am yellow. I'm going out."

Kate held up her hand. "Wait one minute." After he nodded, she headed east, fording the river of hot, sweaty bodies until, after much trouble, she reached the jukebox. She pressed nine numbers—three songs—then hit reset.

By the time she was halfway back to T.J., Salt-N-Pepa had ceased singing and the new record started with a scratch. Elvis took their place to a chorus of groans from the floor.

T.J. gave her his most brilliant smile as he came toward her. They met in the middle of the dance floor and he took hold of her hand.

The kids nearest to them backed away, staring at this remarkable event. She looked from her hand to his eyes and that's when he started. Dancing. Really dancing, like Travolta in *Grease*.

He pulled her forward, then under his arm, then twirled her around to face him again. What could she do but join in?

"It's been a long time," she yelled, as he grabbed her other hand and pulled her toward him.

"It's like riding a bike," he said, then spun her again.

She heard clapping, shouting, catcalls. Several of the girls were pointing at their hands, yelling "Touching! Touching!" In one brief pass, she saw Alice Dee's murderous glare, but she didn't care one bit. No one was going to step on her blue suede shoes right now.

"Where did you learn this?"

"Right here. The nuns taught me," he said, releasing her and taking several steps back, clapping to the beat.

"You're lying."

He walked toward her again, capturing her gaze. "I don't lie to my friends." Taking both hands in his again, he pulled her close. Then he just stood there, breathing hard, staring at her like no friend she'd ever had before. Her heart hammered in her chest and she wasn't sure of her breath.

There was only one thing she was sure of—she was falling for T.J. Russo like a ton of bricks.

The arsonist struck again two weeks later. The convenience store owner, Reuben Sanchez, was killed with a single bullet from a .45. The cash register was empty and the store consumed by fire by the time the Harbor Bay Fire Department arrived. Mrs. Sanchez and her six children had been in Los Angeles for the night.

T.J. put the newspaper down. He'd read the front-page article twice, even though he'd heard about the fire and the murder from the police at five this morning. Someone had left an anonymous tip that Bobby had been at the scene, so they'd come to talk to him. Only Bobby hadn't been here. He'd snuck out of the center sometime after eleven. T.J. glanced at the clock on the wall. It was 6:48 and still no one had heard from the boy. Maybe he was on his way to Mexico. Maybe he was dead.

"How long have you been sitting here?"

He didn't have the energy to turn, even at the sound of Kate's voice. "A while."

"How about I make some more coffee?"

He nodded. She came around in back of him and touched his shoulder lightly as she passed. He recognized the gesture of friendship and concern, but it was an intellectual knowledge that had nothing to do with him.

"You don't know that he's involved," Kate said softly as she poured the water into the coffee maker.

"Don't," he said. "It's damn clear where he was last night."

"Not necessarily."

"Sure," he said, flinching at his own sarcasm.

The sound of the coffee can hitting the counter jarred him, then he just settled further down on the chair and stared once again at the picture of the burned shell of a building that had already ended one life and would probably end more before it was over.

Kate pulled out the chair next to him. "Look at me."

He did. He wanted to fall into the green, sympathetic eyes. To hide there and never come back.

"This isn't the only time Bobby's been out all night. It's happened before. I know, I probably should have told you, but I learned it in confidence and I thought it best to keep it that way."

"You what? You didn't think it was important to tell me my brother's been out running with that damn gang? What the hell am I doing here, then? Will you tell me that?"

She shook her head and reached for his hand. He pulled it back.

"I don't think he's been with the gang," she said.

"Oh, come on."

"I think he's been staying with your mother."

T.J. stood up, sending his chair crashing backward. "You can't tell me you believe that."

"I do."

"Did you ask her?"

"No."

"Then how—"

"Molly told me."

"Ah, well then. No sweat."

Kate stood and moved in on him. He forced himself to stand still.

"Listen to me, damn it. Gus has been acting up. Bobby's been frightened for your mother and he's snuck out a few times to stay with her. That's all. I'm sure that's where he is now."

"Did you call?"

"There was no answer."

"And all this was going on and no one thought I should know. That's what you're saying, right?"

"Molly's been trying to get Bobby to tell you himself. She thought it was important."

"He'll have plenty of time to talk to me from prison."

"He's not going to jail."

T.J. turned away, it was too painful to see her face. "You're being naive," he said.

"There's a difference between trust and naiveté, T.J."

"If wishes were horses, beggars would ride, kiddo. There are no ponies here."

He waited for her to speak again and when the silence became too heavy to bear, he turned. The sadness in her face cut him like a knife; he took no satisfaction in the victory.

"Bobby Sarducci is his father's son," he said softly. "Some things are too big to fight."

Kate closed her eyes briefly, then focused in on him once again. "We're friends, right?"

He nodded.

"All right then. I want you to do something for me. As my friend."

He crossed his arms, waiting.

"I want you to believe in me. I know you can't believe in Bobby yet, so I won't ask you to. But I want you to trust me, even though you have no reason to."

"And?"

"And act as if Bobby is innocent."

"I don't know that I can."

She stepped closer to him. She had on jeans and a tank top and he noticed she wasn't wearing a bra. He could see the sharp points of her nipples through the fabric. His groin tightened even as he knew this wasn't the time or the place. Shifting his gaze, he looked at her face—no makeup, her hair a tousled red mess, her skin pale under the fluorescent lights. The tightness got worse, not better.

"Try," she said softly, touching his arm with her fingers. "Try it for me."

"You're asking a lot."

"No more than you can give."

He shook his head. "You don't know me very well."

"I know you love Bobby. I know you care."

He reached out and touched her bare arm. He ran his fingers lightly down her cool soft flesh. When she didn't back away, he moved up to her cheek and caressed her slowly. He wanted her. So much it was painful.

Before he knew what hit him, his erection was pressing against his jeans, his pulse was racing and his breathing labored. All this from a touch. When he met her gaze, he saw he wasn't the only one. There was desire there, unmistakable, raw, innocent. He moved his hand so it cupped the back of her neck.

Her lips parted.

He pulled her to him, closing his eyes at the last possible second.

Once his mouth touched hers, something seemed to snap inside him. He tightened his hold on her, wrapped his other arm around her waist and pulled her tight. Desperately, urgently, he kissed her, merging with her, using his tongue and his breath and the fire inside him.

He pressed himself against her, and the feel of her body against his was an agony he couldn't resist. Moving his hips, he swayed with her and when he heard her low moan he knew she was burning up, too.

Kate pulled away to catch the breath he'd stolen. His head went down until his lips found the sensitive skin on her neck. She moaned again with the heat and the wet.

"Now. Come with me . . ."

She barely made out the words, but she knew what he wanted. She wanted him, too, with a stunning need. But it wasn't right. He wanted to escape through her, not be with her. That was a difference she couldn't live with.

"Stop," she said. And then she said it again and again until he heard her.

He pulled back, holding on to her with tight hands, and searched her face for clues. He must have seen her doubt and fear, because then he wrapped his arms around her in a hug that wasn't sexual, just achingly sad.

"I'll tell you a secret," he said, his mouth close to her ear. "I still don't know what the hell to do."

She ran her hand over his back, feeling the tightly bunched muscles underneath his T-shirt. He was still pressed against her and his desire for her was as evident physically as it was emotionally. The pull she felt was strong. Stronger than anything she'd felt for any man. Even the man she'd loved all those years ago. Still, that wasn't enough. She would be patient and wait for his brain to take over from his body.

In a move that came from some place she didn't understand, she rocked him. Like a child. Back and forth they swayed, holding on to each other, feeding each other. She petted his head and whispered words that had no meaning and all the meaning in the world. She felt his chest rise and fall, his shoulders relax, his sexual desire diminish. Finally the madness was gone.

T.J. was the first to step back. He let her go and smiled shyly. It wasn't an expression he was used to, she would wager. But the moment had been innocent and so it was right.

"I trust you," she said. "I trust you enough to ask you to believe in me."

"How am I supposed to fight this?" he asked. "Every time I make a jerk of myself, you end up turning it around so that I come out smelling like a rose. How do you do that?"

"It's a gift," she said, smiling.

He nodded. "I'd better warn you. My, uh, reaction to you wasn't all that surprising. I think there may be more here than friendship. You know?"

"Uh-huh. That doesn't mean we have to—"

"Right, right. We're adults and all that."

"Exactly."

"But still. Maybe one time—"

She shook her head and moved toward the counter, needing the space between them. "T.J., I'm here for the duration. I have the center and the kids. My dance card is full."

"Sure," he said a little too quickly. "I've got my job and my place back in L.A. It wouldn't work."

"No." She turned to him and waited until he was looking right at her. "Not just because of logistics."

His smile was bittersweet and for that she was glad. "No," he said. "Not just logistics."

She went back to the counter, surprised by the lump in her throat. It was important that she concentrate on the cup in her hand, the spoon, the sugar—not the tightness inside her that urged her to go back to him.

"So what do we do now?"

She swallowed so that her voice would sound normal. "We wait. Bobby will be back. When he comes, we listen to him. Just listen. No arguments. No accusations."

"I wasn't talking about Bobby."

"I know."

THE EDITOR'S "THANK YOU" FREE GIFTS INCLUDE:

▶ Four BRAND-NEW romance novels
▶ A Cuddly Teddy Bear

PLACE
FREE GIFT
SEAL
HERE

YES! I have placed my Editor's "thank you" seal in the space provided above. Please send me 4 free books and a Cuddly Teddy Bear. I understand I am under no obligation to purchase any books, as explained on the back and on the opposite page.

345 CIS A4UM (C-SIL-IM-10/96)

_____

NAME

_____

ADDRESS   APT.

_____

CITY   PROVINCE   POSTAL CODE

Thank you!

THE SILHOUETTE READER SERVICE™: HERE'S HOW IT WORKS

Accepting free books places you under no obligation to buy anything. You may keep the books and gift and return the shipping statement marked "cancel". If you do not cancel, about a month later we will send you 6 additional novels, and bill you just $3.71 each plus 25¢ delivery and GST*. That's the complete price, and—compared to cover prices of $4.50 each—quite a bargain! You may cancel at any time, but if you choose to continue, every month we'll send you 6 more books, which you may either purchase at the discount price…or return to us and cancel your subscription.

*Terms and prices subject to change without notice. Canadian residents add applicable provincial taxes and GST.

SILHOUETTE READER SERVICE
PO BOX 609
FORT ERIE, ONT L2A 9Z9

019561919199-L2A5X3-BR01

Chapter 9

T.J. stood in the cool morning air, sipping his coffee, staring at the empty street in front of the center. The doors wouldn't open for another hour, which was a tremendous relief. He didn't want to deal with that mess. Not now.

His thoughts were on Bobby and about the past couple of weeks. How he'd thought the kid had changed. Each day T.J. had grown more convinced that Kate's approach was working. His brother had become less belligerent, more open. Of course, Molly was responsible for a lot of that. She was something. She didn't give the poor kid an inch. And Bobby had responded like a lovesick puppy. So what had gone wrong?

Even though he'd promised his trust to Kate, he couldn't stop his doubts. She didn't understand the kind of life Bobby had led. What Gus and his mother had done. Kate would have had to experience that nightmare to really get it. A mother who drank to make it all disappear, a father who drank for no reason at all. Endless nights of violence, screaming and pain that couldn't be wiped away in a few weeks at summer camp. Bobby's mold was cast.

He thought about the families he'd dealt with in his work, how the patterns had become so predictable. The father beats up the kid, the kid becomes an abuser. Time after time after time. He didn't know if it was genetics or not, just that it was a basic truth. One that Kate didn't understand.

"Hey, Cap'n."

T.J. turned at Molly's voice. She stood just inside the front door, a coffee mug in her hand.

"Morning."

"You busy?"

He shook his head and she walked out to join him in the middle of the basketball court.

"I wanted to talk to you," she said, "about Bobby."

T.J. nodded. "Kate told me."

"He swore he was going to tell you. We discussed it the other night. He just wasn't sure you'd believe him."

"Not believe Gus was an abusive jerk? Why wouldn't I?"

"No, not that. Bobby thought you wouldn't believe that he was trying to get Teresa to leave him. That he was trying to get her to walk out and never go back."

"He was right. I don't believe it."

Molly sighed. "Haven't you learned anything from Kate?"

"Pardon?"

"Kate. Hasn't she taught you anything? About people, about how they can change."

He eyed her for a moment. She was a beauty in her own right, with those striking eyes and that toned body. Even wearing men's boxer shorts and a T-shirt, she was pretty and it was easy to see why Bobby had fallen for her. "Don't you get it?" he said. "People don't change. They adopt behaviors that serve a purpose. When that purpose is over, they revert to type. You can dress a wolf in sheep's clothing, but it's still a wolf.''

''No wonder Kate hasn't slept with you.''

''What?'' That one took him by surprise.

''It's clear you two have the hots for each other. Any dummy could see that. I wondered why Kate wasn't doing something about it. Now I know.''

''Uh-huh.''

''You're a fatalist. Gloom and doom and why bother. She's not.''

''And that's why she hasn't slept with me?''

Molly nodded. ''Of course. In case you haven't noticed, she's a very remarkable woman. She saved my sorry butt and Peter's, too. And we're not the only ones. She isn't about to give up the goodies to someone who doesn't see who she is.''

''Goodies?''

''Men have asked her out. Lot's of 'em. But she keeps to herself and spends all her energy on the center. It's not healthy, but that's her. I figured you would be the one to unlock the gate, but now I see that she *can't* sleep with you. It would be like consorting with the enemy.''

''Molly, I think that's enough, don't you?''

T.J. spun around, sloshing his coffee so it spilled on his hand. Kate was behind them, close enough to have heard every word.

''But, Kate—''

''Please go inside,'' she said.

Molly shrugged and walked slowly past her boss into the center.

After she was clearly gone, Kate took a step toward him although she couldn't meet his eye. ''Sorry about that. You know Molly.''

''Yeah. She's a pretty smart cookie.''

''She's got a mouth the size of Nebraska.''

''Is she right?''

Kate, arms crossed, head down, found a pebble and kicked it with her toe. "The views expressed are not necessarily those of the management," she said.

"I see. So why *aren't* you sleeping with me?"

She looked up then. "I'm not going to discuss this."

He started toward her. "Why not? It's a perfectly reasonable question."

"Knock it off, T.J. We've got other issues on the table."

"You're such a spoilsport."

That made her smile at least and let her off the hook. Molly had hit the nail on the head and they both knew it. Oil and water, light and dark. They just had no meeting ground. Friendship? Maybe. More? Uh-uh.

"If Bobby doesn't come back in the next half hour, I want us both to go over to your mother's house."

"And do what?"

"With any luck, find out what happened last night. Where he was when the robbery took place."

"Looking for an alibi, huh?"

"Here's what I think," she said, ignoring his baiting tone. "I think Danny's gang committed the crime, then someone, maybe even Danny himself, called the cops. It would be real convenient for them to have a scapegoat and I'm quite sure Danny would be tickled pink to see Bobby take the blame."

T.J. couldn't find any holes in her logic, assuming Bobby was innocent. "Maybe we should go after the source. Find Arcola."

"We can try, but it won't be easy. He doesn't have a permanent address. He lives wherever he can find a couch to sleep on. But first, I think we should find Bobby before the police do."

T.J. walked with her into the center, closing the door behind them. He knew he should be thinking about his brother, but Molly's talk kept swimming in his head.

He took a sidelong glance at Kate. What would a relationship with her be like? Intense, that's for sure. Fun, too. But the important thing for her would be respect. She would have to respect the man she loved, not just understand him. Believe in what he believed in and vice versa. With Kate, there was no middle ground. She needed a hero to love.

If wishes were horses...

They reached the kitchen and T.J. let Kate walk through the door first. She stopped suddenly and he nearly bumped into her. When he saw Bobby sitting at the table, he stopped, too.

"Are you okay?" Kate asked.

Bobby nodded. He sure didn't look okay. He had a doozy of a shiner and his shirt was torn at the neck. T.J. glanced down and saw that the knuckles on his brother's right fist were swollen. "Who won?"

Bobby looked at him bitterly. "Guess."

"Danny?"

His brother's eyebrows went down in a look of utter confusion. "What the hell are you talking about?"

"You didn't have a fight with Arcola?"

"I haven't seen him in a week. Gus beat the crap out of me, okay? You remember Gus, don't you?"

Kate moved from the door into the kitchen and T.J. followed. She went over to Bobby and tilted his face up, turning it slightly so she could get a good look at his black eye. "I've got an ice pack in the freezer," she said. "T.J., would you mind?"

She sat down across from Bobby and lifted his hand. It was swollen, red and bruised, but when she moved his fingers and his wrist she found nothing broken. "Want to talk about it?"

Bobby looked from her to his brother. T.J. was next to him, holding the blue ice pack.

"Go on," T.J. said. "Take it."

Bobby got the pack and put it gingerly on his eye. "I been going to see her. Trying to tell her to get the hell out. The bastard's been picking on her more since I been here."

Kate kept her attention on Bobby, even though she could feel T.J. tense beside her. She wanted to tell him to keep calm, to listen without judgment. It was out of her hands now.

"Why won't she go?" T.J. asked, his voice brittle.

"She thinks it's her fault. That she asks for it."

T.J. swore. He moved behind Kate so she couldn't feel him anymore. "Why didn't she tell me what was going on? I saw her five days ago and she didn't say one damn thing."

"She don't want to bother you."

"Bother me?"

Bobby was staring at his brother, the accusation inescapable. Kate turned to look at T.J. He had taken a seat on the other side of the table. His face was passive, but his hands were clenched in tight fists.

"She knows you don't give a damn about her."

There was a long stretch of silence. Kate could hear the clock above the sink tick away the seconds. She wanted to ease the situation, to give comfort, but her instincts told her now was not the time. This conversation was long overdue.

"That's not true," T.J. said. "You wouldn't understand."

"Understand?" Bobby's voice rose higher and louder. "What do I have to understand? He's a son of a bitch and if she don't get out of there, he's not going to be happy with screaming at her. He's gonna hit her again. You and I both know that." Bobby stood and tossed the ice pack onto the table.

Kate moved forward, ready with a hand to hold him back, but he stepped out of her reach toward T.J.

"He gets drunk—hell, he's never not drunk and then he goes home and rags on her until she cries herself to sleep. What's so hard to understand about that?"

"You don't think I tried to get her away from him?"

"When? Nine years ago?"

"I learned my lesson." T.J. stood up and paced. "She doesn't listen."

"So you just gave up?"

"What was I supposed to do?" He wasn't even pretending to be calm anymore. His arm shot out wildly and his voice got louder. "Stay there for the rest of my damn life and watch her destroy herself? She loves playing the martyr. She gets all that wonderful attention from the neighbors and her sisters and most of all, her loving sons. She's not the innocent victim here, Bobby. All she's done is trap you in her sick little web."

"You're one sorry bastard," Bobby said. "She's your mother."

T.J. walked to the sink and leaned against the counter. "Were you with her all night? Did you go anywhere else at all?"

Bobby looked at Kate, surprised. "What's he talking about? I told you."

"There was another arson fire, Bobby. Someone called the police and told them you were there."

Bobby sat down again and looked briefly at T.J., then back at her. "Who?"

"We don't know. It was an anonymous tip. The police were here."

He swore. "I was with her. You can ask."

"I called this morning," Kate said. "Several times. There was no answer."

He shook his head. "We, uh, she fell asleep, so I unplugged the phone. I went for a walk..."

T.J. turned. "Did you go near the fire? Could someone have seen you?"

Bobby looked terrified. He sought out Kate's gaze and pleaded for her sympathy. "I don't know. I guess."

"Why didn't you say so?" T.J. came toward the table. "Why did you lie?"

"I don't know!"

"What do you mean, you don't know?"

Kate stood. "Hold it." She reached out and grabbed T.J.'s arm. His muscles were taut beneath her hand. "Sit down."

It took a few seconds for T.J. to hear her. Finally he stopped glaring at his brother and looked at her.

"Sit down. We're going to talk about this calmly. Understand?"

His mouth tightened to a thin line, but then he nodded. He walked carefully to the chair across from Bobby and sat.

"Bobby, I want you to tell us exactly what happened last night. Then we're going to call the police and tell them. Everything will be all right if we keep our cool. Got it?"

Bobby nodded.

Kate positioned her chair so that she could look at both brothers. She thought about getting coffee, but then Bobby started to talk.

Kate smiled at the last of the kids to leave the building, then shut and bolted the door. She was so tired she could barely see straight. Still, there was cleanup left and it was her turn to make dinner. The thought made her groan.

What a hell of a day. After Bobby had told them about his night and the police had come and questioned him to their satisfaction, she'd still had to referee basketball, stop two fistfights, counsel a sixteen-year-old girl who thought she might be pregnant, and be nursemaid to two feverish babies until their mothers could pick them up. A drink—an ice-cold martini with three olives—sounded awfully good right now. Then a dip in a clear blue pool. A massage. Sleep. Was it so much to ask for?

On top of everything else, she'd had to keep her eye on T.J. She had to admit he'd handled himself well this morning. No outbursts, no posturing. He'd listened, although she didn't think he believed Bobby. That would take time.

She started the rounds, picking up empty soda cans and assorted candy wrappers. Something shiny winked at her from the bottom of the corner pocket of the pool table. Another condom. Why would someone put a condom there? She shook her head and slipped the silver packet into her pocket. Another few minutes and the room was clean. Well, clean enough.

She shut off the lights. Peter was still cleaning up his area, but Molly had closed the nursery. Kate found her in the kitchen, sitting with Bobby. His eye looked worse, now there was a good deal of purple mixed with the black, but that was to be expected.

Just as Kate was about to open the fridge, T.J. came in from the back. He'd changed into a pair of worn jeans and a western shirt. His hair was damp from a shower and his cheeks freshly shaved. "Going on a date?" she asked.

His brows went up and he turned to Molly. "Hey—"

"It's a surprise," Molly said, cutting off T.J.'s question. "You and Captain Marvel here are going to dinner. On us."

Kate leaned back against the fridge. "That is a surprise. May I ask why you've suddenly become so generous?"

Molly smiled and shot a conspiratorial glance at Bobby. "It's been a tough day. You deserve a break."

"So you're sending us to McDonald's, right?"

"Nope. The Charthouse."

"You mean she didn't know about any of this?" T.J. walked over to Molly and scowled at her. "You little—"

"Chill, Cap'n," Molly said, patting him on the arm in the most patronizing way possible. "This is a nice thing. A good thing. Just think. Real plates. Matching silverware. Dessert."

T.J. caught Kate's gaze, then shrugged. "What do you think?"

She turned to her protégée. "What are you two going to do?"

"Don't worry," Molly said. "I won't let him out of my sight. We'll eat all our spinach and we'll do our chores."

Kate shook her head. "Bobby? Do you promise to stay here tonight? To take it easy and go to bed early?"

His smile had just enough mischief in it for Kate to add, "Alone?"

"I promise. Jeez. Can't even do a nice thing for people around here."

"Well, then. I guess that's that. I best go change."

"You'd best," Molly said, mocking her gently. She walked Kate to the kitchen door and into the hallway. "I really do have things under control. So don't you worry and come back early. Go to a movie. Take a walk on the beach. Go to a motel."

"Molly!"

She grinned. "It's not healthy, you know."

"And just how would you know this?"

"*Cosmo,* of course. You don't think *I* would *ever*—"

"I think you have entirely too much free time."

Molly laughed and twirled in a complete circle, both hands high over her head like some demented ballerina.

Kate shook her head and went on to her bedroom.

Sipping her wine, Kate stared out the restaurant window at the night sky. The cool liquid turned warm in her throat and all the way down, filling her with an amazing sense of well-being.

"Should I get another bottle?" T.J. asked. "We've done this one in."

She turned away from the window and smiled at the view right across from her. He'd been on his best behavior tonight. She'd laughed a lot, learned a few things and even more than that, she'd felt like a girl. A flirty, feminine, pretty girl with batting eyelashes and pink cheeks. The moment he'd held her chair for her, she'd decided she was on a date. It didn't matter that she wasn't really. She needed a date and a guy paying attention to her and damn it, she'd even giggled. She might even giggle again, if she felt like it.

"Sure," she said. "I'm in no rush."

He signaled the waiter and asked for another bottle of Chablis, then turned his attention fully on her again. That was part of the magic. He'd listened to her all evening. Every word. He'd asked questions, paid attention.

"So, you were telling me about your brothers," he said. "Five of them, right?"

She nodded. "All super-jocks. You ever hear of Caleb Dugan? He's with the Houston Rockets."

"Basketball? Can't say I follow the game."

"Smart man. Stay clear of those pro sports."

"Had enough of them growing up, huh?"

"Morning, noon and night. It was a religion in my family. We said our nightly prayers to Vince Lombardi. Everything we did, we did for the Gipper."

"It must have been hard for you."

The waiter brought the second bottle of wine and made a production of showing the label, pulling the cork and pouring that little taste for T.J. After his nod, the waiter filled their glasses, bowed and left.

"It wasn't hard. It was all I knew. My father did a hell of a job raising us on his own. Believe me, we were a handful."

"You're the youngest?"

"Yep. You wouldn't believe how they spoiled me. I think they all felt responsible for me, after Mom died. You should have seen them. I remember my grammar school graduation. It was no big deal, I mean, everyone passed. But when they called out my name, this huge roar came from the back of the auditorium. It was my family, of course. Shouting and hollering as if I'd just won the Heisman."

"It must have been great."

She studied T.J.'s eyes for a minute. She saw pleasure there, interest. And a little sadness, too. "Not like your family, eh?"

He laughed. "You could say that."

She sipped again and leaned forward, resting her elbows on the table. "You are a very fine looking man," she said. "Despite the fact that you know it."

T.J. leaned forward too, until they were eye-to-eye. "I think you're drunk."

She shook her head. "Maybe. But that doesn't change anything. You really are gorgeous."

His smile sort of blossomed and it was contagious, because then she had to smile, too.

"You're pretty gorgeous yourself."

"No I'm not, but thanks anyway."

"You calling me a liar?"

She put her glass down. "Yeah. But a polite liar."

He reached across the table until his fingers touched her arm. Then he drew a lazy line all the way up and back down again. She shivered with the contact, the closeness, the warmth in her belly that wine had nothing to do with.

"Maybe we should get out of here," he whispered. "Too many people, you know."

"Uh-uh," she said. "Don't forget the rules. Just because I think you're pretty, doesn't mean I'm going to jump in bed with you."

"We need to talk about that decision. I think we were a bit hasty."

She laughed. "That's the wine talking. And the moon."

"I don't think so. Very specific body parts clearly share this opinion. Important body parts."

"I make your toes curl, do I?"

He blinked a few times. "That's an interesting way to put it."

"Don't forget," she said. "I have five big brothers. You have to be careful with me, Detective. Or else."

"They'll come after me, huh?"

"Yep. And if you aren't perfect, they'll make sure you hit the road." She leaned back, breaking that silken bond between his fingers and her flesh. "They'll chase you right out of town and I'll think you left because of something I did." She turned to the window again and watched the cold, dark ocean.

"The guy in the picture, right? That's what happened?"

"Hmm?" She turned to T.J. again. The room had grown chilly and she rubbed her hands over her arms. "It's late," she said. "We'd better be getting back."

He didn't move. He looked at her so intently she had to lean back.

"I'm sorry," he said. "It must have been hard."

"Do we have the check yet?"

"Kate."

"Hmm? What?"

"Can't we talk about it?"

She got her purse from the back of her chair and put it on the table. "There's nothing to talk about. It was nothing."

"If it was nothing, why do you want to run?"

She sighed, the tightness in her chest making her more uncomfortable than she cared to admit. "It's all ancient history. I don't know why I brought it up."

"Go on."

She almost demurred, but then he gave her a smile. It wasn't much, just a little grin on one side of his mouth. What the hell.

"His name was Kevin Anderson. I met him in college. We fell in love and I thought everything was great up until the day he disappeared. A few days later, I found out why he split. My brothers had made it very clear that he wasn't up to snuff. They told him to get lost and he did. I yelled at my brothers and they yelled back. I mourned for an appropriate amount of time, then moved on. It's all better now. There. That's it. The whole ugly story."

T.J. let out a long breath. "So why haven't there been others?"

"There have been others. Lots of them."

"Yeah? How come I didn't see their pictures?"

"They weren't photogenic."

"Your nose is getting longer, Pinocchio."

"Can we just leave? This isn't fun."

His look made her feel like a coward. "Okay, sorry," she said. "You're right. I am avoiding the real issues, but it's been a long, hard day. All I want to do is forget the rest of the world and take a walk on the beach. I promise, we can talk about this tomorrow. I'll even cry, if you like."

"I don't want to see you cry. I want you to be happy."

She was about to make a snide comment, but something about his voice, or maybe his eyes, made her stop. "Thank you," she whispered.

He didn't acknowledge her. He just picked up the check and reached for his wallet." Come on. Let's blow this Popsicle stand."

She let him pay the bill and walk her outside, all the while thinking about Kevin and the pain she'd gone through when he'd left her and her devastation when she'd found out why.

Was he so different from T.J.? Kevin had seemed like a nice guy. Funny, athletic, almost as handsome as the detective here. It never crossed her mind that he could be so ugly. Everything they'd said to each other had meant nothing. The fact that she'd loved him, had made love with him, turned out to be as unimportant as the old T-shirts he'd left behind.

"I thought you wanted to walk on the beach?"

T.J. stared at her quizzically and she realized she was just standing on the sidewalk. "Sorry, I was somewhere else."

"Well, be here, okay? With me? My ego is just big enough to insist that I be the center of attention."

She smiled, knowing his words were meant to perk her up, to forget that little trip down memory lane. "Right," she said. "Let's go."

He took her hand in his. She stiffened, almost pulled away, then forced herself to calm down. This was a friendly walk, nothing more. Holding hands was not a commitment, no matter how you sliced it.

They reached the pier, but she shook her head and pointed to the beach. "I need to feel the water on my toes." She led him to a bench and she took off her sandals while he removed his running shoes and socks.

"Did I tell you how pretty you look in that dress?"

She almost argued. "Thanks."

"I mean it. You're something of a knockout, you know."

"Are we going to talk, or go to the beach?"

He stood up and pulled her beside him. "You're right. What was I thinking?"

"No offense, Captain Marvel. I just want some quiet time, okay?"

He nodded. In the dark, she couldn't see the details of his face. All the same, she knew his expression, the consideration in his eyes, the slight, almost sad smile. She didn't want to think about that. It was dangerous territory and she wasn't up for it.

They went down the steps and onto the cool sand. He led her past the pilings, right to the breakwater. Then they walked. Slowly, silently. Holding hands like lovers. She was grateful for the night. He wouldn't be able to see the tears in her eyes.

By the time they got back to the center, T.J. was beat. He wanted to fall into bed, preferably with the lady, but barring that little miracle, to go right to sleep. He'd wanted to ask her more questions, of course, but he'd kept his promise. They'd walked a long time without talking. He'd enjoyed being next to her all the same. She felt good there. Her strong hand in his, her long legs keeping up with his strides. Her bare feet more erotic then he cared to admit. He found himself thinking of ways to bring her out of her mood. It wasn't the time for jokes, that was clear. Talking about himself wasn't the ticket either. Just being there for her, letting her set the pace, the mood, seemed to be all she wanted of him.

And damn, he wanted to please her. Not just tonight, either. He'd realized, halfway back to the car, that he wanted to be the kind of man this woman would not only like, but respect. He wanted her to look up to him, to seek his advice, to turn to him in a crisis.

He might want it, but that didn't mean it was going to happen. There was still the matter of who he really was to contend with. Ed Russo's son. Teresa—

"Thanks for everything, T.J."

Kate was looking at him, holding the back door to the center open.

"It was my pleasure," he said. "It was nice to get out, wasn't it?"

She nodded. "I'm awfully tired. I'm going in. Don't hurry on my account."

He leaned forward to kiss her, but she ducked inside, leaving him alone, feeling a little foolish, in the parking lot. He grabbed the door just before it closed.

"Hey, police man."

T.J. spun around, reaching for a gun that wasn't there. Danny Arcola. He would recognize that voice anywhere.

The light from the center was perfect for Danny. It made T.J. an excellent target. He closed the door, unlocking it first. Once it was shut, he struggled to adjust to the darkness.

"What do you want, Arcola?"

"Just thought I'd let you know something the cops didn't find out."

T.J. searched the space behind his car, the dark next to the Dumpster. Arcola's voice seemed to be coming from there, but he couldn't see, damn it. "And what would that be?"

"Your little brother is in this up to his neck. He's mine, police man. All mine."

"Why don't you come say that to my face, instead of hiding like a girl?"

Arcola laughed. "Check it out. The old man had a cross on his neck. It wasn't there when he died."

"You want me to believe Bobby took it?"

There was no response and T.J. knew Arcola was gone. He waited another few minutes, still searching the shadows for the son of a bitch, but it was no use. Danny had come on his own terms and T.J. had been helpless to stop him.

There was only one question now. Had he told the truth about Bobby?

Chapter 10

The alarm startled him, but didn't wake him. T.J. hadn't slept much. His thoughts had him by the throat and wouldn't let up. The problem was those thoughts hadn't been about Bobby, but Kate.

What was he going to do about her? Last night, they'd crossed a line. They'd moved to new ground where the stakes were damn high. If it had been any other woman, now would be the perfect time to jump ship. But it wasn't another woman. It was Kate.

If he screwed things up now, he would hurt her. It didn't seem to matter that they hadn't slept together. She'd given him a secret and, in a way, that was more intimate. The smart thing to do was nothing. To act as if they were still pals. Joke around, flirt a little, then get the hell out of Dodge.

After all, she knew he wasn't staying after the summer.

He flipped the covers back and got up, anxious to get the day underway. He wanted to talk to Bobby, to find out once and for all if he'd been involved with the fire. T.J. would even follow Kate's advice and listen to the kid, no matter what. But Danny'd had a reason for coming last night. Maybe it was just to make T.J. wonder, to put a wedge firmly between him and his brother. On the other hand, the visit could have been a victory announcement.

He slipped on his robe and grabbed his toiletry kit, then walked quickly down the hall. Kate's door was closed, so was Bobby's. No one was in the bathroom and, heaven be praised, there was hot water.

By the time he was dressed and aching for coffee, the others had all gotten up. The bedroom doors were open, the rooms empty. T.J. thought Bobby might be in the shower.

Taking no chances, he went to the kitchen. Kate was eating cereal and reading the comics. Peter found a word in his puzzle. Molly poured herself a cup of coffee. No one noticed T.J. He ducked back out and headed for Bobby's room. There would only be a moment.

His brother's room was a mess, which actually comforted T.J. in some weird way. It was so typical of a teenager. Magazines and cassettes littered the floor next to dirty T-shirts and pants. Several soda cans lined the windowsill. The bed itself was a jumble of sheets, pillows and a comforter.

He began the search with Bobby's discarded jeans. He patted them down one after another and, for the first time in a long while, he felt like a cop. It felt lousy. He didn't want to suspect Bobby, but what were his choices?

After he'd checked the four pairs of jeans, he moved to the head of the bed and the junk beside it. Two more minutes and he would have to leave, even if he hadn't searched everything. He moved aside an empty pizza box, knocked over a *Sports Illustrated Swimsuit Issue*. And there it was. A gold crucifix on a gold chain. T.J. had never seen it before. He lifted it slowly, the metal cool in his hand. It wasn't ornate or inscribed, except for the eighteen-karat stamp on the back.

A door slammed shut. T.J. closed his fist around the necklace and darted into the hall. No one was there. He went back to his room and put the crucifix in his top drawer. He would hold on to it for a while, think about what he was going to do. Kate had made him promise not to jump to any conclusions, although this didn't seem like a jump to him, just a hop.

He would talk to her about it. Listen to her advice. When all that was done, he would confront Bobby. The game would be over. Danny would win.

"You want to tell me what's wrong?"

T.J. looked up at the sound of Kate's voice. She stood in his doorway, leaning against the frame.

"I thought you had to meet with the city council tonight," he said.

"I did. I'm back."

He looked at his watch. It was after eight-thirty. He'd been sitting here, staring at the walls, for over an hour. "How'd it go?"

"Swell. Now, you wanna talk?"

She looked great. Her hair was up, showing off that neck of hers. She even had earrings, little pearls on her perfect lobes. He couldn't tell if she had makeup on. It didn't matter. The dress was something new, at least to him. Soft and kind of large, it flowed on her curves like water flows around a rock.

"Last night," he began, shifting his gaze to the wall once more, "after we got back from dinner, Danny came by."

"What?" She came into his room, shutting the door behind her. "When?"

"Just after you went inside. He was in the parking lot."

"What did he say?" Without an invitation, she sat next to him on the bed. He felt the dip when she sat, although he didn't turn to look at her. She smelled good.

"He said that Bobby was his. That the cops didn't know it, but Bobby had stolen a crucifix necklace off Sanchez."

"Whoa."

"Exactly."

"Have you asked him? Bobby, I mean?"

He shook his head as he stood and went to the dresser. "I didn't need to." He opened the drawer slowly, as if there were something lethal inside. The gold chain caught the light from the overhead bulb and glinted at him. He took it out of the drawer and went back to the bed. "I found this in his room," he said, handing her the cross. "It's not Bobby's."

She took it and looked at it for a long time. "How do you know?" she asked quietly.

"I don't."

"Then why assume—"

"When do you give up? Do you have to watch him pull the trigger? See the smoking gun yourself? This is known as circumstantial evidence. Bobby admitted he was at the fire, he was seen there. The cross was in his bedroom. It all adds up."

"Only if he's guilty."

He walked across the room to the far wall, kicking his boot as he went. Leaning his head on the cool white surface, he took several deep breaths. Then he turned to her. "I like your world," he said. "It's nice and it's neat and there's a bow on every package. But it's not real. At least it's not any world I've ever lived in."

"Stop it," she said. "You're not going to make me the crazy one in this. Just because I don't believe that everything is a portent of doom doesn't make me nuts."

"Fine, we'll do it your way." He went to the bed again and held out his hand. Kate hesitated for a moment, then put the cross in his palm. He didn't acknowledge the worried look on her face. "Come on. Let's go ask him."

Crossing the room quickly, he opened the door and went into the hall. He didn't hear Kate's footsteps behind him, but he knew she would follow. Bobby's door was closed. T.J. heard music. He knocked. Loudly.

"Come in."

Just as T.J. opened the door, Kate came up behind him. She put her hand on his arm, not to stop him, just to warn him to take it easy. He nodded, consciously tamping down his anger.

Bobby was sitting cross-legged on the bed. The *Sports Illustrated* was on his lap. He looked so young.

"What?" he said, suspicion clear in his voice and on his face.

T.J. took a breath. "Danny Arcola came by last night."

"So?"

"So he told me something that's got me concerned." He held out the crucifix by the chain, the cross swaying at Bobby's eye level. "Where did you get this?"

The boy reached out and grabbed for the cross, but T.J. stepped back and away.

"It's mine. Give it back."

"I asked you a question."

Bobby looked from T.J. to Kate. "Make him give it to me."

"Just tell him where you got it, Bobby. It's all right."

His mouth tightened and his anger expanded to include both of them. "My mother gave it to me, okay? Is that a crime?"

"When?" T.J. took a step toward the bed. "When did she give it to you?"

Bobby moved sideways, away from his brother and off the bed. He stood, arms crossed over his chest, his face a mask of defiance. "What the hell's going on?"

"Just answer the goddamn question." T.J. felt his own fury building. He tried to take it down a notch, but when he looked at Bobby, something snapped. It wasn't just Bobby standing there. It was Gus and Ed and even himself. His whole family, his history, was right there in front of him.

Stubborn, stupid, belligerent. He wanted to knock some sense into the boy, make him see that this was no game. That his life was on the line and if he didn't do something right now, he would end up like the rest of them.

"I tell you she gave it to me. Ask her if you don't believe me."

"You think I won't? You think I'm gonna just let this pass, don't you? Well, I've got news for you." He stepped toward the boy, forcing him to back away. "You may be able to snow the others, but I know you. I *am* you." He turned to Kate. "Keep him away from the phone."

She moved toward T.J., but he slipped past her, heading out the door.

"Where are you going?" she asked, her voice high and tight.

"To visit my dear mother."

He knew she was following him, heard her ask him to wait, but he didn't. He'd gone as far as he could doing things Kate's way. Now it was time for him to take action.

Kate watched T.J. drive off, fighting the urge to chase after him. She was afraid of what he would do when he got to Teresa's. Not that he would hurt her, but that he would damage the relationship irreparably.

Molly came up behind her. "Boy, howdy," she said softly. "This is some pickle, hmm?"

Kate nodded. "You've said a mouthful, kiddo."

"So go on after him. What are you waiting for?"

Kate turned. Molly looked like a refugee from *Terminator II*. She had on an olive green tank top tucked into camouflage pants. Instead of army boots, however, she wore orange high-tops.

"Tell me something," Kate said as she led her assistant down the hall. "Had you seen the crucifix? Before the fire, I mean?"

Molly stuck her hands into her pockets and frowned. "Can't say that I have. Not that I believe Bobby was involved with the fire. 'Cause I don't. But I can't lie about that necklace, either."

"Something tells me this isn't going to go well. I think that necklace is going to hurt us."

"What are we gonna do?"

Kate stopped at her door. "I'm going after him. You stay here and talk to Bobby, okay? See if you can find out when he got the cross."

Molly nodded. "Go for it." Then she headed toward Bobby's room.

Kate grabbed her purse and went down the hall to the back door. She made sure it was locked before she walked to her station wagon. She tried to remember where the Sarduccis lived. She'd been there twice before and thought she remembered the way.

The drive gave her too much time to think. Trouble with T.J. had been inevitable, but damn it, she'd hoped for a longer period of grace. It had been really great there, for a while. Now she feared with all this hoopla about Bobby, T.J. would find his mask again, the one he'd worked so hard to lose. If it did turn out that Bobby was responsible for the fire and Mr. Sanchez's death, it would kill him. It would be the proof he'd looked a lifetime for—that he and Bobby were destined to come to a bad end.

She turned left on Welby Way and headed toward the old part of town. This had been a strictly agricultural area, up until the 1970s, when some smart developers had figured out that Harbor Bay had the best weather in the U.S. The boom had lasted well into the eighties and hadn't slowed down much even with the recession. Now oceanfront real estate was sky-high. Property values fell each mile from the beach and the houses grew older, the graffiti grew worse and gang activity wasn't sporadic, but the norm.

Three more long blocks and she turned left at San Paolo, then just a short stretch until she found the apartment complex where Teresa Sarducci lived.

T.J.'s car was parked crookedly on the street. Trash barrels had been left on the curb and someone's dog searched for a snack amid the garbage. She had to go another block until she found an empty spot.

What was he doing in there?

She locked the car and walked slowly toward the two-story building. The air was warm here; it felt as if it were in the high seventies, at least ten degrees warmer than at the center. Street lamps illuminated circles of broken sidewalk and rap music caromed off high walls.

Was he listening to her?

The door to the apartment house had a broken lock and she was able to enter without buzzing. Inside, the temperature rose another ten degrees and she felt clammy and uncomfortable as she walked to the stairs. What was she going to say? If T.J. wanted to fight with his mother, how could she stop him? He was a big boy now, able to cross the street all by himself. It wasn't her business and he had every right to toss her out on her keister.

She arrived at 2B, the Sarducci home. The paint was peeling from the warped door and it scratched her knuckles as she knocked. She couldn't hear anything but the sound of a vacuum cleaner across the way.

The door swung open. T.J. looked surprised to see her.

"May I come in?"

His eyes narrowed. He wasn't too glad to see her. But he stepped back, holding the door open.

The apartment was neat as a pin. The furniture was old, scarred, weary. Kate smelled cabbage. "Where's your mother?"

"In her room."

"Is she all right?"

He closed the door and walked across the mottled carpet to the kitchen. "My guess would be she's praying."

"What did she say about the crucifix?"

T.J. closed his eyes and shook his head in a moment of pure disbelief. "She doesn't remember. Can you beat that? She says she doesn't remember."

"Have you considered that it might be true?"

He opened a cupboard above the sink and nodded for her to look. "See that? Jelly glasses. Do you know how many years I spent drinking milk out of jelly glasses?"

"But—"

He moved to the next cupboard and opened it with such force it banged loudly against the wall and swung back. He shoved it aside. "See this? No two plates alike. Every one of them some piece of crap given to the church. Other people's trash. That's what she's lived with her whole life. Worked two jobs, just to keep up with the booze bills."

He turned to the cupboard and moved some plates to the side so roughly she felt sure they would break.

"There's probably a pint or two in here. This was always a favorite hiding place." When he didn't see any liquor, he went to the cupboard under the sink, flung it open and started going through the cleaning supplies and folded paper bags. "She hid them everywhere," he said, his anger making his voice quaver. "I used to find Scotch bottles in my T-shirt drawers, in my closet, in my tennis shoes. I don't know who the hell she was hiding them from. Ed drank. Gus drank. It's the only thing this family has ever done well."

No longer satisfied to just shove things aside, T.J. tossed a bottle of detergent on the kitchen floor, then cleanser, spray wax, bags. He was a wild man, insane, searching for evidence of the pain of his childhood. Kate felt like crying, like running out of here and not stopping till she got to the center.

She took a step toward him, then heard a soft moan behind her. It was Teresa Sarducci. She watched her son with a hurt beyond words. Her shoulders slumped forward, her eyes filled with tears. Her fingers played lightly on her rosary. Kate couldn't stand it.

"T.J.," she said, turning again to him. He had left the kitchen for the living room, right across from Teresa. If he'd seen his mother, he gave no sign. He was too busy throwing books from the bookcase to the floor, a steady stream of curses setting his tempo.

"T.J.," she said again, taking a step toward him. A hand stopped her. She glanced back at Teresa, who said nothing, just shook her head.

"But he doesn't know—"

"It's all right, Miss Kate. Don't say anything. Let him do this."

"I can't, Teresa, it's not fair."

The woman looked at her oldest boy, watched him tear her house apart looking for bottles. "Not much in this life is fair. When he's through, listen to him. He never had anyone to listen to him." She squeezed Kate's arm, then turned to walk back to her room. The sound of a heavy book hitting the floor made the old woman jerk, but she didn't look back. Kate could see, even from where she stood, that her shoulders trembled.

When Teresa closed her door, Kate faced T.J. once again. "Are you going to tear down the entire apartment?"

He paused at the last bookshelf, but didn't turn to face her. "Maybe."

"Then what?"

"I don't know. Maybe I'll go start some fires myself."

"Fine," she said. "Have a great time. While you're at it, you'd better figure out where you're going to stay tonight, because it's not going to be the center."

She headed for the door. There was no way she was going to stand here and watch this, or even try to get T.J. to listen to sense. It wasn't her job to be his keeper, or his conscience.

"Wait."

She grasped the doorknob.

"Wait, damn it. Wait."

She stood very still, not sure if she should head on out and not look back, or—

"Please, don't go," he whispered. "I can't get through this without you."

Her hand dropped to her side. "Yes, you can. You have to. Until you've made peace with this, you can't do anything else."

"You seem to have an awful lot to give to Bobby and the others."

She closed her eyes and forced herself to stay at the door and not go to him. "They're kids, T.J. You're not."

She felt him behind her and turned to face up to him. To stand by her beliefs, even if it meant the dream would be over. That he would hate her for this. "I'm sorry you had a rough childhood. I'm sorry your father hurt you and that your mother drank. But you know what? It doesn't matter. If your life is a mess now, it's because you want it that way. Every time you blame your past or your genes or your history, you buy into a mythology that you've created. You have a choice here. One you'll have to make by yourself."

"I see," he said, his voice quiet and hurt. "Thanks for the advice."

She waited for him to say something else. To yell at her or defend himself or tell her to go to hell. But he just stood there, in the middle of his past, not making a move.

She turned and walked out the door.

Kate knew she should go inside. It was very late, after midnight, and Molly and Peter were worried about her. But she couldn't. She framed her shot and threw the basketball. It hit the rim and bounced to her right. She took her time retrieving it.

Maybe T.J. would never come back, she thought. It was a very real possibility that she'd crossed the line with him, that he would never be able to forgive her. She took another shot, making the basket this time.

The night was cool, the sea breeze caressed her bare arms and legs. The sound of a car stopped her, but it wasn't his. She'd been like that for the past hour, pausing at the sound of every car, hoping it was the Camaro bringing T.J. home.

Except it wasn't his home. His home was in Hollywood, not here. No matter what, he would have left her. But damn, she hadn't wanted it to end like this.

Bobby had never changed his story. Even Molly hadn't been able to get him to recant. He swore his mother had given him the cross, that he'd never seen Reuben Sanchez. Kate believed him, but that had done nothing to make him feel better. He felt utterly betrayed by T.J. She couldn't blame him.

Why was it so hard for T.J. to give up his position, to give Bobby the benefit of the doubt? She knew the answer to that, even as the question formed. T.J. would never be able to believe the best of Bobby as long as he believed the worst about himself. He was trapped in a mind-set full of blame and anger and Bobby was just an extension of that canon.

She went to the free-throw line and held the basketball just above head level. Her concentration was rotten and she had to struggle to aim. Just as she let the ball go, she heard a step behind her and she spun around.

One corner of her mind heard the ball swish through the hoop. The rest of her attention focused on the man in front of her.

"Can anyone get in this game?" T.J. asked.

She nodded.

He walked to the ball and picked it up, then came back to the court. The lights that lit up the front of the center were good enough to play in, but they didn't let her see his eyes.

It was clear he wasn't smiling, but she couldn't get a handle on his mood.

"It's late," she said.

"Yeah, well, it took a while to repair the damage." He took another step toward her. "Wanna play shirts and skins?"

She breathed a bit. "Sure."

"You be skins." As he bounced the ball, she saw him smile and to her surprise she felt her eyes tear up.

"I don't think so, Captain," she said, struggling to keep her voice calm and playful, even though she wanted to run right into his arms.

"Spoilsport. Have it your way." He tossed her the ball and she caught it. "Twenty-one wins, two-point spread?"

She nodded and he came toward her, lifting his arms to guard her. She bounced the ball a few times, then broke off to her left, leaving him in the dust. She made the basket and caught the rebound.

He made the next two baskets and then the game got serious. She forgot the scene at his mother's house, forgot about Bobby and the cross and just enjoyed the sport. T.J. was a good player, but not good enough.

He got in a few extra points after he took his shirt off, though. He claimed it was because he was hot, but she had the feeling he knew just what he was doing. It wasn't fair, really. She tried to ignore him, to keep her eyes on the ball. But then she would brush against him, feel the hard muscle and the sheen of sweat on his pecs. For a minute, she thought about taking off her own shirt. That would even the score. But they were on a public street and she didn't feel like getting arrested.

He made a bad shot and she got control of the ball again. He looked at her with that cocky grin of his, like he knew his buff bod was too much for her delicate little heart to handle. That's all it took.

There was nothing he could do to stop her. She hit every shot, blocked his every move. After ten straight points, he had trouble coming up with original curses.

"One more, Russo," she said, wiping the sweat from her forehead. "Then you are history."

"Don't count your chickens," he said, circling her as she kept the ball in motion.

She darted to her right and he anticipated the move. He nearly stole the ball, but she spun and recovered, moving quickly to her left and behind him. He swore and she felt him in back of her, so close she heard his rapid breathing.

"Too little, too late, bub. I've got you beat by a mile."

"Never," he said, then leapt to block her shot.

He missed. The ball came down in a poetic arc, right down the center of the hoop. Kate pumped her arm, exhilarated by the win, the game and, mostly, her opponent. "What do you say to that, hotshot?"

He stood square in the middle of a circle of light. This time she could see his face, his eyes. His smile was warm, his gaze steady. "You win," he said.

She picked up the basketball and went to his side. For a moment she just looked at him and let her heartbeat slow a bit. Then she held out her hand. He took it. They walked to the door slowly, saying nothing. If she'd had a better moment, she couldn't remember when.

Chapter 11

T.J. was in serious trouble. He'd thought the game would have lessened his desire for her, but it had done just the opposite. He wanted her in his bed and he wanted her now.

He thought about going to his room. Shutting the door. Sensing Kate on the other side of the wall. He knew if he did that he would go nuts. He didn't *want* her in his bed—he *needed* her.

He needed to see her naked, to feel every inch of her body, to have her cry out from his thrusts. She might say no. He would respect that, of course. But something told him she wouldn't.

They moved through the big, dark main room, the squeak of rubber soles the only sound. Why was this so difficult? It wasn't as if he'd never seduced a woman before. But he'd never seduced Kate. He didn't want it to be like that with her. A parlor trick, a smooth move. He felt like a kid on his first date. His body was sure behaving like he was.

He slowed his step until finally Kate stopped and turned to him.

"What's wrong?"

"I don't know."

"You're not moping because I won, are you?"

He nodded. "Yeah. I'm all broken up about it."

A shaft of blue moonlight came through the high windows to illuminate her face. Her smile made his groin tighten even further.

"Come on, Captain. What's really going on?"

He let go of her hand and moved his fingers up her arm, tracing the delicate skin all the way to her shoulder. "We've got a problem here, ma'am."

She stepped back. The pool table stopped her. T.J. moved in, slowly, until the lower third of his body met hers. He saw her clearly in the moonlight. Her eyes wide and shiny, a little afraid, but excited, too. Her skin pale and glowing, her hair a wild halo. "A big problem," he whispered. Then he moved that last inch.

Her mouth opened beneath his. Willing, hot, ready. First just lips, soft, pliant. It wasn't enough and he used his tongue to explore her heat, her taste. He moved his hips, pressing his erection against the juncture of her thighs, feeling the heat there, too.

She moved her hand down his back and he felt electrified and the kiss wasn't nearly enough. He found the bottom of her T-shirt and slipped his hands underneath.

Her skin was soft and damp, warm and sleek and he explored her back until he couldn't stand it and he undid the clasp of her bra. Her gasp urged him on and he slid his hands to her chest, her breasts. Perfect beneath his palms, he felt the hard buds of her nipples. He brushed them lightly and when she pressed herself against him, he cupped her firmly with both hands. Perfect, perfect. The word played over and over and it didn't do them justice at all.

Breaking away from the kiss, he moved his body down while he lifted her shirt. His lips found the rigid peak of her right breast and his tongue flicked until he heard her moan.

Then he took the nipple in his mouth and sucked until he felt her tremble. Her hands grabbed at his back and her hips moved in undulating circles and she smelled hot and sweet and ready.

One last flick of his tongue and then he stood again and kissed her mouth, her cheek, her jaw and then that exquisite neck. It was his turn to moan.

"Shh," she said. "They'll hear you."

"Who?" he said, then went back to the important business of nibbling her earlobe.

"The kids."

He felt her open palms on his chest, pushing. Not hard, though. More for show than results. "They're asleep," he said.

"What if Molly wakes up? She does that, you know."

T.J. moved from Kate's ears to her mouth again. He kissed her, tickled her lips with his tongue and then she was tasting him and they didn't speak for a long, long time.

When she absolutely had to breathe, she gasped, then said, "Someone's going to catch us."

"Then let's go to your room."

"No! That's right next to Molly's."

"Then let's go to my room."

"No. It's not—"

He didn't let her finish. He kissed her again and she couldn't help herself, she had to kiss him back. What was he doing to her?

His hand was on her breast again. Touching, caressing, tickling until she squirmed. She felt his arousal, the hot thick pressure right up against her sex. Her hips seemed to have an agenda of their own and no matter how hard she tried to be still, it was no use. She pressed against him and when that wasn't enough, she lifted her leg around his backside and pulled him closer.

She ran her hands over his back, the muscles beneath her fingers alive with tension and strength.

The next thing she knew, he'd lifted her and sat her on the edge of the pool table. She wrapped both legs around him and squeezed, while he showed her the wonderful advantages of this new position.

His hands found the waistband of her shorts and he pushed down. Just as he got them as far as he could go, the sound of a siren pierced the silence and they both jumped. She stood up quickly while he stepped back. In a second she had her pants up and her shirt down.

She heard his soft chuckle. "I don't think that was the sex police."

"No," she whispered. "But probably an omen."

"It's a sign that you and I should be making love right now."

"No," she said again, backing away from him. "Not here."

"Where?"

"I don't know. Just not here."

"Your office?"

"Uh-uh."

"The kitchen?"

She shook her head. He kept coming toward her and she kept backing up. Eventually they would run out of room. She held out a hand and stopped him. "Look," she said. "We can't do this. It wouldn't work. You and I, we're friends. We shouldn't mess that up. We're both adults, right? We can be strong."

"Right." But then he did a magic trick with his hands. Touched her side and turned her mind to mush.

"Molly is just inside," she said, barely recognizing her own voice. "So is Peter. And Bobby."

"They're not invited."

"We'd have to be quiet."

"I can do that." He stepped toward her again. Her arm weakened just a bit.

"No, you can't. You'll yell."

He took her hand in his and brought it down past his waist. "I don't think I'm the one who's going to do the yelling."

"That's pretty arrogant, don't you think?"

"Just the facts, ma'am."

"You are too much."

"Nope. Just enough."

Then he kissed her again and as she closed her eyes she knew he'd won. Darn.

The second she had that thought, he broke the kiss, then grabbed her hand and led her past the pool table, out of the main room, past the preschool area, all at a clip that was nearly running. She laughed and he shushed her. She felt like a naughty kid, sneaking into the barn for a roll in the hay.

Just before they left the kitchen, he stopped, kissed her once hard on the lips, then opened the fridge. The light nearly blinded her, but then he shut the door again, a big bottle of Gatorade in his hand.

Then he took her arm and they went down the hall as fast as they could tiptoe. She didn't think, didn't dare. For once she let her excitement rule, her heart lead, her body have its way.

Finally they were in his room, the one farthest from the others, and the door was shut. There was no lock, but it was really late and everything had been really quiet out there and damn it— She kissed him and he flailed a bit until he found the dresser and put the sports drink down. Then his hands were all over her, pulling and tugging until her shirt was off and her bra was somewhere else.

She found the top button of his jeans and she got that open, then she fumbled a bit with his zipper. He yelped, she laughed, he growled, then she heard the unmistakable sound that can only by made by a zipper in the middle of the night. While he got rid of his pants, she got rid of hers, both of them kicking off shoes at the same time.

It was just light enough in the room for her to make out the important parts of his body. That world-class chest. His muscled arms. The rather astonishing evidence of his desire.

"You are gorgeous," he said. "I'm humbled."

"That doesn't look humbled to me."

He looked down and grinned. She wasn't quite sure how but he moved that portion of his body and only that portion, in a jaunty little wave.

"How do you do that?" she asked.

"Practice, practice, practice," he said. Then he grabbed her again and she was flush against him, feeling everything from an entirely new perspective.

She wasn't sure how they got there, but they reached the bed. She sat and he leaned over to kiss her and then they were both on the bed and he was lying on top of her.

He stared at her, locking her gaze to his. "You know I've wanted you for a very long time," he whispered.

She nodded.

"I've given a lot of thought to what I wanted to do."

She nodded again. But this time, she ran her foot up his leg and back down again.

"I dreamed about this. Every night. You being in the next room and all."

"T.J.?"

"Hmm?"

"Shut up."

He laughed and she felt him shake from his feet all the way through his chest. Then he kissed her and the laughter became a soft groan. His touch went down the length of her and he lifted off her just enough so that his hand could sneak between them. He tickled her belly, then lower, until his fingers slipped inside her and she trembled.

The pressure built slowly and she felt as though she were caught in a tornado of sensation. Every place she touched she found hot, willing flesh. Every place he touched simply wanted more.

She brought her hand down his back, then down his side and underneath. Taking him in her palm, she stroked him evenly, his whole length. His gasp was loud and she shushed him, and when that didn't work she silenced him with a kiss.

He lifted his hips and spread her legs with his knees.

"Wait," she said. "We have to—"

He cursed, then rolled quickly to his left and opened the drawer of the bedside table. She heard him move things around then shove the drawer closed again. He hadn't even looked.

"Boy, you were sure prepared," she said.

"It wasn't hard. I kept finding the little buggers all around the place." He ripped the packet open and she had to scoot over so he could lie flat on his back.

"You want to give me a hand here?" he asked as he tried to put the condom on.

She applauded softly.

"Cute," he said. "Never mind. I did it all by myself."

"Well, I hope you're not going to do the next part all by yourself."

"Uh-uh. That wouldn't be fun." Then he was on his side and he swung his leg over hers and moved so he was on top once more.

He looked at her for a long minute and even in the dark room, she realized how inevitable this moment had been. The first time she'd seen him he'd cast a spell, and every second since then had been leading to this man, this night, this bed.

He moved. Slowly, surely, his hips came down and he slipped inside her. Without thinking, she lifted her legs and wrapped them around his waist. Her arms went around his neck. Her lips found his and as he continued the forward pressure, her kiss turned into a long, low moan.

"Oh, damn," he said. "Oh, damn."

"Shh."

"Kate you're so—"

"Shh. Kiss me."

"But oh, this is—"

"Shh. T.J. Don't."

"Don't what?"

"Talk."

"I'm not. But damn it."

She heard a clunk. Something loud. She froze. "Wait."

"What?"

She grabbed his hips and stopped him. "I heard something."

"It was me, dying."

"No. I think it was one of the kids."

"Screw 'em"

"T.J.!"

He didn't say anything for a moment. Neither did she. There was no sound. When he moved inside her again, she relaxed and brought her attention right back where it belonged.

He was moving faster now, the pressure inside her building. She wanted him closer, tighter, not separate at all and she lifted her own hips to the rhythm he'd set. It had been so long. So worth the wait.

They moved together as if they'd known each other a lifetime. Somehow he knew just when to slow down, to speed up, just where to touch and when to kiss. He knew everything there was to know about her.

She knew him, too. The softness, the confusion, the anger. And she loved him. She loved him in a way that was totally new, with a different heart, a different mind. He'd changed her forever.

The thoughts flew away until she was all sensation. It would be soon. She was climbing and he was going faster and deeper. She moaned and he moaned and then there was a thump.

She froze.

He groaned.

She shushed him.

"Don't make me beg," he whispered.

"Quiet."

Nothing. Long seconds of nothing but the agony of staying still.

Then she couldn't wait. Not a heartbeat longer. She moved her hips up. He whimpered. It started again, the slow, steady, rising buildup. But it was harder this time. Hotter. More urgent. Desperate. She was almost there. Almost.

A door closed. T.J. stopped. "What was that?"

"I don't care," she said.

"But—"

She pushed her hips up hard. "Don't make me beg."

He didn't.

It took a long time for her heart to stop thumping in her chest, to catch her breath. He lay beside her, his chest rising and falling rapidly. His arm was under her neck and she felt his body pressed against her side. She was satisfied beyond words and anxious for more all at the same time.

"Wow," he said.

"Yeah."

"The East German judge gave that a perfect ten."

"I should hope so," she said, smiling.

"The only problem is, our drinks are all the way over there."

"Thirsty, eh?"

"Hell, yeah."

She thought about getting him the drink, about moving at all, and decided he would live. "T.J.?"

"Uh-huh?"

"How come we did this?"

He shifted beside her, just a little move of his hips and her stomach clenched at the thought of his leaving. When he didn't move for another few seconds, she relaxed again.

"I think it's a function of biology," he said. "Man, woman, hormones."

"No, I mean why now? I wasn't going to, you know."

There was a long pause and finally she turned her head to look at him. He was staring up at the ceiling. "I'm not sure. Maybe you did it because I needed you." He looked at her now and although it was still dark, she could see his face. The gentleness there made her swallow hard. More than that, his openness, his vulnerability, were heart wrenching. This from a man who'd lived behind his mask for so many years.

"I think I needed you, too."

He shook his head. "Not in the same way. You're a hell of a strong woman, Kate."

"Not so much."

"Yeah, so much. You're the strongest woman I've ever met."

"Yeah, me and Schwarzenegger."

"You know what I mean."

She did. Hadn't she worked at being strong? Wasn't that just what she wanted to be? Then why did she feel so—

"What's wrong?"

She sighed, then turned on her side. She snuggled close putting her arm and her leg over his body. A quick shiver of cold went through her and by some strange magic he reached to his side to grab the comforter and tossed it over them both. Closing her eyes, she wallowed in the warmth. His body felt so good, so right. It was as if she'd found the other piece of the puzzle, the exact matching piece. Together they made a complete picture.

"Hey," he said. "Tell me."

"I'm not always strong, you know. I can be hurt and I can be wrong."

"You think I'm going to leave? That all I wanted was a toss in the sheets?"

She shook her head, at least as much as she could without disturbing her position. "No. I know we're friends. And that means a lot to you, too."

"Then what?"

She sighed again. She twirled some soft hairs on his chest. "I had it all figured out. I didn't need sex. I was perfectly fine without it."

"Hmm?"

"Really. I haven't done it in—well, a long time. It's not that hard, you know. Lots of people are celibate."

"I don't even like to hear that word."

"It's just that I've never been able to separate sex and love. And I've never been any good at love."

His chest kept rising and falling, moving her head with him. She could hear his heartbeat, a steady strong pulse that seemed incredibly intimate to her.

The longer he stayed silent, the more she thought she shouldn't have said anything. Now he would think she was out to trap him or something. "Forget it. It's not important."

"I've never been any good at it, either," he said, his voice soft and kind. "Maybe this is better. Being friends, I mean."

"Maybe."

"You're my first, you know."

"First what?"

"Friend that I've had sex with."

"I see."

"Hey, this is a big deal."

He rubbed her arm and she closed her eyes.

"The women I've known, I don't know, have all had this schedule. First dating, then sex, then marriage. Like it was all written up beforehand in some secret women's manual. So having sex was like this test. To see if I could do it, then escape. You know?"

"I think so."

"But with you, I can just enjoy it. No pressure."

"Right."

"So I'm thinking this might be a good thing for both of us."

"How do you know I don't have a schedule?"

"You wouldn't have said what you did at my mother's house if that were true."

"What do you mean?"

"Basically, you told me to grow the hell up. To stop whining and get on with it."

"And that meant I didn't have marriage in mind?"

"No. Just that I was more important to you than that. It was a risk. I might not have come back, you know."

"Sure you would have."

"I thought about leaving. Just getting in my car and going back home."

"Why didn't you?"

"Because I'm not through here."

"With Bobby?"

"Among other things."

She stopped playing with his chest hair, nearly stopped breathing. "What other things?"

"You."

His fingers came under her chin and urged her to look at him. "I don't know where this is going," he said softly. "I care a lot about you, more than I've ever cared for any woman. But I've got a lot more questions than answers right now. About Bobby, me, you, everything. I don't know who I am anymore, Kate."

She reached over and touched his cheek with her fingers. "I do. You're a good man, Captain Marvel. Maybe you aren't comfortable with that, but I know it's true. I want you to understand something. I see you. I do. All of it."

"And here you are."

"And here I am."

Chapter 12

T.J. stood under the hot shower. For once, he didn't try to rush. Kate had already washed up and the kids would just have to deal with the cold water. He closed his eyes and thought about last night. About what the hell he was doing.

Kate was in love with him. He knew it as surely as he knew he didn't know what to do about it. She hadn't said the words, but that didn't matter. She'd given herself to him. Opened herself up to rejection, to pain—the kind of pain he was an expert in. Giving, not getting.

His thoughts turned to other women in his life. Sandra, Debbi, Caroline. They'd all been good people, nice. They'd each offered him a future and a home and he'd run like hell.

It hadn't been hard to make those decisions, there hadn't been a moment's hesitation. The police department was his family, his apartment the only home he needed. The thought of having a child scared the hell out of him. What did he know about raising a kid? His role models hadn't been Ozzie and Harriet. Look how well he was handling Bobby and he wasn't even his father.

Everything he knew about life, about how things worked, told him that family patterns were nearly impossible to break. How many times had he watched some poor schmuck cry his eyes out after he'd smacked his kid around. If he had a dollar for every time he'd heard "I swore I'd never hit my kids" he would be a rich man by now.

It was easy to pretend that everything with Kate would be different. But he knew better. There was no pressure here, at least not the kind that led to abuse. No long nights filled with crying babies, where sleep was forgotten and tempers flared. No day after day of the same four walls, the same discussions, the same person across the table. Loving her wasn't hard. It wasn't real.

His beat, homicide, *that* was real. Ninety percent of all murders were committed by a loved one. Those were some kind of odds.

He picked up the shampoo and the fragrance made him think of Kate. In his bed, in his arms. He didn't want to remember that, or wrestle with the fact that something had happened last night that he couldn't explain. Sex had never been like that before. All those women for all those years had been shadowboxing. There had always been a part of his mind outside, observing, keeping him from feeling. Ready to run.

Kate had stripped away that safety net. For the first time in his life, he'd felt complete. It scared the hell out of him.

"Love the outfit," Molly said, staring fixedly at Kate's feet. "It's a new look for you, isn't it?"

Kate followed her gaze. She had on one white sock and one yellow sock. Her face filled with a rush of heat. "I was, uh, distracted this morning."

"I'll bet."

She looked up at Molly's insinuating tone. "What is that supposed to mean?"

Molly picked up her big cup and held it in front of her mouth. "Nothing."

Kate knew she was grinning, that Molly suspected the worst. Had T.J. been too loud last night? Did Peter know? Bobby? What had she been *thinking?* Was she insane?

"It's not just the socks," Molly said.

Kate touched her cheek with her fingertips. How could it show? Was she blushing differently?

"Cold," Molly said. "Ice-cold."

Kate moved her hands to her throat. Had he given her a hickey?

"Warmer."

"What? Just tell me already!"

Molly laughed, spilling coffee all over her lap. "Your T-shirt," she said, grabbing for a napkin. "Look at it."

Kate looked down. She saw nothing remarkable. It was just a white crew neck T-shirt, the same one she wore at least once a week. There were no big stains, no rips or tears.

"Some of us like to wear the tags on the inside," Molly said.

Kate saw it now. The shirt was inside out. It wasn't possible to blush any harder. She'd reached maximum redness. "I like it this way."

"Yeah, uh-huh. And did we practice safe sex?"

"Cut it out, Molly," Kate said, turning back to the sink.

"Hey, I think it's great."

"What's great?"

Kate heard Peter and groaned inwardly. There was no way Molly was going to keep quiet about this.

"Check out Kate's fashion statement," Molly said.

Kate grabbed a bagel and a knife, not sure whether to slice the bread or stab her assistant.

"Holy underwear, Batman," Peter said. "Somebody got laid."

"Peter!" Kate spun around, the knife feeling better and better in her hand.

His grin broadened. "Don't look at me. I'm a damn monk. I'm just glad you kids finally got it out of your system."

"Stop it!" Kate slammed the knife down on the counter. "Stop it, both of you."

Molly batted her lashes. "What do you mean?"

"Fine. We had sex, okay? Not that it's anyone's business. But we did it. Happy now? Nothing's changed, got it? Nothing."

"Why Kate," Molly said. "I'm surprised at you. Such a private matter."

"I'm stunned," Peter said. "I never would have guessed."

"Look," she said. "My life is just the way I want it, okay? I'm happy just the way I am. I'm not in love. I don't do love. It only screws things up. Besides, he's going home. He's going back to his life and I'm going back to mine and I wish to hell you people would mind your own business."

"You don't *do* love?" Molly said, arching her eyebrows. "What does that mean?"

"It means that I have no intention of becoming a lovesick puppy." Kate sighed. This was not going well. "Not that you shouldn't. Fall in love I mean. I think it's a good thing, a noble institution."

"But not for you, huh?" Molly's voice had softened. There was a trace of pity in it that Kate couldn't abide.

"That's right. It's no tragedy. I've tried it. It just didn't work out. Just like some people aren't good at sports or are tone deaf. Don't look at me like that. I haven't got a problem with it, so you can just get that sorrowful little frown off your face. Don't you have work to do?"

"Kate," Molly said. "With all due respect, you're full of sh—"

"Morning."

Kate jerked her gaze to the door. T.J. stood there looking as if he'd been there awhile. What had he heard?

T.J. looked from Kate to Molly, his expression giving nothing away. "I didn't mean to interrupt," he said.

Molly grinned wickedly. "Way to go, Captain."

"Molly," Kate said, glaring for all she was worth. "Don't you dare—"

"What'd I do?" He sounded innocent enough, but Kate didn't buy it. He'd heard.

"Nothing. Not a thing." Molly didn't look up, didn't blink an eye. She took another sip of coffee, then turned to Peter. "I had the weirdest dream last night. All about a train going into a tunnel."

"Oh, man. I hate that. I had a strange one, too. Snakes. Lots of 'em. Big slimy snakes." He gave an exaggerated shudder.

"Really?" T.J. pulled out his chair and sat down.

Molly stood up and walked to the fridge. "*National Geographic* special on tonight, Pete. About volcanic eruptions. You know, all that lava and hot air?"

"Hey, maybe we can pop the cork on some champagne while we watch."

T.J. shook his head. "You two need round-the-clock care. A whole team of psychiatrists."

Kate held her breath, hoping, praying that Molly and Peter would let it go.

Leave. Vanish.

"News flash, Captain," Molly said. "From radio station DUH. We're not the ones who have our heads in the sand. We've known for weeks you guys had the hots for each other. It's all perfectly natural. There's no reason to get all huffy about it."

"Huffy?" He stood then, his gaze shifting between Molly, Peter and Kate. "I haven't got a clue what you're talking about. And I've never been huffy a day in my life." He shook his head. "Huffy. Humph."

"Yeah, right." Molly walked next to him and patted him gently on the back. "Just don't listen to her bull, okay? She talks the talk, but she don't walk the walk."

"As enjoyable as this has been," Peter said, "I've got to get the room ready for the monsters." He walked toward the door, grabbing Molly's hand as he went. "Come on, Beavis. You've caused enough havoc for one day."

"Beavis?" she said, following him out the door. "You know who that makes you, don't you?"

Kate stared after them for a long while. She couldn't make herself look at T.J. She would kill that girl. Then she would kill Peter and go back and kill Molly again.

"Think they might have guessed?" T.J. asked, the sarcasm dripping.

Her head fell forward into her hands. "Is it too late to join a convent?"

"After last night? Oh, yeah."

"What did you hear?" She spread two fingers and peeked at him.

"Nothing I didn't already know."

She relaxed and brought her hands down.

"Not that I believed any of it."

"Oh?"

He shook his head as he walked toward her. Something about his gaze made her step back.

"Don't."

"Don't what?"

"Look at me like that."

"Now you're sounding like Molly."

"Fine. Don't look at me like that, *Captain*."

"I must say, I don't think I've ever done this to a woman before."

She backed up farther and hit the counter. "What?"

"Turned her inside out."

Kate looked down at her T-shirt again. "This? Oh, please. Just because I—"

He took another step. Close enough for her to feel his sweet breath on her face. Close enough for the heat of his body to warm her to the bone.

"I—"

The moment his lips touched hers, all of the sensations from last night rushed through her, as if the kiss had opened the floodgates. Her arms went around his neck of their own accord. Her insides grew moist and her knees weak. Coherent thought disappeared and in its stead came a hunger for this man, this kiss. For more.

His hands moved down her back, pressing her closer, tighter. The sway of his hips provoked her into readiness. But more than that, his taste, his smell, the feel of him was a hypnotic drug that took her balance and her senses.

"Wait," she said, breaking away. "Stop."

"Why?" His voice had gone all gruff and throaty.

"We can't. I can't."

"Sure you can. The cat's out of the bag, Kate. They know."

"This has nothing to do with them." She put her hands on his chest, then slipped sideways, out of his embrace.

"Then why?"

"Because it's not appropriate."

"We're over eighteen."

"Knock it off, T.J. You know what I'm saying."

"That last night didn't matter?"

"Of course it mattered. But it was a one-time phenomenon. We both had a lot of angst to get out of our systems. It was completely understandable that it manifested physically. But we're both intelligent adults who can curb that predilection. And we must."

"Thank you, Sybil. Can I speak to Kate now?"

She sighed, taking another step away from him. "Okay. It was a one-night stand, T.J. We were both hot to trot and we wound up between the sheets. It was great. Wonderful. And the only event of its kind."

He grinned at her. That wasn't the effect she was going for.

"I'm serious."

"I know."

"Then why the hell are you grinning like that?"

"You snore."

"What?"

"You do. It's pretty cute though. Not a window-rattler or anything like that. Just this soft little snort every once in a while."

She looked him over, from head to toe. He looked like a normal man. With his combed hair, his clean, neat shorts and T-shirt. *He* had even managed to find a matching pair of socks. But it was quite clear he was totally insane.

"And you mumble, too. I couldn't make out the words, but I'm pretty sure you were talking about me."

"What does this have to do with anything?"

His smile broadened. He folded his arms across his chest and leaned against the fridge, somehow managing to infuriate her with his stance alone.

"Well?"

"Don't kid yourself, sweetheart. We both know this was more than a quickie. Something happened last night. I was there, remember? I don't know what we're in for, but there's no way it's not going to happen again. Not while we're both under the same roof."

"Then what? We shake hands and say goodbye? You go your way, I go mine?"

He nodded. "That's what you want, isn't it? You don't do love, remember?"

She couldn't seem to swallow. Or look him in the eye. "The kids will be here any minute. I need to get ready." Before he had a chance to say another word, she was out of there.

* * *

T.J. went on the morning run, but the old competitive spirit wasn't in full gear. Kate ran like the wind, leaving them all in the dust and he stayed with the herd. Well, slightly apart from them. He needed to think. Why had he baited her like that? She'd given him the perfect opportunity to bow out gracefully and instead he'd jumped in with both feet.

A horrible thought niggled at him. He held it at bay as they crossed the street to the pier. But once he was on the sand, running past the pilings where his dagger hung like an old master, he gave in.

He'd egged her on because of his ego. He couldn't stand the thought that she found him so dismissable. How could she have gone through what he had last night and been so willing to chalk it up to a one-night stand? He *knew* one-night stands and damn it, that wasn't one.

He'd been so sure she was in love with him, that she'd press for a relationship, a commitment. And then she says she doesn't *do love*. What the hell did that mean, anyway?

His leg muscles ached from running in the soft sand. It would be a lot easier to move over a few feet to the wet sand, but somehow this morning, the pain worked. He wanted to hurt, to keep his brain busy with that. Once again, Kate had managed to mess him up but good. What was he supposed to do now?

His question was answered as soon as he rounded the corner to the center. A police car, bubble light circling, was parked in front and every kid who hadn't been on the run stood gawking. They were here for Bobby. He knew it with a certainty that was physical.

T.J. urged his body to move faster, but by the time he got to the center he was walking. The crowd parted for him as if he were Moses. The kids that had been so friendly just yesterday, talking, joking, laughing, stared at him with saucer eyes. He was used to that look. The bystander stare, he called it. As if the murder or robbery or accident created a shield, like a television screen, between the participants and observers. The rules of etiquette no longer applied. The nicest people turned into insensitive jerks. As if their voices didn't carry, didn't wound.

Bobby, flanked on either side by uniformed officers, came outside. He looked too young to T.J., like a nine-year-old. A child. His kid brother. The pain set in his stomach, a great low ache. He wanted to rip the handcuffs off, beat the policemen until someone was dead. How had he ever believed Bobby could have set those fires? It was insane. The realization hit him with the force of a blow.

Bobby was innocent. No question remained, no doubt at all. It wasn't possible for his kid brother to commit murder, not even manslaughter. Why had it taken this to get him to see that? Kate had been right from day one. Damn it all to hell, he'd tripped up somewhere and now Bobby was facing murder charges.

"Hold it," he said.

The cops stopped and looked him over. The blond kid, he wasn't that much older than Bobby, stared for a minute at the LAPD logo on his chest.

"I'm Detective T.J. Russo. Hollywood homicide."

"Looks like we solved this one, Detective," the shorter cop said. T.J. looked at his name plate. Officer J. Freed.

"What's the charge?"

"Murder two. Arson."

T.J. turned his attention to Bobby. "Did they read you your rights?"

T.J. didn't think he would answer. His stare was so full of hatred, it could peel paint. As it was, it took a few years off T.J.'s life.

The silence grew and then there was a little commotion from inside. It was Kate. She wasn't in shorts anymore. She wore a simple dress with plain pumps. The latest in jailhouse chic. Molly was beside her, and the look she shot T.J.

didn't make him feel any better. It was clear she blamed him, too.

"Bobby, remember," Kate said, walking right to him. "You don't say a word until you talk to the attorney. I've called him and he'll meet us at the station."

Bobby nodded, still staring hard at T.J. Kate followed his gaze. "Go get changed," she said. "I'll wait for you."

"I don't want him there," Bobby said, practically spitting the words.

She turned back to him. "Bobby—"

"He put me here. I won't cooperate if he's there. I swear to God. I'll clam up so tight you won't know what to do. I mean it. Just keep him the hell away from me."

She hesitated. Then she nodded. "Go on. I'll see you in a few minutes."

The officers had watched this little slice of human drama with serene indifference. But before they reached the car, Freed turned to T.J. "Who are you?"

T.J. swallowed. He couldn't find his voice for a second and had to cough. "I'm his brother," he said.

"No, he's not," Bobby said. "He's nothing to me. I don't even know his name."

The smaller cop opened the door to the black-and-white, then put his hand on Bobby's head so he wouldn't bang his head against the window frame. T.J. couldn't watch.

He heard the engine start. He heard the car move into gear and take off. His guilt felt like a noose around his neck.

"Go on. Get dressed."

It was Kate, beside him. He didn't move. She touched his shoulder and he winced.

"It's going to be all right. Just get yourself dressed."

"He said he didn't want me there."

"We'll see about that."

"I don't want to do any more damage."

"You're going to have to trust me. I know you don't want to, but that's just too darn bad." She walked in front of him, forcing him to look at her. Her face was filled with determination, not defeat. She didn't hate him, even though she had good reason.

"Will you trust me?" she said in a whisper only he could hear.

"Yes."

"Good. You have three minutes. Wear a suit."

When he didn't move, she took his hand in hers. "I don't want your mother getting to the station first. Understand?"

He nodded, squeezed her palm, then went inside.

The really great thing about knowing everyone at the police station was that they let her sit in with Charley McKeague and Bobby.

Charley was an old friend, an attorney who reserved his *pro bono* work for her kids. He was in his sixties and sharp as a tack. She enjoyed being with him. His speech was slow and very calm. He soothed the way classical music soothed, working on a part of the brain she couldn't name. Charley was also the happiest married man she'd ever met. He'd been with his wife for over forty years and he talked about her as if they were newlyweds.

Today he'd worn a necktie that was bright, to say the least, and she knew without asking that he'd done it for Sara. One of the grandkids had probably given him the awful thing for Christmas and Sara had probably said it was only right that he should show how much he loved the thought, if not the gift itself.

He sat across from Bobby, on her right. He leaned forward a bit, giving Bobby his whole attention. Every so often, he would write on his yellow legal pad, then pause and ask another question.

Kate tried to follow the conversation, make sure every angle was covered, but thoughts of T.J. sitting in the hallway on that small bench kept crowding in. He'd been silent the whole drive over, silent when he'd met Charley. She was pretty sure she knew what he was thinking, how worried he was about Bobby, but the silence bothered her a lot. It wasn't like him. He should be on a tear right now, demanding Bobby's release, throwing his weight around. Not sitting there so quiet. So disheartened.

"Tell me about this necklace, Bobby," Charley said, that liquid voice of his unsuited to the ugly room and uglier circumstances.

"My mother gave it to me. I told you that already."

"You sure you can't remember when?"

Bobby shook his head. "It was a long time ago. When I was a kid."

Kate saw the slight smile whisper over Charley. "For a birthday present?"

Bobby stared at the scarred table. "I don't know. Maybe."

"Does it have any special significance? Perhaps for your confirmation?"

He looked up then, the fear so apparent in him it made Kate's stomach tighten. "Look, she gave it to me so I wouldn't tell, okay? That she'd been drinking. It was a bribe. I didn't even want the friggin' thing. Can't we just let it go?"

Charley gave Kate a questioning look.

"Let's skip it for now, can't we? Move on to something else?"

Charley nodded. "When you were watching the fire, did you see anyone? Anyone at all?"

"Sure. Firemen. Rubberneckers. There was a bunch of people all over the place."

"Did anyone see you?"

Bobby shrugged. "I don't know."

"It's important. They say there are eyewitnesses, son. Three of them."

"They're lying scum." Bobby's voice was loud and tinged with panic. Kate reached over, but he moved his hand away. "I didn't start that fire!"

"It's going to be our job to prove that, young man. And if we keep our cool, we can do just that."

"Yeah, well, you just let me out of here. I'll find that rat bastard."

"Who?"

"Danny Arcola. He's been trying to get me in his gang for months. Trying to make me do his dirty work. When I turned him down he said I'd be sorry. The goddammed son of a bitch."

"Let's watch the colorful language, shall we?" Charley said. "It won't help you any."

"I have been watching it."

Charley smiled at that one. "Well, keep working on it." Then he reached down and brought his briefcase to the table.

"Is that it?" Bobby asked.

"For now. I'm going to see about bail procedures."

"When can I get out of here?"

Charley put his notepad in the briefcase, closed it and put it down on the ground again. He folded his hands on the table and smiled once more at his client. "I'm going to do everything I can to make bail. This is your first serious offense and that's in your favor. But it's murder and that means the bail is going to be high. I know your mother and father are coming down here, so we'll put our heads together to see what we can see."

Bobby looked at Kate. "Why is Gus coming? I thought you weren't going to call him."

"I didn't, Bobby. Your mother did."

Bobby's curse made Charley cough.

"You keep him away, Kate. He'll screw things up. I know it."

"I'll do my best."

Bobby nodded. He looked so young. So innocent. He shouldn't go to prison. It would be terribly ugly for him.

Charley rose and held Kate's chair for her as she stood. He moved his hand to her arm, giving her a gentle, reassuring squeeze. "Come on, dear. Let's go tilt at some windmills."

"I'll be right there."

"I'm going to have to notify the guard."

She nodded. "I'll only be a second."

Charley got his briefcase and walked to the door. Kate held out her hand to stop Bobby, but she didn't touch him.

"Yeah?" he asked.

"It's about T.J."

A darkness came over his face like a shroud. "I already said—"

"He wants to help."

"Look where his help has got me."

"He didn't do this to you, Bobby. It's not his fault."

Bobby's eyes narrowed. "I heard you two last night. I know what you were doing."

She felt her face fill with heat. This was no time for embarrassment. "What we did has nothing to do with you."

"Nothing *he* does has anything to do with me. Just tell him to go back where he came from. Tell him to leave me alone."

"I'm not going to do that."

"Then why the hell are you asking me, if you don't want to listen?"

"Because you need him. You don't realize it right now, but you do."

"I think you got me mixed up with you. I haven't needed him for a long time. Not since he left without looking back."

She closed her eyes briefly, wondering what she could say that would make any difference at all.

"He's gonna leave you, too, you know. One day, he'll just take off. You'll think you did something wrong. You'll think about it for a long damn time. You'll learn to hate him, just like I do."

She shook her head. "No. I don't think—"

"Look, I don't got time to worry about your love life, okay? I'm in jail. They want to blame me for killing a guy."

"Of course," she said, then she heard the guard open the door behind her. "I'm here for you, Bobby. Not because of T.J. I'm here because I care about you."

"Then get me out."

The guard was next to him now, putting on handcuffs. Kate waited until he was gone before she let herself fall back in her chair.

"Kate? You all right?"

She looked up to see Charley standing by the door. "No, I'm not. I'm worried sick."

"You let me do that for you, okay? That's what I'm paid for."

She smiled. It felt phony and she was certain he knew it. But it would have to do.

It was like watching a rerun of a bad TV show. Gus stood in front of him, swaying to keep from falling. The smell of liquor was so strong it nearly choked T.J.

"You sonomobich," Gus said, his words slurred and wet. "I tol' you to keep outa here. You did this to my boy, you sonomobich. I oughta kill you righ' now."

T.J. thought of telling him to go ahead, but dismissed the idea as too satisfying to Gus. "Where's Teresa?"

"None o' your damn bidness."

"Gus, get out of here before they throw you in the drunk tank."

"Let'm try." He swung out with his right arm, trying to connect with T.J.'s jaw but missing by a mile. He lost his

balance and T.J. had to steady him. He got a good whiff of
that breath and nearly retched.

"Go on. Go home. You can't do anything for Bobby in
this condition.

"I don' have to listen to you. You're evil. Jus' like your
father. Shot him like a dog. Righ' on the street. In the gut-
ter. Tha's wha' they'll do to you. Shoot you like a dog."

"Shut up, old man." T.J. looked down the hall, but the
two of them were alone. Where was a cop when you needed
one? Maybe he should leave. No, not until he talked to Kate
and the attorney. They should be coming out soon. He
didn't want Kate to see Gus, but short of knocking the bastard's block off, he didn't know how to get rid of him.

The door to the interrogation room opened and Kate
walked out. She saw Gus first, then she stopped to speak to
the lawyer. T.J. couldn't hear her.

He felt Gus move in on him again and just as he turned
he heard Kate yell his name. That's when he saw the gun.

The old drunk had a .32 in his hand and he was waving it
around, trying to aim at T.J.

"I'll shoot you myself. You rotten—"

T.J. ducked and moved as fast as he knew how around the
old man. He got behind him and grabbed for the gun. Gus
was quick, though, and lurched away.

"Get out of here, Kate! Get a goddamned cop!"

He couldn't see her now. Gus had turned to face him
again. He held the gun in both hands, trying to aim but
shaking so hard the barrel was all over the place. T.J. went
straight for his gut, moving like a tackle, with his right
shoulder leading.

He hit Gus square in the solar plexus and heard the old
man's "Oof" as the air rushed out of his body. They both
went down and then he heard the sound of shoes, lots of
them, heading their way. He grappled again for the gun,
getting an elbow in his eye for his trouble. Gus struggled
more, kicking, wiggling, shoving.

T.J. got the gun in his hand and pushed, but the old man was stronger than he could have imagined. He found himself staring straight down the barrel of the .32.

T.J. rolled just as the gun went off.

Chapter 13

Memories came crashing around him like waves. He was barely aware of being yanked to his feet. That night in the liquor store. His father. Gus. The gunshots. He shook his head as if that would erase the images, but he could still see them as clearly as if it had happened an hour ago.

"Marcus, hold on," Kate said, rushing to his side. "Let him go. It's Detective Russo."

Her voice. He locked onto Kate, listened to her with everything he had. Her hand went to his arm and he felt he was waking from a bad dream.

"Then he should know better than to play with guns in here."

T.J. looked around. He saw two guys on Gus. One on each side. The gun was nowhere in sight.

"It was him," Kate said, pointing at the old man. "He brought it in. T.J. was trying to stop him from killing someone."

Marcus eyed T.J. the way a butcher would look at a side of beef. He shook his head, then let go of T.J.'s arm. The moment he was free, T.J. stepped away and worked on curbing his urge to pop good old Marcus in the mouth.

"Lemme go." Gus struggled with his cops, trying to break free. Neither one budged. "Lemme at that bastard."

"Book him." Marcus pointed at Gus, then turned to Kate. "And get your friend out of here, okay?"

She nodded, taking T.J.'s arm in her hand. "Thanks a million. Do you need us to press charges?"

"I think we got that covered, Kate."

She didn't hang around to hear any more. She walked quickly, pulling T.J. behind her like an errant child. When they got to the visitors' lobby, he stopped, forcing her to stop too.

"Hold it. I'm not finished in here."

"Yes, you are."

"I want to talk to that attorney of yours. Then I want to talk to Bobby."

"Later. We can do it all later. Right now, I just want to get you away from here."

He shook his head. "I'm glad he pulled the gun on me. Glad they locked him up. It should have happened a long time ago."

"Don't say that. I was scared to death." Her glance shifted to something behind him. "Oh, no."

He turned to follow her gaze. It was Teresa. She looked like a washerwoman, with her hair in a scarf, her skirt nearly down to her ankles and those white hospital shoes. The bags in her hand, one from Neiman Marcus, the other from Pic-N-Save, looked filled to the brim with rags. He felt like shoving his fist through a wall.

"My boy," she said. "Is he all right?"

"He's in trouble," T.J. said, wishing he could walk out the door and never come back. How was he going to tell her about Gus? Maybe she would be glad to know the drunk would be out of her hair for a while, but probably not. If ever there was cause for a bender, this was it. Her youngest in jail for murder, her husband in jail on a weapons charge. Time to find the bottle in the tennis shoes, the bottle in the bathroom vanity, the bottle in the freezer, behind the vanilla ice cream.

Teresa put down her bags. He saw the creases in her palms from the cords, deep and raw looking. She rubbed her hands together and he remembered how she used to get the shakes in the morning, so badly that she couldn't help him with his buttons. She would try and he would close his eyes, because he didn't want to see the confusion on her face.

"He's innocent. Did you tell them, Theo? Did you tell them?"

Hearing her call him Theo was a jolt. He hadn't been called that since he was a small boy. "It's too late for that."

The look on her face held a lifetime of disappointment—that he'd run off the moment he could, that he never came back to help her, that he didn't save Bobby. That he was so much like his father.

He should never have come home. That would have made his record perfect.

Kate knew she should keep out of this, that it wasn't her business, but she couldn't. She cared too much about T.J., about this whole family. She turned to him, shocked at the hardness of his expression. "T.J., don't do this. Talk to her."

He looked at her with stranger's eyes. She didn't know this man. She'd met him once, long ago, when he'd come to her center looking for Bobby. But he'd disappeared, she'd thought, for good.

"Talk about what? You want me to tell her that Gus tried to kill me?"

Teresa moaned and for a moment, Kate thought she might fall down. Hurrying to her side, she took the old woman by the shoulders and led her to a chair. When she was settled, she looked up to Kate for an explanation. But Kate wasn't going to give her one. She turned to T.J., anger chasing away her pity. "Damn it, don't you do this. You'll regret it for the rest of your life. She needs you. You're her son. You have to forgive her, T.J. If not for her, then for yourself. It'll kill you if you don't."

"How am I supposed to do that? Huh? Just forget about all those years when I didn't have a mother because she was nursing a bottle? Forget that she let my father beat the hell out of me, that she let Gus beat the hell out of me?"

"Yes," Kate said. "What good does it do to remember? It was a long time ago. People change."

He laughed. It was an ugly sound. "Oh yeah? Ask her where she hides the booze now."

Kate glanced at Teresa. She could see the woman wasn't going to fight, wasn't going to stand up for herself. She turned back to T.J. "Let me ask you something. How come you didn't know your mother's been sober for five years?"

"What the hell are you talking about?" He looked at his mother, but she said nothing. No confirmation, no denial.

"Didn't you wonder why you couldn't find any liquor bottles when you tore up her house? Did you even bother to *look* at her? To see she wasn't a practicing alcoholic anymore?"

His mouth opened as if he were going to say something, but he didn't. He just stared at her unbelievingly.

"Ask her."

He was silent for a long time. Teresa sat quietly. Kate saw she'd pulled her rosary beads from her pocket.

Finally T.J. turned to face his mother head-on. "Are you sober, Mama?" he asked. "Did you stop drinking?"

She nodded slowly. "Yes, Theo."

"Why didn't you tell me?"

"You wouldn't have believed me."

"That's not—"

At least, Kate thought, he couldn't finish the lie. She didn't understand why Teresa had kept quiet. Maybe it was her way of atoning for her sins. But it had gone on long enough. This family needed to start telling the truth, whether it was comfortable or not. Enough games. The games had nearly destroyed them.

T.J. moved closer to his mother. That didn't seem to be enough and he sat down, pulling the chair right next to her. "Why? What made you stop?"

"You. Bobby. When I realized what I'd done."

"And you stayed with Gus anyway? Why didn't you leave him?"

She looked at the beads in her hand. "I couldn't. It's not his fault he drinks. He didn't mean to hurt us."

"Yes, he did. He's always meant to hurt us. You don't know how much."

"I couldn't run out on him."

"Even if it was for your own good?"

"I said a vow. I can't break that kind of promise."

T.J. shook his head. "I don't understand you."

Teresa reached over and took his hand in hers. "It's enough that we're talking now, isn't it? That you came back when I asked."

Kate stepped back. She shouldn't listen to this. It was too private.

"Don't go," T.J. said.

"This is between you and your mother."

He smiled. "It's a little late to butt out now, wouldn't you say?"

"I'll be right over there." She nodded to the other side of the room. "You call me when you're through."

He looked at his mother's hands, then back to her. "It'll just be a minute."

Kate gave his shoulder a quick squeeze, then walked to the far side of the lobby. No one was around and for that she was grateful. It would give the two of them a chance to talk.

She sat in a leather chair that had seen better days. Her stomach was in knots and she still hadn't gotten over hearing that gunshot. The fear that T.J. had been hurt, or even killed, made her want to scream. She'd wanted to rush over to him but the police officers had been on him like white on rice. There weren't words to describe her relief when he stood up all in one piece.

Now there was a different fear inside her. As much as she ached for Bobby and Teresa, part of her wanted them to just disappear. To vanish, along with all their troubles. It was a rotten thing to think and she tried not to, but there it was.

Something told her this was the end of her relationship with T.J. They'd been in a sort of limbo for the past few weeks, dealing with the kids at the center, learning about each other. It had been the nicest time she'd had since, well, forever. Now it was over. No matter what the outcome, their time together was at an end. T.J. would go home. Back to his job, his life. Leaving her behind.

She looked at him now, sitting there, head bent close so he could hear Teresa. His suit was nice, but she liked him better in his jeans, casual, smiling. She'd made a mistake sleeping with him. It would have been better if she didn't know the texture of his skin, the way he looked naked. For the rest of her life, she would remember how he made her feel. How even when she was more turned on than she'd ever been before, he'd made her laugh. And how that laughter had made everything sweeter.

Maybe it was for the best, him leaving. The relationship wouldn't have to go through the inevitable breakdown. He would never grow tired of her basketball playing or her running. She'd never have to watch him become disillusioned or bitter. She wouldn't have to spend another fifteen years agonizing over what she'd done wrong. How her love wasn't enough.

Maybe in a few months she would stop hurting and the memories would come to comfort her. She would be able to look back at her days with T.J. as a gift, an extraordinary time when things had been perfect.

She focused in again on T.J. and Teresa. She wondered if they were telling each other the truth. If he realized how much he loved his mother and how that love didn't need to be destructive.

He'd moved closer to her. Now her hand moved from her lap to his head. The old woman petted him with her gnarled fingers and even from here, Kate could see that something big was happening. He was crying. She could tell from the way his shoulders shook, the swipe of his eyes with the back of his hand. Good. He needed to cry. He needed to get rid of all those years of confusion and betrayal. He needed to make amends and he needed to forgive himself.

T.J. leaned forward and kissed his mother's cheek. Then he hugged her and they rocked for a long time.

Kate sniffed and went into her purse for a tissue.

"Are you okay?"

She looked up to see Charley. She hadn't heard him come in. Nodding, she wiped away her tears and smiled. "I'm fine. What's the story?"

"His bond is being set right now. The charge is a first-degree felony, so I'm pretty sure bail will be twenty thousand. Can you take care of that?

She nodded.

"I'll want to go over the case with you, after Bobby's back at the center. Find out what I can about this other boy."

"Danny?"

He nodded. "Can you find him?"

She stood up. "I can try."

Charley nodded at Teresa. "Is that his mother?"

"Yes," she said as she led him to where Teresa was sitting. She made the introductions and while Charley was explaining the legal situation to her, T.J. took Kate aside.

"I'm going to find Arcola," he said.

"Where will you look?"

"I used to live here, remember? I think I know where to start."

It wouldn't do any good to argue with him. She could see he was completely determined to do this. Who knows, maybe he could find Danny and get some evidence that he was the arsonist. "He won't come easily, you know."

T.J. nodded.

"He'll have a gun."

"So will I."

She studied him for a long while. Lord, she didn't want to lose him. "Hey, Captain?"

"What?"

"You know that pony I've been looking for?"

He smiled sweetly. "Yeah?"

"Don't let him get hurt, okay?"

He reached over and cupped the back of her neck, gently folding her into his arms. He held her tight and she held him right back and she didn't cry, not one drop.

When he kissed her gently on the mouth, she knew he'd discovered her secret. He knew she loved him.

"I'll be back," he said. "I promise."

"Is Bobby okay? When can he come home? Is he scared to death?"

Kate took Molly's hand in hers as they walked through the crowd in the main room. The soft hum of whispered conversations buzzed around them like flies. She was quite sure Bobby's arrest had been the only topic of conversation and that no one had bothered to play the morning basketball game.

Molly went into Kate's office first and waited impatiently for her to close the door, walk to her desk and sit down.

"He's fine," Kate said, trying to sound as positive as she could. "He's going to be released on bail in about an hour, then he'll come back here."

Molly pulled up the plastic chair and sat directly across from her. "They can't really convict him of murder, can they? He didn't do anything. I know he didn't. He would have told me."

"I hope not, honey. But I can't kid you. He's in pretty big trouble."

"But he didn't *do* anything."

"I believe that, too. It's the D.A. we have to convince."

Molly sat back so hard she nearly tipped the chair over. Kate knew just how she felt. "Charley's with him. If anyone can get him out of this, it's Charley."

Molly stared at the wall for a long time. She didn't move, barely even blinked. Finally she looked at Kate. "How's the Captain dealing with all this?"

Kate studied her fingernails. "He's gone off to find Danny."

"Lone Ranger time, huh?"

Kate looked up and smiled. "You really do have an acute understanding of men. It's a real gift."

"So what's going to happen with you two? After this is over, I mean."

"Nothing. T.J. will go home. I'll stay here."

"Come on, Kate. Don't play dumb with me. I have a gift, remember?"

She studied her assistant, then shrugged. Why not tell her? "I don't want him to go. But I don't get a vote."

"Have you told him?"

She shook her head. "He knows, though."

"So why not talk about it? He might surprise you."

The sound of laughter drew her gaze to the window. The kids, her kids, were on about their business. Flirting, joking, complaining about their parents. There was Ted Lynsky surrounded by adoring fifteen-year-old girls, each of them vying for his attention. And Alice Dee leaning just so against a bookshelf, completely aware of how her young body inflamed the imaginations of the hormonally challenged boys. The twins were busy, as always, little mothers themselves. She knew these kids, cared about them. But they weren't going to stick around, either.

Even Molly and Peter would leave. Not tomorrow, but soon. Every serious relationship in her life was transitory. She'd planned it that way, so why should it surprise her that T.J. would go back home? "It's not meant to be, Molly." She smiled at her young protégée. "Some people just aren't supposed to have long-term relationships. I'm one of them. I don't mind. Really."

Molly stood up and moved closer to the desk. She bent and crooked her finger for Kate to lean forward. When they were just two inches apart and Kate was listening for the secret, Molly said, "Bull." Then she stood up straight. "That's a crock and you know it."

Kate laughed. How could she help it? Molly didn't see the humor, however.

"This isn't funny," she said.

"Don't worry, Molly. I'm not laughing at you. I'm laughing near you."

"Ha. Don't change the subject."

"What do you want me to say?"

"How about telling him the truth? For God's sake, Kate, aren't you a little old for this high school crap? You're reasonably intelligent, the Captain isn't too stupid, for a guy. This might be your last chance at happiness!"

"I'm not a hundred and eight, Molly. Besides, there are things you don't know about T.J."

"Like what?"

"It's not my place to tell you. I will say that he's got a lot of things to work through. He didn't exactly have the best childhood, you know."

"And?"

"And he walked in here with a lot of baggage. That's not something that can be changed overnight."

"That's swell, but what the heck does it have to do with loving you?"

"You're too young to under—"

"You finish that sentence and I'm going to have to bop you."

"Look, kiddo. I appreciate the sentiment, but it's late, I'm beat and I still have a roomful of kids to take care of. Which reminds me. Who's in the nursery?"

"Peter. He's got Bonnie and Kathy in there with him."

Kate stood up and walked Molly to the door. "I'm going to change, then I'll be out to help. She paused with her hand on the knob. "Don't worry about me, okay? I'm fine."

Molly leaned over and gave her a tight hug. "I'll just say one more thing. He's not the only one with baggage to unload. You're living in the past, too, Wonder Woman. You have to do something about Captain Marvel. If you let him go, you'll regret it the rest of your life." She let go and hurried into the crowd.

Kate watched Molly thread her way to the back room. A weariness came over her that was unlike anything she'd experienced before. She was soul tired. Tired of making decisions, tired of struggling to make a difference with the kids. Tired of playing games.

Molly's intentions were good, she appreciated that, but the girl didn't understand. She was still young enough to believe in happily ever after. She'd never gone through the kind of heartbreak that cripples. Kate could have told her the real reason she didn't dare tell T.J. she loved him. But she'd grown used to Molly's admiration and even though she knew it was vain, she wasn't willing to give that up. Some things were meant to be secret, to be locked away in the dark recesses.

She chased those thoughts away and headed for her room. She had work to do.

* * *

T.J. pulled into the dark parking lot of the youth center and turned off the engine. It seemed a monumental task to open the car door and walk the few steps to the back door, but he managed. Of course, the door was locked and it took several minutes for someone to hear him banging away. Finally he heard the turn of the dead bolt and then Kate was there, backlit like a movie star. Just seeing her eased the heaviness in his chest and when he walked inside and saw the concern in her eyes he felt almost human again.

"Any luck?" she asked as she locked the door behind him.

"Well, I found out that our friend Danny has been shaking down most of the convenience stores in Harbor Bay. He's got a regular racket out there. If he doesn't have an apartment, it's not for lack of money. The kid's grafting a mint."

"That's good. We can use that in court, can't we?"

"Nope. That would require testimony and no one was willing to do that. They only talked because they didn't know I was a cop."

She'd led him down the hall to the kitchen. He pulled out a chair and flopped into it. He might just sleep right there. The thought of changing clothes, washing up, even brushing his teeth was too much to contemplate.

"Did you find Danny?"

He shook his head. "I followed a lot of wild geese today." She passed him on her way to the fridge and he touched her arm. "Bobby. Is he here?"

She nodded. "He's fine. Scared, but that's understandable. Molly's been with him most of the night." She moved to the fridge and pulled out a couple of casserole dishes, then closed the door with her elbow. "We posted bail about an hour after you left. The arraignment is tomorrow. Charley's going to handle that. Bobby'll plead innocent and ask for time."

"I'll need a lot of it. Danny knows we're looking for him. For all we know he's in Mexico by now."

"I don't think so." Kate went to the microwave and popped in one of the covered dishes. "I've got some macaroni and cheese for you. And a salad. Is that okay?"

He smiled. "That's nice, but I'm too tired to eat."

"No, you're not. You'll feel better once you do. What do you want to drink?"

"Beer. Lots of it. Ice-cold."

"Will you settle for apple juice?"

He sighed. "Sure. What do you mean, you don't think so?"

After getting a glass and pouring his juice, she sat down next to him. "This is his ballet. He's not going to want to miss the finale."

"Translate, please."

She leaned forward, near enough for him to study her beautiful green eyes.

"Danny set this whole thing up. He set Bobby up. He set *us* up. He's not going to skip town and miss the fireworks. He's going to want to gloat."

"Even though it means he could get caught?"

"Yeah. His ego is almost as big as yours."

"Very funny."

"Very true." She smiled then, letting him know that she liked him despite his swelled head.

"Okay, I'll give you that. He's here. But where?"

"I don't know. I should know, but I don't."

"Why should you?"

"Because I care about him. More than that, I'm responsible for him."

"How do you figure?"

"There's no one else. He didn't start out being a gangbanger. His parents, poverty, drugs, they all did that to him. I wanted this center to be a safe place, a second home. I wanted the kids to feel free to confide in me. I wanted to make a difference."

"You did. You do."

"Not with Danny."

He leaned forward and took her hand in his. "Don't you dare blame yourself for this. You do so much good."

She looked away and he caught her chin with his finger and brought her back.

"I admire you, you know that? I think you're a remarkable woman."

Her gaze skittered over his face, but finally met his straight on. "Thank you," she whispered.

"If it wasn't for you, I never would have talked to Teresa. You did that."

"I may have helped a little, but you did the talking."

"No. The person I was before I met you would have walked out of that jail and never looked back. I'm not the same man. I never will be again."

"So you're saying people *can* change?"

"Is that what I said?"

She nodded.

"Damn. I guess I did."

"So maybe Bobby isn't destined to come to a bad end?"

He leaned back. "I suppose he's got a shot."

"But?"

"It's not that simple. He's got to want to change. He's got to work hard at it."

"With you to help him, I don't see a problem."

"Me?"

"You're his big brother."

"I'm no role model, Kate. I thought you knew that by now."

"I know no such thing."

The ding of the microwave made Kate look away. He didn't want to admit it, but he was grateful. He'd thought about her so much today. How extraordinary she was. But he'd also realized that when the business of Bobby was settled, he had to go home.

He had to go back to his world, where he knew the rules and the players. Being here with Kate was the best time he'd ever had, but it wasn't real. It wasn't permanent. He couldn't be like this forever.

Kate finally got up and fixed him a plate of food. He could tell she wanted to talk more, that she was waiting for him to go on. Instead, he ate.

Surprisingly, he found he was hungry after all. It wasn't hard to concentrate on his plate and avoid looking her in the eye, even though she'd taken her seat again and was so close.

Finally she got up. "Rinse your dishes, okay?" she said, her voice tinged with sadness.

He finished his juice and watched her walk away. When she was nearly at the door, he said, "It's not you, Kate. It's me. I'm no good for the long haul. It would end badly." He turned away and closed his eyes.

Then, without knowing how, he knew she was gone.

T.J. finished washing up and headed to his room. He'd already taken off his clothes, except his shorts, so he could fall into bed as soon as possible. He couldn't remember being this tired. Ever.

He didn't want to think anymore. About anything. He didn't even bother to flip on the light in his bedroom. His toiletry kit hit the floor, followed instantly by his robe. Two seconds later, he was under the covers.

Just as he was drifting off, his door opened. He reached out to the side table for his gun, but when he saw Kate's silhouette, he stopped.

"Are you asleep?" she whispered.

This wasn't a good idea. He ought to say yes, to make her go back to her room. To stop this speeding train before it killed them both.

Instead, he said "No."

Chapter 14

She didn't turn on the light. Even so, he could see she was dressed in an oversized T-shirt and nothing else. Walking slowly to the bed, she paused and he held up the covers and scooted over. She climbed in beside him, so her back was to him, spoon-style. His arm went around her waist and his legs bent to accommodate hers as if they'd slept like this a hundred times. Why did she have to feel so right?

For a while, all he did was listen to her breathe and enjoy her sweet flower scent. His eyes closed, but he didn't fall asleep.

"Can I tell you something?"

He knew what she was going to say. That she loved him. He thought about stopping her, but he couldn't. In some misguided way, he wanted to hear the words, just the once. "Okay."

"I just wanted you to know that you've changed me, too." She found his hand and wrapped him tighter around her. "You made me look at some things I've been avoiding for a long time."

"Yeah?"

"I didn't tell you the whole truth about Kevin Anderson. He didn't just leave because of my brothers. In fact, my brothers tried to hide the real reason from me. They did, too, for a long time."

He chased away the disappointment. Maybe he was wrong about her. Maybe she didn't love him. Or maybe this confession was her way of telling him she did.

"It was Kevin himself that straightened me out," she said softly.

He rubbed the back of her hand with his thumb, amazed that he could be so blown away by the feel of her even when his concentration was so focused on other things. The silence grew, but he didn't try to hurry her. She sniffed and he wondered if she was crying.

"I ran into him about four years after he left. He was surprised to see me and I could tell he wanted to get away. But I needed to explain about my brothers, so I sort of trapped him into staying. We were at UCLA for a women's basketball tournament, sitting in a stairwell that had no air-conditioning. I remember it was sweltering in there."

She lay very still now. He could barely feel her breathe.

"Anyway, I asked Kevin what they'd said to run him off. I guess I wanted to know that they'd offered him something big, something worth the pain. He didn't know what I was talking about. I kept pressing. Finally he just told me. He said he hadn't left because of my brothers, but because of me."

She was crying now. He could feel the soft quiver of her chest.

"He said he never felt like he was with a woman when he was with me. That I was too strong, too masculine. That I was just using him as a shill, that I really was more of a man than he was. He said he needed a real woman, not an Amazon. My brothers—"

He held her tighter, wrapping his legs around her, slipping his left arm under her neck so he could hold her closer. He had to watch it, though, and not squeeze too much. What he wanted to do was wring Kevin Anderson's neck.

"My brothers had gone after him, not to chase him away, but to make him stop saying horrible things about me. The big goofs were defending my honor. And I had no idea."

Kate shifted a bit more, and by the feel of it, she was wiping her face. Then she settled down again.

"Before Kevin, I'd been fine about my sexuality. Sure, I was tall, but I always thought of myself as being *female*. The damnedest thing was, I'd never suspected a thing. I thought he loved me. I was sure I loved him."

"He was a jerk," T.J. said. "You're more woman than anyone I've ever known."

"I wasn't fishing. I know you think I'm..."

"Beautiful? Sensual? Magnificent?"

She sniffed again. "Feminine enough."

"Sweetheart, you look up 'female' in the dictionary and you'll find your picture."

Kate rubbed his arm. "The thing is, I let that one guy, that one experience change the whole rest of my life. I made a decision all those years ago that I couldn't do love. You made me see that it was all a lie. A big, fat, hairy lie that made me run from men and from myself."

"Hey—"

"Wait," she said. "Let me finish. I was doing the exact same thing as you, don't you see? I was using my past to frame my future. I was cutting myself off from love and joy and even sex just because I believed one horrible man. I let his words eat into me, brand me. Until I met you."

"I—"

"Shh. Not yet. I also want you to know that I don't expect you to stay. I'm not asking you to. You have to discover your path for yourself. I'll respect whatever you decide to do. And I'll always be your friend. Always. Got it?"

"Can I talk now?"

"Yeah."

"You have to turn around first."

"Oh, I don't—"

"Come on. I want to look at you." He scooted back and waited for her to turn over. When she did and she settled comfortably next to him, he brought his hand to her cheek and wiped the remnants of her tears away. Then he kissed her, gently, on the forehead.

She closed her eyes.

"I want you to know one thing. I care about you. More than I ever thought I could. I think I care more about you than I do about myself. That's a biggie, coming from the original Mister Selfish."

She looked at him and the smile she gave him made him swallow so he could speak again.

"I want the best for you. In every way. I want to see you happy and fulfilled. I want all your dreams to come true. I even want you to find a guy who can give you everything you deserve. That part won't be easy for me. I'll be jealous as hell. But I'll give him my blessings, as long as he treats you right."

Her smile faded. He knew he'd hurt her, but it was important to tell the truth. He owed her that. "For a long time, I've wished I could be different. That I could trust myself to do the right thing, to be hopeful about the future. But I've never wanted it more than right now. I'd give my left arm to be the man for you."

She leaned over and kissed him on the cheek, then settled back down on the pillow. "I think we both have a lot to learn about ourselves, Captain Marvel. A whole heck of a lot."

As tired as he was, he didn't sleep right away. He watched her. He tried to picture her years from now. She'd be beautiful no matter how old she was. Imagine waking up to that face every day. To that long, sleek body. It wasn't to be, and thinking about it was stupid. Yet he couldn't stop looking at her. Wondering. He knew the second she'd fallen asleep. He hadn't lied about caring more for her than he did for himself.

His last thought was that this just might be love.

She awoke in his arms. He was still asleep. She could see his eyes move behind his lids and she wondered if she was in his dreams. He'd been in hers.

It was time for her to get up, but she didn't want to move. This time with him was too precious to waste. It was important to memorize him, to be able to recall everything about him in the months and years ahead.

His beard had grown overnight. Not all that much, but enough to scratch. There was that little scar above his eyebrow. How had he gotten that? From his job, probably. She didn't like to think of him that way—as a homicide detective. It was too dangerous, even though she knew he must be a very good detective.

His nose was a little crooked, too. Surprising that she hadn't noticed that before. Just a bit, at the bridge. A fight perhaps, or just an imperfection that made his whole face more interesting. His lips, of course, were perfect.

If she closed her eyes she could feel them on her own. It would be hard living without his kisses. She'd never realized how great kissing could be, until T.J. She would like to take him to a drive-in movie and make out with him for two hours. Hell, make it a double feature. That would be nice.

"What's that smile for?"

Kate hadn't noticed him awaken. Now she lifted her gaze to meet his. "I was thinking about a movie," she said.

"Must have been a good one."

She nodded. "It was." Then she reached for the top of the comforter. "I should go."

He looked past her to the clock on his side table while he stilled her hand. "It's early yet."

"But the kids will be getting up."

"They've already discovered our secret." He put his arm around her back and scooted her closer. When he shifted she felt his arousal press against her thigh. It was obvious, a physical reaction to their closeness. Hers was internal, in her heart and in her stomach. The ache she felt for him made her chest feel heavy and her vision dim.

As if he'd read her mind, he leaned forward and kissed her forehead. A sweet, gentle kiss. Slowly, very slowly, his hand traveled down her back until he found the bottom of her sleep shirt. He lifted it, then got hold of the waistband of her panties. His hand slipped down her bottom, softly caressing her as he undressed her.

"What are you doing?" she asked.

"What do you think?

"Is that a good idea?"

"Best one I've had in ages."

He had to sit up to get the panties all the way down, but she barely noticed the movement. Then he was back and she was in his arms again, touching him, exploring him with her hands, just as he was exploring her.

Remember me, she thought. *Remember that you touched me and made me whole again.*

His hand went to her hip and then down her stomach and quickly to her thigh. Lifting her leg, he brought it over his hip and she turned a little bit more to get comfortable. By then his fingers had gone back to the juncture of her thighs and then inside and she trembled at his touch.

How could she have denied this part of herself for so long? The way he made her feel was completely female and utterly wanton. Her hips moved in a rhythm of their own and she had to touch him everywhere. Her hand moved down his back and she kneaded his muscles and felt them flex beneath her palm.

His fingers worked their magic until the pleasure was too much to bear. She reached down and realized he was naked. When had he done that? The thought flew away as she circled him with her hand and guided him inside her.

There was no laughter this time. No sweet, silly games. Just slow, deep thrusts that went beyond sex, beyond anything she'd ever known before.

He brought her closer to him, almost hurting her with his intensity. She used her leg to press him tighter, tighter. She wanted it to hurt. To hurt him. Leaving her shouldn't be easy, damn it. It should tear him apart and wound him forever. Just as it was going to wound her.

His moan came from deep inside, a mournful ache that had no beginning or end. He pulled away, almost breaking the connection, then slid back in again, filling her with his thick, hot passion.

It wasn't fair. None of it was fair. He'd awakened her with a kiss, just like Sleeping Beauty, and now he was going to leave her.

T.J. couldn't go deep enough inside her. He wanted to merge with her, melt into her. He wanted to brand her with his sex so she would never forget.

If only things were different, if only *he* were different. Then he could stay and learn everything there was to know about her.

She tightened around him and he nearly lost control. It was almost impossible to slow down, to breathe deeply and forestall the inevitable, but he did it. This would not be rushed. It had to last a lifetime.

Why not stay with her? Live here. Marry her. The thoughts washed over him and he almost said yes! Then he remembered that he'd been Captain Marvel for four weeks and T.J. Russo for thirty-eight years.

What could he offer her? His ugly apartment? Long nights alone? All he had to give was himself and he was damaged goods. Besides, she wouldn't leave the center. She shouldn't leave. She was important here, she was alive here. Taking her away would be like clipping the wings of an eagle.

This was it then. His last time inside her.

He studied her beautiful face, memorizing every curve, every line. When she met his gaze, he saw his own torment reflected in her eyes.

"Don't be sad," he whispered. "It can't be sad to have found this, even for a day."

She smiled then. A brave, shaky smile that broke his heart. He closed his eyes and thrust again, concentrating on the sex, because the love was too hard to think about. He moved his hand so he could touch her. All his energy was on her happiness, her fulfillment.

When she came, it was stunning, incredible, to know he gave her that. His climax was all the more powerful after giving her such pleasure. White heat surrounded him and then it was over and he was still in her arms, still inside her.

He was home.

No one said anything when Kate entered the kitchen. Molly had finished her bagel, Peter had folded his newspaper and Bobby sat stiffly and still, watching her. She thought at first that the silent treatment was because she'd been with T.J., but when Molly reached over and took Bobby's hand, she realized the quiet was because of his arraignment.

"How you holding up, kiddo?" She asked him.

He shrugged.

"He didn't get much sleep last night," Molly said.

"I can understand why." Kate got her coffee and brought it to the table. She sat across from the boy. "Charley is a wonderful attorney," she said. "He's worked magic for me in the past. I don't want you to worry about it. Our emergency funds have taken care of the bail. Today, Charley's going to plead you innocent and ask for time."

"They won't believe me. They all think I killed him."

"They're going to believe you, because we're going to find Danny and we're going to find evidence to prove you didn't do it."

"He won't let you find him."

T.J. walked to the table. She hadn't heard him come in. "Tell me where to look, Bobby," he said. "Where does he hang out?"

Bobby turned away from him.

"Don't be a fool, kid." T.J. went to the counter but he didn't get a cup, yet. He faced Bobby, arms crossed over his chest. "I'm doing this for you."

"Don't do me no favors," Bobby said harshly.

Kate stood up. "Hold it. We're not going to do this. I won't have it."

Both T.J. and Bobby looked at her as if she weren't welcome in their private little war. Her own anger bubbled up almost before she realized it. "Grow the hell up, both of you! This isn't about who's right or justified. Bobby Sarducci, you're facing prison. Got it? Real life prison. You'd better take his help and be grateful for it. No one else is on your side but us. That includes T.J. He's putting his ass on the line for you. So quit the smart remarks and tell him what you know."

"But—"

She turned to T.J. "And you're no better. Quit treating him like he's five. He's old enough to be tried as an adult, the least you could do is treat him like one. Standing there like you know everything. Just knock it off. Try behaving like a brother instead of a cop."

He unfolded his arms and moved as if he were going to argue with her, but she put up her hands and said, "No. I don't want to hear anything from you except an apology to Bobby."

"Go, girlfriend," Molly said.

Kate gave her a look. "You keep out of this."

"Excuse me."

Molly slunk a little in her chair and Kate felt bad, but only for a second. She turned her attention to T.J. again. "Well?"

"Okay," he said. "You're right." He walked slowly to where Bobby sat. "Listen, kid. I know you got a bum deal. I should have been there for you. I can't change that, but I'm here now. And I want to help."

Kate breathed again. She hadn't realized how desperately she wanted the two of them to reconcile. She dropped into her chair again and picked up her coffee. Her hand trembled slightly and that troubled her.

"You listen, man," Bobby said.

Kate put her cup down, her pulse instantly racing again. Maybe she'd known it couldn't be that simple.

"You can go right to hell. You think some words will make things okay? Bullshit. You're the one who left us. You didn't want nothing to do with us. So stay the hell away."

"Bobby," T.J. said, taking a step toward him.

Bobby bolted up and shoved T.J. in the chest. "I said stay away. Where were you when he was beating the crap out of me, huh? I was a little kid! She never did nothing, except drink and pray with her beads. She was crazy and he was nuts and you left me there. There's nothing you can say to me, man. There's nothing I want from you."

"You don't understand."

"What's there to understand? That you were a traitor? I got that."

"No. You don't know why I left."

"You left because you were yellow. Because you didn't give a damn about anyone but yourself."

"That's not true."

"Then why?"

Kate saw tears well in Bobby's eyes and fall down his cheeks. He didn't wipe them away. She wondered if he even knew he was crying.

"Because he would have killed you if I stayed."

"Who?"

"Gus."

"What are you talking about?"

"He swore he was going to kill you, just like he killed my father."

Kate jerked to look at T.J. The silence in the room was as deep as a bombshell crater.

"What?" Bobby's voice sounded strangled.

"Gus was with Ed the night they robbed the liquor store. It wasn't the cops who killed him. It was Gus. I saw it. I was there."

Bobby swayed like a drunk and for a moment, Kate thought he was going to fall. She stood, afraid for both of them.

"He shot my father right in front of me. He didn't know I was there. Everyone thought the cops did it. He got out the back way and so did I. No one knew."

T.J. walked to the far wall, as far as he could get away from Bobby. He slammed his hand on the side of the fridge, then turned again to face his brother.

"I was scared to death. I stayed away," he said. "I got in trouble with the law. I stole a car and they sent me to live in juvenile hall. I hardly saw them after that.

"I never dreamed that ten years later, Gus would go after Teresa. They got married before I knew a thing. I just got a phone call that she was going to have a baby. I tried to tell her about Gus, but she wouldn't listen."

Bobby leaned forward and put his head in his hands. Before Kate could move, Molly was next to him, arm around his back. T.J. didn't seem to notice.

His voice had grown quieter and somehow that seemed worse to Kate. Why hadn't he told her? She remembered Gus's threat at the police station and suddenly things seemed to fall into place. She'd known there were secrets. She just didn't know how awful they were.

"I moved back to town when you were seven. Got a place on the same damn street. Gus thought it was too close. He started beating up on me then." T.J. took a step toward Bobby. "I told him one night, what I'd seen. I threatened to turn him in. He didn't believe me at first, but I told him where I'd been hiding, how I'd seen him tell Ed that he would cover him and then how he shot him in the back. He knew I was telling the truth. He said if I ever told anyone, he would kill you. Not me. You."

"How could he—"

"He's a sick bastard, Bobby. He always was. He knew I couldn't stand to see you get hurt. And he used that to keep me in line. I'd do something he didn't like and you'd pay for it. I couldn't stay after that. I thought if I left, he would leave you alone."

"Mom?"

T.J. shook his head. "She never knew. At least I don't think so. With her, it's hard to say."

Bobby reached out for his chair like a blind man, waving his hand until it connected with the wooden back. He sat down, staring straight ahead.

Kate walked over to T.J. The pain on his face pierced her heart and she reached over to take him in her arms. He backed up, knocking her hand away. "Don't you get it? That's my family. That's what I come from. I can't wash it off, or wish it away. It's who I am. It's who I'll always be."

"No," she said. "You're not Gus. You're not your father. You didn't do anything wrong."

"No? I left my kid brother. I left my mother. I ran off with my tail between my legs. I couldn't stop him. I became a cop so I could stop him and I didn't."

"He's in jail now," she said. "He can't hurt anyone anymore."

"He'll get out. Teresa will go back to him. I know she will. He'll take it out on her, next."

"We won't let him."

He laughed then. The sound made her break out in a rash of goose bumps.

"You still think people can change, huh? You think you can make it better by saying nice, comforting words. But the truth is underneath all that. It's lying in a liquor store, shot in the back like a dog."

"You didn't pull the trigger."

"I should have. I should have taken care of Gus when I had the chance."

"No. You're better than that. You're not like him."

"That's just it. I'm afraid I am." He moved quickly, then. So fast, she couldn't catch him. He didn't look back, didn't say anything more. He just walked away.

She had the awful feeling he was leaving for good.

Chapter 15

T.J. got to his room and went right to the closet. He pulled his suitcase out and tossed it on the bed. Damn it all to hell, why had he opened his big mouth?

The zipper stuck and he nearly ripped the stupid thing before he got it open. Then he turned and yanked open the top dresser drawer and gathered his clothes with both hands. He threw them into the case and opened the next drawer.

"Where are you going?"

He jerked around to stare at Kate. She stood in his doorway looking concerned and a little bit frightened.

"Away."

"Why?"

He laughed, although there was no humor left in him. "I've told you before. I don't belong here. I should never have come."

"Am I that easy to leave?"

He winced. "No fair hitting below the belt."

"I can be pretty ruthless."

"You can also be pretty smart. You don't want me, Kate. You don't want me at all."

She walked toward him and as she got nearer he saw he'd been wrong a moment ago. She wasn't frightened, she was angry.

"How dare you tell me what I want," she said, standing right next to him, looking at him dead-on. "What am I, some kind of child that I need you to tell me what I think and feel?"

"I didn't mean—"

"That's exactly what you meant. You think I can't see you. That I don't really know who you are. That you have this dark side that will come out when I least expect it, like a werewolf during a full moon. You know what I think?"

She took one more step. Now she was close enough for him to see the fire in her eyes.

"I think you're afraid that *won't* happen. I think you've lived with this image of yourself for so long, it's become your safety zone. So safe that you don't have to love anyone but yourself. You don't have to commit to anything but your credo. I think you're afraid to live, Detective. Afraid that all you are is a regular guy. A guy who makes mistakes, not because it's your destiny, but because you're human.

"That's very interesting, Kate, but you don't know what I've seen, what I've—"

"Oh, can it. I know your father's death was awful. It was brutal and it shouldn't have happened, but *it wasn't your fault.* You did the best you could with what you had. Don't you get it? You left Harbor Bay because you are, you've always been, a decent human being. You wanted to protect your brother. Your instincts were right on the money. Maybe you could have done something more effective, who knows? The point is your motivation was good. You didn't become a cop to get back at Gus. You became a cop because you're a good guy and you always have been.''

He shook his head, marveling at every single thing about her. Her intensity, her passion, her beauty. If only she were right. ''You're determined to find that pony, no matter what, huh?''

''That's not the issue here.''

He reached over and took her by the arms, holding her steady. ''Listen to me, Kate. When I was on that floor in the police station, struggling with Gus over the gun, I wasn't trying to just get it away from him. I wanted to hurt him. Like he hurt me.''

''And?''

''There is no *and*. You're not listening. You want me to be someone I'm not. I wish I could be, but I can't. It's too big a leap. People don't change like that. It's too fundamental a shift. Your vision is skewed because you deal with kids. I'm not a kid anymore. I'm coming on forty. Not that I like it, but it's a fact. I've been Theodore J. Russo, son of Ed and Teresa Russo, with all attendant baggage for a long, long time.''

''You listen,'' she said. ''Listen up good. I'm not saying you have to change. You're already there. All you have to do is recognize it.''

He dropped his arms. For the first time since they'd become friends he felt a great distance between them, an unbridgeable chasm. He turned and went back to the dresser. ''I've got to go find Danny,'' he said.

''That's it? End of discussion?''

''I don't want either of us to get hurt,'' he said.

''Too late.''

He faced her one more time, hoping, praying, she would believe him. ''I'm sorry for that. I never meant for that to happen.''

Her back stiffened and somewhere inside her a light clicked off. "Fine. There's no reason for you to leave, yet. Go on. Find Danny. I'll look for him, too. I want this over with."

"Kate—"

She turned and walked out of the bedroom. That same light went out inside him and he knew the darkness would last forever.

Kate went to her room. She didn't want anyone to see her right now. She closed her door and went to her dresser. There was the picture of Kevin Anderson taken all those years ago. Why had she kept the damn thing? To remind her of her failure? To torture herself with her shortcomings?

She lifted the curled photo and ripped it neatly in half. Both pieces floated to the trash can as she said goodbye to him once and for all. At least that issue had been handled. Being with T.J. hadn't been a total loss.

Would he be so easy to forget? She had the feeling that T.J.'s memory would linger a long time, maybe forever. He'd taken her heart hostage and there was no ransom to be found. This was love, real love. She'd never expected it to happen to her. The idea had always scared her and now it was clear why. It hurt.

She felt different inside, as if he'd carved the vital parts out of her and replaced them with pain. Her image in the mirror hadn't changed and that was probably for the best. If she looked the way she felt people would run screaming.

Why? Why had he come here? Why had he taken her life and turned it inside out? It wasn't fair. She might have been numb before, but that was better than this.

She turned and saw her whistle hanging from the hook by her door. The kids. They were surely here by now, waiting for her to come lead them on the run. Good. Being busy would be a blessing. There was no way she was going to cry about this. No way. Wasn't she the toughest lady in town? Couldn't she outrun, outjump, outfox anyone in the city?

Wasn't she strong enough to say goodbye?

Just after twelve noon, T.J. got lucky. It was at Selco's, a mom-and-pop grocery store he'd been going to since he was a little kid. Mr. Selco had always run the place and even then he'd been an old man. Now he had a stoop to his back and he'd lost all his hair, but he was the same man who'd chased him down the block countless times, yelling for him to quit stealing his fruit. T.J. had suspected more than once that Selco could have caught him if he'd wanted to.

"Do you have any idea where I could find Danny now?" T.J. asked. He was standing right next to the nectarines and he had an almost unbearable urge to slip one into his pocket.

"Not for certain," Selco said, his thick Yiddish accent more pronounced than T.J. had remembered. "But I t'ink . . . you know the building mit the picture on it?"

"The mural?"

"Yeah, the picture. The one mit the dog and the horse."

T.J. nodded. That mural was on Pine and Fourth, right by the pawnshop.

"The little bastard goes there. He hangs out mit his hoodlum friends. The music they play, so damn loud it would make my Bubba rise from the grave just to tell them to shut up."

T.J. smiled. "I know just what you mean."

Selco nodded. "You go by there. You see him."

"Thank you."

"You get him, okay? You put him behind bars. Little pisher is trying to do extortion on me. Can you believe it? The schmuck."

"I'll do my best." He shook the old man's hand and turned to leave.

"Hey, kid."

T.J. stopped.

"Take the damn piece of fruit."

T.J. grinned again and grabbed a nectarine from the pile. "You old softy."

"Get the hell out of here."

It was the best nectarine he'd ever had. He threw the pit in a garbage can once he got to Fourth. He'd parked the car behind the big metal bin behind the pawnshop so Danny wouldn't see the Camaro.

Now he made his way carefully up the alley, making sure his jacket was unbuttoned and his holster unsnapped. There was a good possibility the whole gang could be just around the corner and he needed to be ready.

Slowing his pace and keeping his back to the wall, he tried to look everywhere at once. He'd been in situations like this before, so how come his heart was thudding like a damn bass drum in his chest? It couldn't be because he was afraid of Danny. He could take out that punk in five seconds. So what was the deal here? He was acting like a rookie, like a rube.

Concentrate. That's what he needed to do. Get the world down to size. Step over the brick, watch out for the nail sticking out of the wall, check to his right. Breathe, damn it.

He felt the music before he heard it. It was a slight vibration, just around his shoulders, but he recognized the feel of it from the center. Not only was Danny on the other side of the pawnshop, but he had his boom box up against the wall.

T.J. reached for his gun. The moment it was in his hand he felt better, grounded. This was what he knew.

He inched his way closer to the empty lot. Now he heard the words to the song. Something about a cop killer. How appropriate.

There was the edge, the final inch between himself and the bastard who was trying to frame his brother. Holding his breath, he stole a look. Quick and then his back was up against the wall again.

Danny wasn't alone. Six, maybe seven guys were with him. Most were standing around a trash barrel, but some were sitting on the hood of a beat-up old car. If he turned that corner, he wouldn't last a moment. The odds of taking Arcola out before he bought it were slim to none. Damn it, why didn't they turn that music off?

What if he looked one more time? Fixed Danny in his sights? Memorized his position and went for the good kill? Sure he would be dead, but so would Arcola. It might just be worth it.

At the thought, his heart picked up again. The drum was back, beating like a son of a bitch. And right along with it, an image of Kate burst into his head. Right there. Clear as a bell. He could see every line, every curve. The picture left as quickly as it had come, but the feeling of her lingered and that's when he knew. He knew why his heart pounded. Why this was unlike any other bust he'd ever been on.

For the first time in his life, he had something to lose.

Kate ran out the door, searching for Charley's car. She saw him at the corner and she waved him back, even though she knew it was useless. He drove away and her thoughts went right back to her conversation with Alice Dee.

After Bobby had come from the arraignment and Charley had filled her in on the details, she'd gone to the nursery to check on Molly. Alice was playing with a baby. When Molly went out after Bobby, Kate had hung around and found herself studying Little Miss Hot Pants. Only something was different. Alice was different. She wasn't parading around the boys or trying to suck up to her. As a matter of fact, the girl was subdued, right down to her baggy jeans and T-shirt.

The dance had been a complicated one—Kate had approached her and Alice had pretty much ignored her. One conversation after another had died on the vine, what with Alice giving those one syllable answers. Finally Molly had returned, Bobby in hand, and Kate started to leave. That's when Alice had grabbed her arm.

"I think I know where Danny is," she'd said.

Kate waited, fighting off the urge to grab the girl and shake the information out of her.

"I think he's going to the Stop-N-Go. By the high school."

"How do you know?"

Alice had looked at her feet, then. "I was with someone last night. Banger. I mean Tony Bandara. He didn't really say. I'm probably wrong. Forget it."

"When? When is he going to be there?"

She shrugged. "I don't know. I'm sorry I said anything. I'm probably crazy."

Kate had grabbed Alice then, but not to shake her. She'd given her a mighty hug. "You did the right thing, Alice."

Then she'd run for Charley. Now that he was gone, she wasted no more time. She went back to the nursery and found Molly. Bobby wasn't around and she assumed he was changing clothes.

"I need you to take over. I'm leaving for a while."

"What's wrong?"

"Nothing. I've got to find T.J., that's all."

Molly put her hands on her hips and started to say something else, but Kate was out the door before she heard it. Walking didn't cut it and she jogged to her room and grabbed her purse. By the time she reached the parking lot, she was shaking.

She finally unlocked the wagon door and slid behind the wheel. Before she put the key in the ignition, she took a deep breath. Alice hadn't been sure. Maybe nothing was going to happen at the Stop-N-Go. But she needed to tell T.J. about it nonetheless.

How was she going to find him? He could be anywhere. But she hoped he was by the high school.

T.J. hadn't moved for five minutes. He listened harder than he ever had, trying to hear the words underneath that blanket of music. It was useless.

He put his gun hand down by his side. No use fooling himself, he wasn't about to go out there like Dirty Harry. Kate wouldn't like that. He smiled. No, she wouldn't like that at all.

What he would do was hang tight, keep low. Wait for an opportunity. The gang would move out sometime. And he'd be right on their tai—

The music stopped. T.J. couldn't believe the depth of the silence that followed. It was nearly as deafening as the music had been. Voices came to him after a moment. He scooted closer to the corner.

"How we gonna do it in the daytime?"

T.J. didn't know that voice.

"Just like always. No sweat."

That one he knew. Danny Arcola himself. He almost expected to hear him say "police man" in that slow, cynical drawl.

"But—"

"You don't want to come, then you stay here, little girl."

"Shut up."

"You shut up."

"Aw, man."

The voice he didn't recognize was weaker. Were they moving? He snuck another look. Yep, they were climbing into the car. Danny behind the wheel. Two of them, kids he'd seen at the center, were heading his way.

He was off like a shot and in his car before they rounded he corner. He grabbed his visor and swung it toward the ide of the window so they wouldn't see his face. They might ecognize the car, but he didn't think so.

He started the engine and drove slowly, watching the two ɔoys on his right. One of them banged his fist on the trunk ind he jumped. Then they were gone and he caught the tail ɛnd of the Chevy turning on to Fourth.

Following them wasn't difficult. The car was distinctive ind not just because of the rust stains. It had been lowered ind any small bump caught the rear end with a spray of parks. It also had the words "Hell Raiser" in elegant script ɩcross the back window.

He'd just see about that. No hell would be raised on his vatch.

They turned on Pacific and headed east. T.J. kept about ɔur cars between them. It wasn't hard, the streets were busy ɩere in front of the mall. On Twelfth Street he got caught at . long red, but he snaked his way through the traffic again ɛfore Danny turned.

The neighborhood was more familiar to T.J. now. They vere heading toward Harbor Bay High School. Home of the ʹellow Jackets, national basketball champions 1975-76. Ie'd been a guard on the team both years. This was his old ɩomping grounds. If he remembered correctly, there was a ฿top-N-Go just a few blocks from here. He would bet the arm that's where they were headed.

Kate parked a block away from the convenience store. If ʹanny showed up, she didn't want her car tipping him off. he locked it then hurried down the street. Just before she ɔt to the small parking lot, she stopped. What if they were lready inside? What if T.J. hadn't found them? He could ɛ across town for all she knew. If they were inside, what vas she going to do about it? Try to stop them? With what?

She looked around and found her answer. There was a public telephone booth on the corner. She peeked around the side, checking the lot. There was a van parked in the handicapped space. No Danny. No T.J.

Still it would be foolish to assume nothing was going to happen. She headed for the phone booth, feeling like a walking target. This was not the fun part.

Finally she made it. She found a quarter in her purse and reached for the receiver. When she put it to her ear, there was no dial tone. She toggled the switch hook a few times. Nothing. She put the quarter in the slot, but it just came out again. Damn. She'd have to call from inside the store.

One more quick look around and then she was inside. There was a woman at the counter buying a pack of cigarettes. She was on her cellular phone and barely looked at the woman behind the counter.

Kate thought about borrowing her phone, but she was afraid the woman would spray her with Mace if she even looked like she would interrupt her call.

The other woman, the owner she assumed, was in a wheelchair. That explained the van. The woman with the phone bumped into Kate on her way out. The glare she sent made Kate glad she hadn't asked to borrow a darn thing.

"Excuse me," Kate said to the woman in the wheelchair. "Is this your store?"

She nodded. She looked to Kate to be in her fifties, heavyset, with blond hair.

"Yeah."

"My name is Kate Dugan. I was wondering if a man had been by here today. T.J. Russo. He's a little over six feet tall, dark hair, dark eyes. Too handsome for his own good?"

The woman smiled. "I woulda remembered that."

"Yes, I think you would. What about a boy, Hispanic, seventeen. His name is Danny Arcola."

The smile disappeared. "You a cop or something?"

"No. I run the youth center."

"Yeah? How do I know that?"

"I'm not here to cause trouble. I heard something through the grapevine about this store. I'm not sure if it's true or not, but I don't think we can afford to ignore it. I think Danny Arcola and his gang are going to come here. I think they're going to set fire to the store."

The little bell above the front door tinkled. The sound shot a bolt of fear straight down Kate's back. When she saw the woman behind the counter pale, she knew her instincts were right.

"Well, look who's here."

She heard the voice, the unmistakable voice, and slowly turned around.

Danny Arcola stood in front of his gang; four of them had guns. His gaze started at her feet and climbed up her body inch by inch. By the time he reached her face, she wondered if arson was the only crime about to be committed.

T.J. pulled his car to the side of the road a block away from the Stop-N-Go. Although he hadn't seen Danny turn into the store's parking lot, he knew that was the target.

He reached into the glove compartment and got his cellular phone out. After plugging it into the cigarette lighter, he waited for the dial tone then punched in the number of the Harbor Bay P.D.

Fleming, the old son of a bitch who had busted T.J. all those years ago, answered the phone. Despite his hatred for the man, there was no time to ask for someone else. Fleming started to give him a hard time, but finally gave in and said he would send out a car. Now all T.J. had to do was make sure nothing happened until the cavalry arrived.

He got out of his car and checked around to see if he could spot the Chevy. When he didn't, he started walking

toward the store. That wasn't good enough and he picked up
the pace. They were inside the place, he felt it.

His instincts had always been good. Hell, he'd been
taught from the inside. This little market was just like the
ones his father had robbed. Just like the one where he'd
been killed by Gus Sarducci.

He was running now. No more time for trips down memory lane. He turned the corner and there was the store. A
van was parked in the handicapped zone. The rest of the lot
was empty. When he looked at the store itself, his muscles
tensed and he reached for his gun.

The shades were down and the sign in the door said
Closed. Danny was inside, all right.

It wouldn't do him any good to storm the place. The door
would be locked, of course, and he would just get shot.
Moving as quickly as he could, he went around to the alley.

It was deserted and T.J. raced to the back entrance. He
grabbed the knob but it didn't budge. He bent low and saw
the dead bolt wasn't engaged, just the lock on the knob itself.

He reached into his pocket and got out his credit card. He
jimmied the lock just like his father had taught him. A small
click and he was inside the storage room.

He heard muffled voices. He smelled gasoline. They were
going to torch this place any minute now. They weren't even
going to wait for nightfall. Was Arcola that confident, or
that stupid? He would bet on the former.

Moving carefully around big boxes of motor oil and dog
food, he made his way to the door. He got a better grip on
his Magnum, then bent low.

"... haven't cooperated with us. We gave you your
chance. This is what happens when you don't play the
game."

It was Arcola.

"Danny, stop. Don't do this."

T.J. froze. Damn it all to hell, that was Kate's voice. What was she doing here? He leaned out until he could see at least part of the room. At first he thought maybe he was nuts, then he saw a leg. There wasn't another woman alive who had a leg like that. Those were her shorts, her shoes and socks. He wasn't insane. She was really here and Danny Arcola had her in his grasp.

Slipping back into the safety of the storeroom, T.J. had to force himself to think calmly and not just rush in with his gun blaring. Above all else, Kate's safety came first. Why the hell had he called the police? The minute those thugs heard the siren, they would have only one use for Kate. Hostage. T.J. doubted Arcola would hesitate to kill her if things didn't go his way.

Somehow he had to get her out of here. In one piece.

"Danny, I mean it. Don't do this. The police know about you."

"So what?"

"There's already a warrant out for your arrest."

"Screw the warrant. They can't touch this."

He moved toward her, taking each step deliberately and slowly, working on her fear. The other boys, Banger, Fast Eddie, Calhoun, those were the ones she recognized, were staring at her lasciviously, but none of them could equal the feral hunger in Danny's eyes.

"Come on, you guys. I know you don't want to spend the rest of your lives behind bars. Calhoun, you've been there. Tell them."

"We ain't goin' to jail, Kate." The way Calhoun said her name made her want to throw up. "Danny's got that covered."

"What do you mean?"

"I mean we ain't in this alone."

Danny turned to Calhoun. "Shut your damn face."

The older boy looked at his shoes.

"Who's in this with you?" Kate asked. "A cop? Is that why you're not afraid?"

"Don't you worry about that, Legs. Don't you even think about that."

He was right in front of her now. She didn't back away, even though she desperately wanted to. If she showed her fear, the game would be over. It might already be over, but damn it, she wasn't going without a fight.

"The problem is, Legs, you dissed me one too many times. I put up with it for a while. But it's gone too far. You get me?"

"I didn't diss you, Danny. All I did was expect the best from you."

He laughed. His hand went out and up as he touched her hair.

She held steady. He wasn't going to get to her.

"You are one tall female," he said. "One hot babe."

"Stop it, Arcola." She knocked his hand away.

"Hey," Fast Eddie whispered. "Someone's coming."

Danny smiled at her before he left her side. The smile held a promise, one she prayed he couldn't keep.

Moving to the front of the store, Danny lifted aside the shade to see who had arrived. It must have been someone he was expecting, because he immediately unlocked the door.

Kate turned to the woman in the wheelchair. She looked utterly petrified. "Move," Kate whispered. "Get behind something. A box or the counter. Try for the storeroom."

While the woman nodded and inched her way back, Kate headed toward the center of the store. She needed to distract the gang and give the owner time to get out the back way.

The front door swung open. The tinkle of the bell sounded foolish in the oppressive tension of the room. Her gaze went to the newcomer and it didn't surprise her one bit to see the black uniform of a Harbor Bay police officer. It wasn't a surprise to see which police officer it was, either. Even though she'd only met him once, that had been enough. It was Fleming. The cop who'd busted T.J. all those years ago.

Chapter 16

"Where is he?" Fleming said as he scanned the group.

"Who?" Danny relocked the front door.

"Russo."

"He ain't here," Danny said. "But his girlfriend is."

Fleming turned on Arcola furiously. "You idiot. He called the station. He knows you're here. He knows everything."

"How?"

Danny's gaze went to Kate, all the lust she'd seen just moments ago replaced by a hatred so fierce she felt burned by it. "You told him?"

She shook her head. "He must have figured it out all by himself."

"Oh yeah? How's he gonna like it when he gets here and finds you dead?"

"Listen up, you morons," Fleming said. "Get on the phone. Get that bastard's little brother out here. Now. Tell him we've got Russo and we'll kill him if he doesn't show up."

Then he looked up and nodded at the lone security camera. "Get rid of that, too." He turned to Danny and nodded toward Kate. "And her." As Calhoun passed him, he said, "Russo is here, dammit. He said he was calling from just down the street. Have you checked the back room?"

Calhoun shook his head.

"Well, do it!" Fleming yelled.

Kate couldn't make her legs move. Everything had changed. She'd never known fear like this. It felt as though her blood had turned to ice water. T.J. was here. He was here! *Please God, at least give me a chance to say goodbye.*

T.J. pulled the old woman's wheelchair the rest of the way into the room. He leaned close to her and whispered, "Get out. Get help."

She didn't move.

"Go!"

She leaned toward him. "I pressed the alarm," she whispered.

It took him a moment to register what she'd said. Help was on the way. Thank God. He nodded and she turned her chair quickly around and headed for the back door. T.J. forgot about her and concentrated on what was going on in the store.

Fleming. He was behind everything. How he must have laughed when he figured out he could frame Bobby for arson and murder. The bastard.

T.J. pushed the thoughts away. Someone was coming into the storeroom to find him and he had to move. Now. He crouched as low as he could get and looked out the door. The way was clear for the moment and he took advantage of it. He ran past the counter to the canned food aisle. Still crouching low, holding his gun steady, he watched as one of the gang went into the storeroom. The sound of breaking glass and tumbling boxes told him the search was on.

His only goal now was to save Kate. She was all that mattered. The thought of losing her was more than he could bear. He'd been so stupid! A world-class jerk. How could he have ever thought of leaving her? He didn't even want to live in a world without Kate. The thought that someone was pointing a gun at her filled him with rage he'd never experienced before. If Danny touched one hair on her head, he would be sorry he'd ever been born.

A flash of memory swept through him. Standing in his room, his suitcase open and half-filled. Kate telling him he was a good guy, and always had been. That the only thing he needed was to see himself clearly.

This was one hell of an attitude adjustment.

T.J. listened as hard as he could to locate Fleming and Arcola. He would take out Arcola first. He was younger and faster. But then he would have to go for Fleming and not miss.

He closed his eyes and calmed his breathing. Although he hadn't prayed in years, he did now. The words were simple, and right to the point. *Don't take her from me. Not now. Not when I've just found her.*

Kate watched as Danny reached into his pocket. Instead of a gun, he pulled out a knife, a dagger. It reminded her of the one on the pier, the one on T.J.'s shoulder, only this one was longer, shinier, deadlier.

"You should have stayed at the center," Danny said, taking a step toward her. "You should have minded your own business."

"Danny, don't. Fleming can't protect you from this." She moved backward until the counter blocked her way. "You'll end up dead."

He shook his head. "Too late, muchacha. It's all over. For you and the police man."

Fleming pounded his fist on the counter just inches away from Kate. She jumped, the sound too much like a gunshot to leave her with any breath at all.

"Just get it over with, Arcola. Stop screwing around."

Danny nodded slowly.

She could see beads of sweat on his forehead and upper lip. He held the dagger steady, though. She had to do something, or that blade was going right into her heart.

A gunshot made T.J. jump up before he was ready, terrified that he'd waited too long. The sound of breaking glass barely registered. As if his gun knew where to point all on its own, he had Arcola in his sights. Just as he squeezed the trigger, he saw that Kate was in the line of fire. He jerked his hand, praying he'd caught it in time.

The bullet missed her. Arcola's knife wouldn't though.

T.J. took a step toward her, then he was sidelined, smashed from the back and thrown against the stacks of cans. The wooden racks fell, and he fell with them, cans, boxes, jars flying around him like shrapnel. His Magnum flew from his hand.

Fleming's fist in his gut took his breath, but he managed to get his leg up and his foot planted on the cop's chest. He shoved him backward and gasped for air.

Where was Kate? He struggled to get to his feet, and just as he caught sight of her, still alive, Fleming was on him again.

T.J. smashed him once in the jaw, sending him reeling. There was his Magnum next to a can of yams. He dove for it, and got a kick in the kidneys for his trouble.

"T.J.!"

He heard Kate's voice, but he couldn't look at her now. The gun was still too far for him to grab. He went for it just as Fleming lifted his own weapon and aimed.

Kate jerked sideways, away from the thrusting knife. Danny grunted in surprise and turned toward her again. She backed away, no longer held in place by the counter.

He lurched at her, and somehow she grabbed his wrist, stopping the blade inches from her chest.

"Calhoun! Damn it, shoot her!" Danny screamed. "Calhoun!"

Kate struggled as she'd never struggled before. Danny was strong, too strong. She felt the sharp tip of the knife on her chest, then the sting as it cut into her flesh.

She heard a shot and she froze, certain she'd feel the bullet enter her body. Instead, a shower of breaking glass hit her like a wave.

T.J. dove for his weapon. He heard the gunshot and felt the bullet hit his leg. Only it didn't feel like a bullet. More like a sledgehammer.

His hand found his Magnum and he turned to search for his target. Another shot rang out, but that was behind him. Fleming aimed his weapon again. This time he couldn't miss. T.J. pulled the trigger, the recoil sending a shock wave of pain down his right shoulder. Fleming jerked backward, the impact of the bullet toppling him like a felled tree. He went down hard.

There was no time to celebrate. T.J. glanced at his leg and saw that Fleming's bullet hadn't hit him. The sledgehammer had actually been a can of motor oil, and the wet pool on the ground wasn't his blood at all. It still hurt like hell to stand.

The first thing he saw was that Kate was alive. But not for long. In the seconds it took him to get to her, he registered the police at the front door. The blue flack jackets, the SWAT team helmets. Then he was on Danny, his arm around the kid's throat, jerking him backward.

Danny gasped and brought the knife straight back. It clipped T.J. on the ear. He let go, and Danny turned on him like a pit bull. He jabbed the knife again, and T.J. looked at the weapon. The jolt of recognition nearly got him killed. He swung to his right, lifted his gun and aimed.

Only Kate got there first. She spun in a perfect circle, lifting that long leg of hers until it caught Danny smack in the head. T.J. heard the concussion and watched as the bastard teetered sideways and then down.

The dagger twirled on the floor, catching a glint from the overhead light.

"Freeze!"

T.J. looked around. They were surrounded. He didn't see the other gang members. They'd probably taken off when they heard the SWAT team arrive.

"Drop it." The cops moved in closer.

T.J. let his gun go. It clattered on the ground right next to Danny Arcola's prone body.

"I'm a police officer," T.J. said. "My ID is in my wallet."

It took forever for the cop to frisk him, to find his wallet and open it up. The whole time, all T.J. could do was stare at Kate. She was alive. She was all right.

The moment he was free, he rushed to her side. He wrapped her in his arms and held her tighter than he'd ever held anyone before. Then he kissed her, broke away to make sure she was okay and when he saw her smile, he kissed her again.

"Thank God," he said, hugging her once more. "I thought I'd lost you."

"I thought he'd killed you," she said breathlessly.

After another kiss, he looked at her again. "Kate, I—"

"Uh, you mind giving us a hand here?"

T.J. looked at the cop behind Kate. He wanted to tell him to go to hell, but that didn't seem possible. The place was a madhouse and he had work to do.

He kissed her one more time and leaned close to her ear. "We'll continue this later, okay?" he whispered.

When he pulled back to look at her, he felt sure the glimmer of tears in her eyes were from relief, not pain. When she nodded, he touched her cheek with his hand, then he got down to business.

An hour later, Kate had calmed down somewhat, but her hands were trembling and they wouldn't stop. Shock, she thought. A delayed reaction. It would pass.

After the medics had patched them up, T.J. and she had both been swamped with questions. She tried to answer truthfully, but her brain was out of sync and she knew her responses were vague and disjointed. All she wanted was to go back to the center, to safety and, of course, T.J.

The way he'd held her when it was all over still made her dizzy. He'd been so *glad*. Almost as glad as she'd been to hold him.

She picked her way over some cans of chili, moving toward the front door. She didn't want to be in here any longer. She wanted to breathe in the wonderful ocean air and feel the sunlight on her face.

Rounding the aisle, she saw the great splash of darkened blood on the floor and she turned quickly and headed in the other direction. Something tripped her and when she bent down to pick it up, she saw it was a box of condoms.

She stood up so fast she knocked over a whole pile of paper towel rolls. T.J. hadn't used a condom. Was it only this morning? It felt like a week ago, a month ago. But no. It had happened today and neither one of them had had any protection.

Her hand went to her stomach. Was it possible? Could she? The idea wasn't at all unpleasant. As a matter of fact, it was pretty damn wonderful.

She turned, scanning the small store to find T.J. He was standing by the storeroom, talking with a plainclothes detective. The two of them laughed about something and she got her second shock in as many minutes.

He'd changed. He'd become the T.J. of his other life. It clearly wasn't the way he looked, but something about him had transformed. The way he held himself, or the shoulder holster, or just the way he seemed so relaxed in the midst of all this horror.

She rubbed her stomach again, the decision forming without hesitation. She wouldn't bring up the condom. In all likelihood she wasn't pregnant and nothing would come of it. If it turned out she was, she would tell him then.

She had to get out. Moments ago that had been a nice idea, now it was imperative. If she looked at T.J. one more time she would come unglued.

There was a crowd outside. The police held them back behind yellow wooden barricades. Channel 13 had a truck just behind the phone booth and she caught a glimpse of a man with a camera.

"Kate!"

Turning at the sound of her name, she searched until she found Molly. Kate almost wept to see her wonderful face. Naturally Molly didn't let anything as quaint as a police barricade stop her and in two seconds she was hugging Kate with a vengeance.

When Kate opened her eyes, she saw Bobby had come through, too. She let go of her assistant and switched her attention to him, giving him a fierce hug of his own.

"What happened?" Molly asked. "We got this phone call. Is T.J. okay?"

Kate nodded. "Yes, he's fine. He's inside with the police. Bobby, you're off the hook, kiddo. It was Danny and his gang who were setting the fires. We've got all the proof we need."

Molly grunted. "I assume you knocked his block off."

"Actually, I did. He's on his way to the hospital. He'll live to stand trial, don't worry about that."

"I wasn't," Molly said. "I just wish I coulda gotten a few licks in, too."

"Yeah, I'll bet. T.J. and I managed to kick some butt. Fleming, I don't remember if you know him, he's a cop. He was in cahoots with the gang. T.J. took care of him. I was busy at the time with Danny. I did a pretty good job of that, if I do say so myself."

"Damn straight."

She spun around at the sound of his voice. T.J. stood behind her. His smile was warm, caring, but there was a distance there she didn't want to see.

T.J. glanced at his brother. "Did she tell you?"

He nodded. "I told you I didn't do anything."

"I know, kid. I'm sorry I didn't believe you sooner."

Bobby frowned, but it wasn't very convincing. "It's okay." Then he met T.J.'s eye. "I didn't know about Gus. I swear I didn't."

"You weren't supposed to."

"I guess I see why you left."

T.J. smiled sadly. He reached over and gave his brother a quick hug. "What do you say I take you over to see Mom?"

"Now?"

"Don't you think she would like to know you've been acquitted?"

Bobby nodded. "Can Molly come?"

T.J. looked at Kate.

"Sure," she said. "You guys go on. I need to get back to the center." She smiled as best she could. "My car's over there. I'll see you in a while."

"Kate—" T.J. held out his hand.

She didn't take it. "I'll see you later." She turned then and fought the urge to run.

The last of the kids went home at seven. It felt to Kate as if this were the longest day in the world. Too much had happened. She needed to sleep, to shut off her brain for as long as possible.

Molly had called over an hour ago to tell her they would be home soon. She said they'd worked a lot of things out, that Bobby and T.J. were actually talking. Wasn't that great?

Kate had done her best to sound enthusiastic, but it was hard. Hard, because now T.J. had finished what he'd set out to do. He could leave with a clear conscience. He'd made up with his mother, put Gus behind bars on a weapons charge, taken care of Bobby. It was all a nice, neat little package. Except, of course, for her.

The cleanup took a long time. She guessed the kids figured if she wasn't there it was all right to toss their empty soda cans on the floor and to leave food wrappers on the tables. Oh, hell, what did it matter? At least she didn't find any condoms this time.

After the last of it was put into the trash, she went to the back bookshelves and picked up some stray novels. It was important not to think right now. Just look at the name of the book and find its rightful place. But the words were blurry. She wiped at her eyes and her hands came away wet. Damn it. She didn't want to cry.

It wasn't the end of the world, for goodness' sake. She still had the center and her work. She'd faced some real demons in the past few weeks and although she didn't feel it, she knew she was stronger. In time the pain would fade and she would have memories to treasure. The laughter, the runs on the beach, the sweet hours in his bed. Even though it hurt like hell, she wasn't sorry. For a while there, she'd had it all.

She put the books on the closest shelf and started walking to the light switch. In the quiet of the empty room, she heard the sound of the jukebox switching on. The music stopped her right beside the pool table. It was Elvis.

She turned slowly. T.J. stood by the old machine. He wasn't wearing his jacket or his holster anymore. Just his worn jeans and a T-shirt. He headed her way.

Elvis asked if she was lonesome tonight and then the lights, in a burst of magic, dimmed to a low, soft glow. T.J. held out his arms.

Then he was with her, holding her tight, kissing away the remnants of her tears. And the only thing she heard was his voice as he said, "I love you, Wonder Woman. Will you marry me?"

The dance began.

"What about your job?"

"You know that detective at the store? He told me they're looking for a new man right here in Harbor Bay. Said I just might fill the bill."

She held him tighter as he spun her around in a lazy circle. "What about—?"

"Shh," he said, touching her lips with his finger. "All I can tell you is that I was a fool. A big old king-sized fool. You're the best thing that's ever happened to me, darlin'. And I want a lifetime to be the best thing that'll ever happen to you."

She nodded. "Well, seeing as how I'm crazy in love with you, that's okay by me, Captain."

He reached down and touched her stomach. "Know what I remembered?"

She nodded again.

"Wouldn't that be a kick in the pants?" he asked, his voice filled with sweet expectation.

She smiled. "It's an awful long shot."

"Then we'll have to better the odds. Say every night for... forever?"

She laid her head on his shoulder.

Elvis kept on singing.

And the dance went on.

Epilogue

Six months later...

"I am not going to name my child Spike," Kate said. "Or Igor."

Molly shook her head and sighed. "You have no adventure in your bones, Kate." She turned at the sound of shoes in the hallway. "Captain?"

T.J. rounded the corner. "Yes, ma'am?"

"Will you kindly tell your wife that an unusual name builds character? It's what sets people apart from the crowd. It's what makes people sit up and take notice."

He stopped and looked at Kate's softly rounded belly. "Hmm... Maybe she's right. What do you think of Captain Marvel, Junior?"

"That's the ticket." Molly got up from the chair she'd been straddling. "Listen to him, Kate. For an old guy, he's got some pretty good ideas."

"Don't you have a movie to go to?" Kate asked, although she wasn't looking at her assistant any more. T.J. had her full attention. His smile held all the satisfaction she felt. How had she gotten so lucky?

"No movie tonight," Molly said. "Bobby has to study."

"And you don't?" Kate got up and walked over to T.J. "You've got mid-terms, don't you?"

"You just want to get rid of me so you two can grope each other."

"The girl is astute," T.J. said, pulling Kate close. "You've got to give her that."

"Comedians," she said. "I'm living with a whole troupe of them."

"Actually," T.J. said as he rubbed the small of her back, "I promised to help Bobby tonight. Algebra. You didn't know I was something of a mathematical genius, did you?"

"Genius?"

Kate turned at Bobby's voice. He stood in the doorway, his mouth tight and his posture rigid. But she wasn't worried. It was all for show.

"He's got the teacher's edition of the textbook. The one with the answers already in it."

"You wound me to my very soul," T.J. said. "As if I would have to look at the answers."

"Uh-huh. So are we gonna do this, or are you gonna play with Kate all night?"

T.J.'s look told her that he'd like to do exactly that. She was in full agreement, but he'd promised. She kissed him once briefly, and when he tried to make it linger, she stepped back. "Go on. I hear isosceles triangles begging for attention."

T.J. narrowed his eyes. "I hate school," he whispered. Then he walked to his brother, put his hands on his shoulders and turned the kid around. "If we're not back in two hours, call the cops," T.J. said, as he disappeared down the hall.

Kate took in a deep breath and rubbed her stomach, hoping her little boy would make a move. Nothing pleased her more than the friendship that had blossomed between T.J. and Bobby. The darkness had left both of them, and although the relationship wasn't perfect, it was solid and good and healthy.

She'd been delighted at Bobby's decision to stay on here, even after school started. Molly, too. This was her family. Unorthodox, yes, but all hers. The baby was going to be surrounded by love. By laughter. What more could she ask for?

"Hey, beautiful."

She turned to the door once more. As always, T.J.'s smile made her melt.

"About that groping thing. Meet me by the jukebox at ten, okay?"

"I'd be delighted."

He nodded, and she went to tackle the dirty dishes in the sink. Who could have guessed she'd keep falling in love with him? That marriage would suit them both so well?"

"Hey."

She jumped at T.J.'s voice so close, then relaxed as his body pressed against her back.

"I got you a present today."

He kissed her neck, so her question turned into a sigh. She closed her eyes, and felt him reach around her.

"There it is."

She opened her eyes. And laughed.

There, on the counter, next to the fruit bowl, was a tiny, silly, impossibly yellow and pink plastic pony.

His hand went to her stomach, to their child. "Who says dreams don't come true?"

*   *   *   *   *

The Calhoun Saga continues...

in November
New York Times bestselling author

NORA ROBERTS

takes us back to the Towers and introduces us to
the newest addition to the Calhoun household,
sister-in-law Megan O'Riley in

MEGAN'S MATE
(Intimate Moments #745)

And in December
look in retail stores for the special collectors'
trade-size edition of

THE
Calhoun
Women

containing all four fabulous Calhoun series books:
COURTING CATHERINE,
A MAN FOR AMANDA, FOR THE LOVE OF LILAH
and *SUZANNA'S SURRENDER.*
Available wherever books are sold.

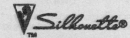

TM
Look us up on-line at: http://www.romance.net   CALHOUN

Take 4 bestselling love stories FREE

Plus get a FREE surprise gift!

Special Limited-time Offer

There's nothing quite like a family

REUNION

HANNAH · MICHAEL · KATE

The new miniseries by
Pat Warren

Three siblings are about to be reunited.
And each finds love along the way....

HANNAH
Her life is about to change now that she's met
the irresistible Joel Merrick in HOME FOR HANNAH
(Special Edition #1048, August 1996).

MICHAEL
He's been on his own all his life. Now he's
going to take a risk on love...and
take part in the reunion he's been
waiting for in MICHAEL'S HOUSE
(Intimate Moments #737, September 1996).

KATE
A job as a nanny leads her to Aaron Carver,
his adorable baby daughter and the
fulfillment of her dreams in KEEPING KATE
(Special Edition #1060, October 1996).

Meet these three siblings from

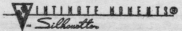

Silhouette SPECIAL EDITION®
and

INTIMATE MOMENTS®
™ *Silhouette*

Look us up on-line at: http://www.romance.net

As seen on TV!
Free Gift Offer

With a Free Gift proof-of-purchase from any Silhouette® book, you can receive a beautiful cubic zirconia pendant.

This gorgeous marquise-shaped stone is a genuine cubic zirconia—accented by an 18" gold tone necklace.

(Approximate retail value $19.95)

Send for yours today...
compliments of ▼ *Silhouette*®
™

To receive your free gift, a cubic zirconia pendant, send us one original proof-of-purchase, photocopies not accepted, from the back of any Silhouette Romance™, Silhouette Desire®, Silhouette Special Edition®, Silhouette Intimate Moments® or Silhouette Yours Truly™ title available in August, September or October at your favorite retail outlet, together with the Free Gift Certificate, plus a check or money order for $1.65 U.S./$2.15 CAN. (do not send cash) to cover postage and handling, payable to Silhouette Free Gift Offer. We will send you the specified gift. Allow 6 to 8 weeks for delivery. Offer good until October 31, 1996 or while quantities last. Offer valid in the U.S. and Canada only.

Free Gift Certificate

Name: _____

Address: _____

City: _____ State/Province: _____ Zip/Postal Code: _____

Mail this certificate, one proof-of-purchase and a check or money order for postage and handling to: SILHOUETTE FREE GIFT OFFER 1996. In the U.S.: 3010 Walden Avenue, P.O. Box 9077, Buffalo NY 14269-9077. In Canada: P.O. Box 613, Fort Erie, Ontario L2Z 5X3.

FREE GIFT OFFER   084-KMD
ONE PROOF-OF-PURCHASE
To collect your fabulous FREE GIFT, a cubic zirconia pendant, you must include this original proof-of-purchase for each gift with the properly completed Free Gift Certificate.

084-KMD

**A brutal murder.
A notorious case.
Twelve people must decide
the fate of one man.**

Jury Duty

an exciting courtroom drama by

Laura Van Wormer

Struggling novelist Libby Winslow has been chosen to sit on the jury of a notorious murder trial dubbed the "Poor Little Rich Boy" case. The man on trial, handsome, wealthy James Bennett Layton, Jr., has been accused of killing a beautiful young model. As Libby and the other jury members sift through the evidence trying to decide the fate of this man, their own lives become jeopardized because someone on the jury has his own agenda....

Find out what the verdict is this October at your favorite retail outlet.

The collection of the year!
NEW YORK TIMES BESTSELLING AUTHORS

Linda Lael Miller
Wild About Harry

Janet Dailey
Sweet Promise

Elizabeth Lowell
Reckless Love

Penny Jordan
Love's Choices

and featuring
Nora Roberts
The Calhoun Women

This special trade-size edition features four of the wildly
popular titles in the Calhoun miniseries together in
one volume—a true collector's item!

Pick up these great authors and a chance to win
a weekend for two in New York City at the
Marriott Marquis Hotel on Broadway! We'll pay
for your flight, your hotel—even a Broadway show!

Available in December at your favorite retail outlet.

NEW YORK
Marriott.
MARQUIS

NYT1296-R

Bestselling Author
BARBARA
BOSWELL

Continues the twelve-book series—FORTUNE'S CHILDREN—
in October 1996 with Book Four

STAND-IN BRIDE

When Fortune Company executive Michael Fortune needed help
warding off female admirers after being named one of the ten most
eligible bachelors in the United States, he turned to his faithful
assistant, Julia Chandler. Julia agreed to a pretend engagement, but
what starts as a charade produces an unexpected Fortune heir....

MEET THE FORTUNES—a family whose legacy is greater than riches.
Because where there's a will...there's a *wedding!*

"Ms. Boswell is one of those rare treasures who combines humor
and romance into sheer magic."   —*Rave Reviews*

*A CASTING CALL TO
ALL FORTUNE'S CHILDREN FANS!*
If you are truly one of the fortunate
you may win a trip to
Los Angeles to audition for
Wheel of Fortune®. Look for
details in all retail Fortune's Children titles!

Look us up on-line at: http://www.romance.net   FC-4-C

You're About to Become a Privileged Woman

Reap the rewards of fabulous free gifts and benefits with proofs-of-purchase from Silhouette and Harlequin books

Pages & Privileges™

It's our way of thanking you for buying our books at your favorite retail stores.

Pages & Privileges ™

PROOF OF PURCHASE
SIM-PP189
Offer expires October 31, 1996

**Harlequin and Silhouette—
the most privileged readers in the world!**

For more information about Harlequin and Silhouette's PAGES & PRIVILEGES program call the Pages & Privileges Benefits Desk: 1-503-794-2499